Surprise Surprise!

Second Edition

Surprise Surprise!

Second Edition

Mike Faricy

Surprise Surprise! Second Edition © Copyright
Mike Faricy 2023

All rights reserved. No part of this publication may be reproduced, stored in a retrieval system, or transmitted, in any form or by any means, electronic, mechanical, photocopying, recording or otherwise, without the prior and express permission of the copyright owner.

This is a work of fiction. All of the characters, organizations, and events portrayed in this novel are either products of the author's imagination or are used fictitiously.

Library of Congress Control Number: 2023918907
paperback ISBN: 978-1-962080-51-4
e-Book ISBN: 978-1-962080-52-1

MJF Publishing books may be purchased for education, Business, or promotional use. For information on bulk purchases, please contact the author directly at mikefaricyauthor@gmail.com

Published by

MJF Publishing
https://www.mikefaricybooks.com

Acknowledgments

I would like to thank the following people for their help and support:

Special thanks to my editors, Kitty, Donna and Rhonda for their hard work, cheerful patience and positive feedback.

I would like to thank Ann and Julie for their creative talent and not slitting their wrists or jumping off the high bridge when dealing with my Neanderthal computer capabilities.

Special thanks to Ann for her patience.

Last, I would like to thank family and friends for their encouragement and unqualified support. Special thanks to Maggie, Jed, Schatz, Pat, Av, Emily and Pat for not rolling their eyes, at least when I was there, and most of all, to my wife Teresa whose belief, support and inspiration has from day one, never waned.

Prologue

Damien Dambella refilled the crystal wine glass almost to the rim and handed it to the sultry blonde stretched out on his bed. "Enjoy the wine, Phoenix."

She adjusted the pillows behind her and reached for the glass. She took a sip, smiled, and then studied his backside while he topped up his glass. He'd probably been an athlete a thousand years and forty pounds ago. That was okay. The bank accounts more than made up for it. He held out his arm and clinked the crystal with her before he climbed back into the four-poster bed.

It wasn't lost on her that his glass was barely half-full, not that it made any difference. Her husband was working late, again. If he did happen to arrive home before her, she'd just tell him she'd been doing a late-night workout, which in a way, wasn't far from the truth.

After a couple of sips and some idiotic comments, Dambella set his glass on the bedside table, raised his eyebrows, and slid beneath the sheet. Phoenix continued to sip. She occasionally let loose with a false moan and more encouragement. She checked the digital clock on the chest of drawers. After a few minutes, she drained her glass and set it on the bedside table next to her. It was time to bring things to a close. She moaned loudly, rolled onto her side, and groaned, "Oh my God. Oh my God."

The wine bottle was empty. Dambella had shoved it into the silver ice bucket upside down. They'd been involved in post-coital chatting for the past thirty minutes, and he had just said, "It's too bad you're married. Think of all the fun we could have together."

She thought for a long moment, *'The bank accounts, his Victorian mansion, the Florida Keys, trips to Europe. Yeah, I can fix that,'* and she proceeded to consider how, exactly.

One

It was going to be another warm summer day, and I was sipping coffee at my desk. My officemate, Louie Laufen, had a court appearance this morning. My golden retriever, Morton, was ensconced on his pillow gnawing on his rawhide bone. At the moment, I was staring through my binoculars at the apartment across the street. The shade was up on a third-floor bedroom window. I'd been enjoying the view as a woman took her time getting dressed.

As I set the binoculars down when she left her bedroom, I noticed the blue BMW convertible pulling in behind my car parked across the street. A very attractive blonde climbed out of the car. She was wearing a short black skirt and a white top. She removed her sunglasses, placed them in her purse, and waited for a bus to pass. Once the street was clear, she strutted across as if she was on a fashion show runway. A car drove by and tooted its horn as she stepped onto the sidewalk.

I figured she must be headed for the hairdressers just across from our office. A moment later, I could hear the stairs creak ever so slightly. I thought I'd been right about the hairdressers when suddenly there was a knock on the office door, and it slowly opened.

The same attractive blonde peeked around the door and said, "Hi, umm, sorry to bother you. I'm looking for Dev Haskell, the private investigator."

"Oh, yeah, that's me. Please, please come on in," I said, standing up behind my desk. I quickly slipped the binoculars into a drawer and closed it with my knee.

The blonde was even more attractive close up. She flashed a sexy smile of sparkling white teeth and extended her hand as she walked toward me. "Hi, I'm Phoenix Starr. I got your name from a friend." As we shook hands, a wonderful perfume scent drifted over me. She gently rubbed her thumb a couple of times over the back of my hand and smiled.

"Please, have a seat, Phoenix. Nice to meet you. Can I interest you in a coffee?"

"Only if you have it made. I don't want to put you to any trouble."

"No trouble at all. I've got a fresh pot on," I lied. I grabbed my mug and headed toward the coffee. Fortunately, there was enough left from yesterday for two cups.

Morton was up off his pillow. He wandered over to Phoenix and sniffed. She reached down and scratched him behind the ears, which gave me the opportunity to empty Louie's coffee mug from yesterday and refill it.

"Here we go, fresh coffee. You take it black?"

"Yeah, that's perfect," she said, which was good because we didn't have any cream or sugar. "What a nice doggy. What's his name?"

I set Louie's refilled mug in front of her. "That's Morton, and now that you've given him a scratch behind the ears, he'll be your friend for life. Please, have a seat. How can I help you?" I said and nodded toward the client chair in front of my desk.

She sat down, took a sip of coffee, and slid the mug off to the side at an arm's length. I noticed a very large set of diamonds on her left hand. She slowly crossed her legs and smiled. "Well, I got your name from Monica Dolan. We both belong to the Town and Country Club."

"Oh, yeah, I've known Monica since we were kids." Which was true since we went to the same grade school. I'd asked her out a half-dozen times in high school. She always said no. I hadn't seen her in at least fifteen years. The two of them belonging to the Town and Country Club put them on a much higher social level than me drinking at The Spot bar.

"Monica suggested you might be able to help me. I'm afraid I've got an embarrassing situation."

"Phoenix, I deal with all sorts of situations. Please, don't feel embarrassed. I had a client once who insisted his neighbor could turn invisible and was knocking over the trash bins. Turns out it was just the wind, but the guy still believed it was his invisible neighbor."

She flashed a quick smile, took a deep breath, and said, "Well, I'm pretty sure my husband is having an affair."

"Oh, I'm sorry to hear that. Can you tell me why you think this?"

"Well, he's always working nights, just about every night. He comes home late, ten, eleven, sometimes even midnight. How can I put this? No matter what I do, he seems to have lost all interest in me," she said and let that last statement just hang out there for a moment.

Based on her appearance, I figured the guy was nuts. "I see. Any idea who the other party might be?"

She shook her head.

"Tell me about your husband. What does he do?"

"He's an accountant. Has his own accounting firm. He's invested heavily, and, I have to say, successfully, in stocks and a couple of start-up companies. He's always been a workaholic, but something's changed in the last year or so, and I'm pretty sure I know what it is. He's found someone else."

"Other than working late, do you have any evidence? Phone calls? Emails? Text messages? Does he come home smelling of perfume?"

"Well, actually, no. There's been nothing of that nature. But then he's always been boring."

"Do you have any children?"

"No. We decided on a childless marriage. It's part of our contract. Sterling Kozlow is my husband's name. We've been married for almost five years."

I grabbed a pen and a legal pad. I pulled off the top sheet where I'd written my grocery list, tossed it in the wastebasket, and began taking a few notes. "And you kept your maiden name when you married?"

"Yes, I did. Phoenix Starr, two 'r's' in my last name."

"Are you living in town?"

"Yes, we have a home on the River Boulevard," she said, mentioning one of the nicer streets in town. Unfortunately, it was also the same street where Tubby Gustafson, the city's local crime lord, resided.

"What would you like me to do?" I asked.

"Well," she said, slowly uncrossing and then crossing her legs again. Out of force of habit, I took a quick glance, red lace. "I'd like you to confirm if Sterling is having an affair. I can pay you, and I'd, well, I'd be *very* grateful." *Did she just raise her eyebrows, or did I imagine that?*

"What kind of car does your husband drive?"

"A red Mercedes. He's told me a million times what kind it is, but I can never remember. A bunch of letters, ABC or something like that. It's a very nice car."

"And you said he has an accounting firm?"

"Sterling Kozlow Finance. Here's his business card," she said and handed me a card.

I recognized the address. The office was in a 1950s strip mall down on West 7th Street, just a couple of blocks from Highway 5 heading out to the airport. Not exactly what I would call high price space, but then maybe that was typical of an accountant.

"I'll check this out and get back to you. My rate is two-fifty a day, plus expenses. I usually ask for two days up front, but how about I check a few things out, and we can discuss what I think this might run in a day or two?"

She smiled and nodded. "I'm sure we'll be able to work something out. Give me that business card back for a minute," she said, then reached into her purse and took out a pen. She wrote down her phone number and an email address on the back and returned it to me. She'd drawn a little heart next to her email address.

"Thanks. Is it all right if I phone or email you?"

"Absolutely. That's my cellphone, so Sterling will never answer. The email address is very private. You can tell me anything. I'll look forward to hearing from you," she said then stood and picked up her purse.

"Very nice to meet you, Ms. Starr," I replied and held out my hand.

"Oh, please. Call me Phoenix, baby. I'm sure we'll be working very closely," she said and this time definitely raised her eyebrows. I followed her to the door and opened it for her. "Oh, you're so kind. A perfect gentleman." She leaned against me, gave me a peck on the cheek, then stepped out of the office and headed down the stairs. I watched her go halfway down the stairs, then closed the door, and hurried to the window. A hint of her lovely perfume still hung in the air.

My office mate Louie had just parked his faded red Ford Fiesta in front of my car and climbed out. He headed across the street, nodded as he passed Phoenix, and then turned and stared. She climbed into her convertible, put her sunglasses on, and started the car. Louie stood on the sidewalk and watched for a long moment as she drove off.

I heard the stairs creaking as Louie made his way up to the office. The door opened, and where sexy Phoenix Starr had kissed me a moment earlier, now a red-faced Louie stood, gasping for air. He stopped, sniffed, and asked, "Was that hot-looking blonde up here?"

Two

Sterling Kozlow Finance was located in Sibley Plaza, a shopping center developed back in 1955. The center was actually two one-story structures featuring a total of twenty-one different suites, twelve of which were vacant. A large parking lot was in the front of the buildings. The office of Sterling Kozlow Finance was set between a Dollar Store and a vacant unit with a large **For Rent** sign.

I was parked in the parking lot, three lanes away from Kozlow's office. I was on my second McDonald's cheeseburger and halfway through my strawberry shake. Other than three employees leaving at the end of the day, there had been no other activity in the office. At exactly 6:00, a guy I pegged at maybe mid-fifties with thinning gray hair stepped out of an office and locked the front door. His tie was loosened, and the sleeves on his white shirt were rolled up to the elbows. If he was Kozlow, he looked old enough to be Phoenix Starr's father. He turned the lights off in the front office and stepped back into what I presumed was his office. A red Mercedes CLS was parked just in front of the office. I presumed that was Kozlow's car and had copied the license number.

I sat in my car for the next three-and-a-half hours, and nothing happened. I drifted off to sleep for maybe a minute or two but woke when my head bounced off the steering wheel. The Mercedes was still parked in front, and light was still drifting out of the open doorway from what I presumed was Kozlow's office.

It was after 9:30 when he finally turned off the light and stepped out of the office. He locked the front door, climbed into the Mercedes, backed out of his parking place, and drove off.

I followed at a respectable distance. He came to a complete stop at each of the four stop signs along the route. He drove up St. Paul Avenue to Cleveland, Cleveland to Randolph, where he took a left turn and headed down to the River Boulevard. He took a right and pulled into a driveway a half-block later.

One of the automatic garage doors on the attached three-stall garage rose as he approached. He drove inside and disappeared. The two-story house, at least from the street, was dark on the first floor. What appeared to be a bedroom light was on in a second-floor room. A minute later, light drifted out through the living room lace curtains. I waited another thirty minutes. Apparently, Kozlow was home for the night. I yawned and headed to my place. Morton met me at the front door. I let him out back for fifteen minutes, and we headed up to bed just after 11:00.

We drove past Sterling Kozlow Finance at 7:30 the following morning. The large parking lot was empty with the exception of Kozlow's red Mercedes and two taxi cabs in front of a coffee shop. I parked at the far end of the parking lot, clipped the leash onto Morton's collar, and we headed toward Kozlow's office.

As we walked past the office, I glanced in through the floor-to-ceiling windows. The front room had a reception desk, four chairs against a wall, and a coffee table with three magazines. No doubt the magazines would be months old. I didn't see Kozlow, but the light was on in the same office from last night. I figured he was already at his desk.

We walked past his car and then stepped into the parking lot. I had a piece of white chalk in my hand, and as we walked alongside the Mercedes, I leaned over and drew a vertical line down the rear tire on the passenger side. If he drove anywhere during the day, the chalk line would be in a different position the next time I was here. We walked back to our car and headed to the office.

I made a fresh pot of coffee, and at one minute after 9:00, I phoned my friend Denny in the department of motor vehicles. "Dennis Glazier," was how he answered the phone.

"Hey, Denny, you're sounding cheerful for first thing in the morning."

"Hi Dev, you just getting home from last night?"

"I only wish. Wondering if you could check a license for me. I've got a client who's looking to buy a car from a private party. I just want to make sure the sale is legit and not something that's going to come back and cause a bunch of problems."

"What's the license number?"

"Minnesota plates," I said and gave him Kozlow's license plate number. "It's a red Mercedes CLS." I could hear the keyboard clicking.

"Yeah, here it is. Actually registered to a company, Sterling Kozlow Finance. A red 2021 Mercedes CLS. Strikes me as strange someone would be selling that privately."

"Oh, it's some sort of shirt tail relative. I'm not sure what the deal is. I just wanted to be sure the deal is legit, and it sounds like it is."

"You owe me a beer for my effort," Denny said.

"You got it, happy to pay up. It's been too long since we were last together."

"Oh man, between work and getting the kids to swimming lessons, the boy's baseball practice, my daughter to ballet, we're exhausted by the end of any given day."

"Well, give my best to your wife. She's obviously very patient and still has a lot of work to do on you."

"Ain't that the truth. Good talking to you, Dev."

"Thanks, Denny, I…" but he'd already hung up.

Louie wandered in about twenty minutes later. I heard the stairs creaking as he slowly climbed up to the second floor. I grabbed his coffee mug off my desk. Lipstick from Phoenix Starr was still on it, and I wiped it off, and filled it just as he stepped into the office. As always, you'd think he ran a couple of miles based on his red face. He gave me a nod and settled in at his picnic table desk. I placed the mug in front of him. He stared at the steaming mug for a minute or two, eventually took a sip, and said, "So what's going on in your world?"

"Not a heck of a lot. I think I did pick up a new client yesterday."

"Don't tell me it was that hot-looking blonde who drove off in the convertible yesterday. Well?" he said after a long moment.

"You told me not to tell you."

"So she was in here. I thought so."

"Yeah, she seems really nice. Thinks her husband might be having an affair."

"Well, based on what I saw, if he's having an affair with someone, he's missing more than a few brain cells."

"I'm going to watch him over the next couple of days and see. She certainly wasn't hard on the eyes."

"Remember to use your brain and charge her the full amount. No discount just because she's hot looking."

"I've already given her my daily rate plus expenses, so you don't have to worry."

"Just make sure you stick to it," Louie said.

I spent the next hour checking out Sterling Kozlow Finance online. There was a website that had, among other things, a number of reviews, all five stars. Three employees were mentioned. Two of whom, a man and a woman, I'd seen leaving the office just after 5:00 last night. I wrote down their names along with the five people who left reviews. I made calls to the reviewers and left four messages. The fifth and last person answered on the second ring.

"Jason Corbin."

"Hi, Jason. Thanks for taking my call. My name is Dev Haskell. I have a small company, and I'm looking for an accountant. I saw the review you wrote on Sterling Kozlow Finance. Have things worked out well for you there?"

"With Kozlow Finance? Yeah, very well. They know what they're doing. What I like about them is they give me options and explain what to expect, given the choices I make. I run a sales firm. I've got eleven employees. We're all hustling. We do a lot of traveling. We have a lot of expenses. With the exception of two office workers, the rest of us are on commission, so there are a lot of gray areas. They really helped out. It seems like one of us is getting audited either by the IRS or the state every other year. I haven't had to pay a fine since I moved my account to Kozlow."

"Pretty good endorsement. You actually deal with Sterling?"

"Yes, although I've had some interaction with Marshal Jones there too. But the vast majority is with Kozlow. I could say he can be boring as hell, but the guy is an accountant. They're all boring. I just want him to keep my ducks in a row, and he does that."

"You know anything about him socially?"

"Socially?"

"Yeah, does he play golf, or fish, follow sports, that kind of thing? Is he a party animal?"

"I've no idea. Well, except I think I can state for a fact he's probably not a party animal. He strikes me as a one glass of wine type of guy. I'm paying him to handle my financial stuff and protect me from getting audited. That's all I care about. I do know that he's married. In fact, he has a photo of his wife behind his desk. I just presumed it was a picture of his daughter and said something to him once. When I found out it was his wife, I was more than a little embarrassed. Anyway, the guy is good at what he does, damn good. Hope I've been some help."

"Yeah, you have. Business good for you?"

"Hey, we're in sales here. There's always something more you can do. No complaints, I can pay my bills and put a little aside."

"Well, Jason, I appreciate your time and recommendation. Wishing you continued success."

"And same to you. Good luck," he said and hung up.

Three

Two of my four messages were returned early in the afternoon. Both with solid reviews on Kozlow. No suggestion of the guy being wild and crazy or a womanizer. But then, if he was involved in an affair, he'd probably be keeping it very quiet.

Louie had a court date at 11:00 and promised to return with some BBQ sandwiches from Roosters. He didn't return until just after 2:30. As I opened the food tray, my stomach growled.

"Yeah, I get it. Sorry I was so late. Some earlier hearing got held up and knocked everyone back a good hour and a half. It was in Devitt's courtroom. He was not a happy camper," Louie said. He draped his tie over his shoulder and took a large bite from his sandwich. BBQ sauce immediately shot onto his chin and then dripped down the front of his white shirt. He looked at the BBQ stain, shrugged, and kept eating.

I had just finished my sandwich when my phone rang. "Good afternoon, Dev Haskell," was how I answered, figuring it was another one of the folks returning my phone call. Wrong, unfortunately.

"Haskell. Get your dumb ass out here. Mr. Gustafson would like a word with you."

I turned in my chair and looked out the window. A black Cadillac Escalade was parked behind my car. I could just make out the rather large image of Fat Freddy Zimmerman in the front passenger seat.

"Actually, Freddy, not that I wouldn't like to see Mr. Gustafson, but I'm working a case right now. How 'bout I give him a call and stop over later this afternoon. Would that work?"

"In a word, no. Bad idea. A really bad idea. I need to see your dumb ass out here in about sixty seconds, or I'm going to send Happy up there to get you. Let me warn you. He was out last night, and he's nursing a hangover. It would not be a pleasant visit."

Happy Hoffman, Fat Freddy's driver. Not a guy to mess with, especially if he had a hangover. "I'll be down in just a minute," I promised and hung up.

"That didn't sound like it went your way," Louie said. At the moment, he was dabbing at the BBQ stain on his shirt with a wet paper towel, which only seemed to be making the stain larger.

"Fat Freddy is out on the street. He wants to take me to see Tubby. God only knows what that will be about."

"You don't know what he wants?"

"I don't know and really don't care. But things will get even worse if I don't go. You going to be around this afternoon?"

"Yeah, I'm here for the rest of the day. If you're not back before 5:00, Morton and I will be over at The Spot."

"Thanks," I said, took a deep breath, and headed down the stairs. As I walked out of the building and crossed the street, Happy Hoffman stepped out from behind the wheel and opened the rear door for me.

"Thanks, Happy. How's the head?"

"I was home watching the game last night. He was just pulling your leg," he said under his breath.

"About damn time," Fat Freddy growled as I climbed in. I took his greeting to mean he was the one nursing the hangover. The trip to Tubby's mansion proceeded in silence. Once Happy turned onto the River Boulevard, I could see Tubby's mansion on the next block. Phoenix Starr and Sterling Kozlow's home was just two blocks behind us.

The iron gate opened automatically as we approached. Happy drove along the circular drive and stopped opposite the front door.

"Let's go. Move it," Fat Freddy snarled as he climbed out.

"Good luck," Happy said under his breath as I climbed out of the back seat. He drove over to the parking area as a security guy named Billy approached me.

"Hold your arms out to the side, and I'll check you. You carrying?" he asked as he waved a handheld metal detector over my left arm and down my side.

"No, I'm not carrying. I've got a strip of metal in my wallet and a pen in my pocket."

Billy nodded and a moment later, the wand beeped as it ran over my wallet.

"Let me see what you've got in your pocket," he ordered.

I pulled my wallet out and handed it to him. "Oh yeah, one of them Dango's," he said, eyeing the wallet. He glanced at the two one-dollar bills behind the black rubber strap and shook his head. "Figures," he said.

"Haskell, are you through screwing around? Come on, you're keeping the boss waiting," Freddy yelled from the front door.

I hurried toward him. A guy on a short three-step ladder was washing the windows and using a squeegee. Freddy held the door with a disgusted look on his face. Once I stepped inside, another security guy set his comic book on his chair and patted me down. "Okay," he said and returned to his comic book.

I followed Freddy across the entry and down the hall toward Tubby's office. A woman was busy mopping the floor in the entryway, and another woman was vacuuming the staircase leading up to the second floor.

Freddy stopped at the office door, took a deep breath, and knocked as he opened the door. Tubby was seated at his desk, wearing a suit, a tie, and a starched white shirt. Instead of a drink, there was a coffee cup and a saucer. Fresh cut flowers, daises, were in a vase on the fireplace mantel. The office smelled of polish and Windex. The usual cadre of semi-naked women giving neck rubs and a lot of attention to Tubby was nowhere to be seen.

"Nice to see you, sir. I get the feeling there are some changes going on. All the cleaning, cut flowers, you're all dressed up. I mean more than you usually are, and let me just say you're always looking good, sir."

Tubby shook his head and mumbled something I probably was better off not hearing. He cleared his throat a couple of times and said, "I'm going to need your help, Haskell."

"My help?"

"It would seem I have a guest arriving tomorrow."

"A guest?"

"Yes, my sister."

"Oh, I guess I didn't know you had a sister, sir. Well, I hope you have a nice visit. Do you see her very often?"

"As little as possible, Haskell, and that's where you're going to come in."

"Me? I'm not following, sir."

"Oh, yes, you are, Haskell. I suspect you're following quite well. Quinnie is arriving at noon tomorrow. Let me thank you in advance for making her trip so enjoyable."

"Enjoyable?"

"Haskell, I'm a busy man. I don't have time to waste like you do. You will mind Quinnie, take her to dinner, show her the town. Drop her off here at night. She'll be staying in one of my guest rooms. I want her to be busy from sunup to sundown, and that task has fallen on you."

"Me? Look, Tub, err, Mr. Gustafson. I'm in the process of working on a case for a new client. It's going to keep me busy until late every day. I'll be doing stakeouts, eating meals in my car, and—"

"No, you won't, Haskell. Oh, and thank you for reminding me. I'll expect you here at 9:00 tomorrow morning. If you're not here, just drive to the emergency room at the Regions Hospital. It will save you the trouble of calling an ambulance. You will be here at 9:00 sharp. You'll trade in that dreadful vehicle you drive, and I'll loan you one of mine. Quinnie will be arriving at the airport on a 10:00 flight from Los Angeles. Thank you in advance for meeting her at the airport. I will be otherwise detained for the entire day. I'll have a schedule and a list of places the two of you can visit."

"Mr. Gustafson, I'm sorry, but I really can't do this. I'm just beginning work for a new client and—"

"Frederick, would you please summon Breaker? It would appear we have an issue here that is going to have to be dealt with, and I—"

"Wait a minute, sir. You don't have to bring Breaker into this. I'll attempt to adjust my schedule and—"

"Attempt?" Tubby said and glared.

"I look forward to being here tomorrow morning and meeting your sister, sir."

"Much better, Haskell. Oh, and if you wouldn't mind. Perhaps something a little more presentable," he said and nodded at my faded t-shirt featuring the Rolling

Stones distressed tongue. "Something a bit more appropriate."

"She doesn't like the Rolling Stones?"

Fat Freddy grabbed my arm and pulled me toward the door.

Tubby glared and pointed. "Out! Remember what I said, Haskell. 9:00 tomorrow morning, and for God's sake, wear something appropriate."

Four

Fat Freddy pulled the door closed behind us and shook his head. "What the hell is wrong with you?"

"Pardon me, gentlemen," a woman said. She hurried past, pulling a vacuum cleaner.

As we followed her down the hall, Fat Freddy proceeded to lecture me. "Do you have any idea how crazy things are around here? Take a damn look. The entire place is getting scrubbed within an inch of its life. You screw this up, and there will be nothing anyone can do to save you. I'm not kidding, Haskell. This is serious. His sister is a major pain in the ass, and he doesn't want anything to do with her. Let me warn you. You goof this up, and the emergency ward is going to look like a vacation spot."

We walked across the entryway and stepped outside. A taxi driver was in front loading three large suitcases into the back of the taxi. Three Asian women were all smiles as they watched their luggage being loaded into the taxi. I recognized them as the women in thongs I'd seen giving Tubby his massages along with other, more personal attention. Who knew they actually owned nice clothes?

Three of the security guys were focused on the women and didn't even notice Fat Freddy and me. One of the guys opened the taxi door, and the women began to slide in. Just the exercise of climbing into a taxi seemed to make them appear super sexy. Once the doors were closed, the taxi slowly made its way around the circular drive. A back window was lowered, and one of the women waved goodbye and blew a sultry kiss. The three security guys all waved back.

"Where are they going?" I asked.

"A three-day work trip in Las Vegas. It's a pity, really. We're all going to be tip-toeing around here for the next few days, and that's where you come in, Haskell. You gotta keep Quinnie out of here."

"Why do I have to—"

"Stop. Do not say another word," Fat Freddy said just as the Escalade pulled up. Happy was behind the wheel. Freddy opened the front passenger door, climbed in, and looked at me. "Get your dumb ass in back," he said, shaking his head and mumbling something I couldn't quite make out.

It was a quiet ride back to my office. Happy pulled to the curb in front of the building and came to a halt at the bus stop.

Fat Freddy turned partway in the passenger seat, but he was so fat, he couldn't face me seated behind him. "Let me just say it one more time, Haskell. For your own good. You screw this up, and there will be nothing anyone can do to save you. So, let's pretend your worthless life depends on it. Be there tomorrow morning at 9:00 and not a minute later. Now get out."

I hadn't quite closed the door when Happy took off down the street. The door was yanked from my hand and slammed shut. I watched them disappear and then just stood there on the sidewalk, shaking my head. I climbed the stairs up to the office. As I stepped inside, Morton opened one eye, saw it was me, and went back to sleep. Louie was snoring lightly in his desk chair. I walked over to my desk and sat down. I debated calling Phoenix Starr and telling her I would be otherwise detained for the next two or three days. But then, the more I thought about it, the more I decided it really wouldn't matter. I could check out Kozlow tonight, and if nothing happened, I'd call her tomorrow and tell her I was going to back off for a couple of days just so he didn't spot me.

The more I thought about it, the more I decided that would not only work, but it sounded like a great plan. I'll show what's-her-name, Tubby's sister, around town. Get a handle on what she's interested in, and Tubby will end up owing me a favor. I input Phoenix Starr's phone number on my contact list.

"Rumph, rumph," Louie mumbled and moved from side to side in his chair. "I must have closed my eyes for a moment. You been back long?"

"Not really," I said and noticed that the BBQ sauce stain on his formerly clean shirt was now about the size of a dessert plate.

"How did things go with Mr. Gustafson?"

"A pain in the butt, but I can deal with it. I have to keep his sister busy for the next couple of days. She's coming in from L.A."

"His sister? Why do you have to do that?"

"I'm guessing because the two of them don't get along. Could you imagine having someone like Tubby for a brother? Or, for that matter, what kind of family raises a kid that grows up to be Tubby Gustafson?"

"Well, yeah, I mean, I get that, Dev. But why do you have to—"

"Oh, it's really simple. If I don't, Tubby is going to have one of his thugs, a guy called Breaker, put me in the hospital. That pretty much got me on board."

"He threatened you?"

"No, it was more of a promise. Anyway, I gotta be at his place tomorrow morning at 9:00. Get this, he's going to loan me one of his cars, and I'm supposed to dress up. So I look nice. If nothing else, it'll be interesting to see what his sister is like. Who knows, maybe I'll learn some deep dark secret about Tubby."

Louie shook his head and turned on his computer. I took Morton for a walk around 4:30, and we met Louie in The Spot. I wanted to check out Sterling Kozlow, so I took a pass on having a beer. Louie fed Morton a bag of pork rinds. We chatted for about ten minutes, and I took

Morton home. I drove over to Sibley Plaza and parked a couple of lanes over from Kozlow's Mercedes. Based on the chalk line I'd left on his rear tire, the car had been in the same place all day.

Once again, Kozlow walked out of his office at 6:00, locked the front door, and went back into his office. He didn't reappear until almost 9:30. I followed him home, watched his house for a half-hour, and then drove back to my place. I let Morton out the back door, ate some leftover pizza from earlier in the week, and we went up to bed at 11:00.

I was up early the following morning. I showered, shaved, and made breakfast. Once I'd eaten, I hurried upstairs and dressed in a nice pair of slacks and a shirt I'd only worn once since it came from the dry cleaners. I thought about a tie; I had three, but they were all Christmas ties and played a carol when you squeezed them, so I took a pass.

I left Morton in the backyard and drove back over to Sibley Plaza. I parked in the almost empty lot at the opposite end from Sterling Kozlow Finance. Kozlow's car was already parked in front of his office. Just like yesterday morning, I walked past his Mercedes. I left a chalk line on his rear tire and headed back to my car. I drove to the office and left Louie a note reminding him I was involved in Tubby Gustafson duty for the day and then headed over to Tubby's.

Five

As I pulled in through the wrought iron gates, I noticed all the security guys were wearing matching navy-blue sports shirts. Billy stepped onto the circular drive and waved me into the parking area. As I climbed out of my car, he said, "Nice outfit, Haskell. Assume the position." I turned toward my car and leaned forward with my hands resting on the roof. He waved the wand over me and then said, "Okay, you're good to go. Hang in there today."

I nodded and made my way to the front door. One of the guys on the front porch bowed toward me and made a show of opening the door. Everyone laughed as I stepped inside. The marble floor in the entryway glistened. All the wood trim and the paneling had been polished. The guy usually reading a comic book in the chair was wearing a suit and shiny brown shoes. I stopped, extended my arms out to the side, and he patted me down.

Fat Freddy came down the hall as I was patted down and said, "Come on, hurry up, Haskell. Mr. Gustafson is waiting."

"Nice suit, Freddy." I nodded at the blue pinstripe suit Fat Freddy was wearing, size double extra-large.

"Shut up, dumb shit, and follow me."

I followed him down the hall and into Tubby's office. This morning there were two vases of cut daises on the fireplace mantel. Tubby was placing a framed photo of two children, a boy and a girl, on the corner of his desk. The little boy looked to be maybe ten years old and was pudgy. He wore blue shorts and a short-sleeve white shirt. The little girl was maybe six months old with a bow taped to her bald head. She was wrapped in a pink blanket and held by young Tubby.

Tubby appeared to study the photo for a moment. Today he had on a three-piece gray suit, a white shirt, and a red tie. He handed me a sheet of paper with his sister's name, Quinnie Gustafson. Her flight information was listed below that. I could only hope the little girl in the pink dress hadn't grown up to look like Tubby.

"That's the flight information," Tubby said, stating the obvious and nodding toward the sheet of paper. "She's scheduled to land just after 10:00. I want you to wait for her at baggage claim. I told her you would meet her at whatever carousel her luggage ends up on. Should she ask, you will tell her you work for my marketing firm."

"You have a marketing firm, sir? I had no idea."

"You idiot," he said and shook his head. "Just follow my directions. You'll return here from the airport. I want you to send me a text message when you learn her plane has landed. I plan to be off the premises. Should she ask, you are to tell her I'm in a meeting. Questions?"

"No, sir."

"Madeline will meet the two of you when you enter the house, and she will show my sister to her room. You are to remain in the entryway. Once she has arranged her luggage in her room, here is a list of sites you can escort her to," he said and handed me a two-page list of various places in town. A number of museums, two zoos, the History Center, the Swedish Institute, the Minneapolis Art Institute, the list went on and on.

I glanced at the first page, looked at the second page, and said, "You want her to see all these places in the next two days?"

"No, you idiot. That's just so you don't run out of places to take her. If she wants to go shopping, I know you'll be only too happy to escort her."

"Shopping?"

"Just do it, Haskell, or else. Any questions?"

"I guess not, sir," I said and nodded.

"Frederick, if you would be so kind as to get Haskell out of my sight and show him to the vehicle he'll be driving for the next few days."

"It would be a pleasure, sir. Let's go, Haskell," Fat Freddy said, and I followed him out of the office. We headed down the hall, outside, and over to the parking area. The Harley Davidson with the XXX sticker that read 'Free Rides' usually parked in the area was nowhere to be seen.

Freddy led me to a dark blue Cadillac CT5. The thing was spotless with about a half dozen coats of wax. I could clearly see my reflection in the waxed body of the car.

"This is what you'll be driving, Haskell. Need I point out there is not so much as a scratch anywhere on the vehicle. Drive it as if your life depends on it because it does."

"Yeah, okay. But just so you know, Freddy, I'm going to have to park this in a ramp at the airport. There's all sorts of idiots coming and going out there. People in a hurry. Folks carrying too much luggage. Kids, teenagers, I'm not going to be able to guard this thing when I'm inside grabbing luggage. Maybe you should come with, and you could even drive. I'll ride in the back seat, and we—"

"Not on your life," Freddy said and handed me the key fob. "Climb in, get yourself oriented, and get your dumb ass out to the airport. She's landing in about forty-five minutes, and if you aren't there waiting for her, there will be hell to pay."

I folded the sheet with the flight information and the two-page list of places to take Tubby's sister. I stuffed both of them in my back pocket. I climbed into the Cadillac and looked around. Actually, it was very nice and obviously a lot more up-to-date than what I was driving. After about five minutes of pushing buttons, adjusting speakers, the temperature control, and the driver's seat, I backed out onto the circular drive. I headed down the

River Boulevard, past Phoenix Starr's house, to the entrance onto Highway 5 and the Fort Snelling bridge. From there, it was less than a five-minute drive to the airport.

    I pulled into the parking ramp, took the circular drive up to the second level, and actually found a place not that far from the entrance into the terminal. I ended up in baggage claim fifteen minutes before Quinnie's plane was scheduled to land. I checked the status of the flight on the Delta screen. It was listed as on time, which was perfect because that gave me a chance to phone Phoenix Starr.

Six

Phoenix answered after two rings, "Hello?"

"Hi Phoenix, this is Dev Haskell checking in."

"Did you get pictures of Sterling and his mystery woman?"

"Actually, no, I haven't, at least not yet. But I've been watching him. I even followed him home the last two nights. He's been at the office both nights until after 9:00, and then I followed him home and waited around, but he never left."

"Interesting," she said.

"You didn't know he was home?"

"We've got separate rooms. What you said makes me think he's probably going out for a nooner," she said.

Separate rooms? "Well, if he's going out at noon, he's not taking his car. I checked it both days, and it hadn't moved since he parked it first thing in the morning." I didn't feel it necessary to tell her I just drew a chalk line on a tire.

"So what are you saying? He's not having an affair?"

"No, what I'm saying is, I've been out in front of his office for the last two days," I said, stretching the truth. "I'm going to back off for the next couple of days. I'll still be checking on him, but I don't want to be too obvious and alert him."

"Oh, well yeah. I guess that maybe makes sense."

"Yes, it does. If he is having an affair, I'll find out."

"Mmm, I'm sure he is. I just need the proof. I could, you know, maybe come down to your office and pay you if you'd like." The way she said it seemed to suggest more than writing me a check.

"You don't have to worry about that, Phoenix. Oh, and by the way, I'll drop my rate for the next couple of days. I just don't want to alert him."

"I get that, I guess. Okay, so you'll keep me posted?"

"Yes, I've already got a tracking device on his car," I said, referring to my chalk line on his tire. "If he goes somewhere, I'll know."

"Oh, you are so good. That's a great idea, Dev."

"Thank you. I'll touch base with you later today or tomorrow. Okay?"

"Can't wait. Mmm-mmm, many thanks. Bye, bye," she said and disconnected.

I checked the Delta screen again. The flight had just landed and was five minutes early according to the scheduled time. I sent a text message to Tubby letting him know his sister's flight had arrived. After a couple of minutes, I wandered over to the screen that listed the appropriate carousel for the flight. Her luggage would be arriving at carousel six. I was standing next to carousel ten, and I headed down to six.

Passengers were beginning to arrive. I pulled out the sheet with Quinnie's flight information. Her assigned seat was 2B which was most likely located in first class. She'd probably be one of the first passengers to arrive at the carousel. I watched the people arriving and standing around waiting for luggage to be lowered onto the carousel. There wasn't a fat woman in the group. Eventually, people were removing their luggage, and I still didn't see anyone remotely resembling Tubby's sister.

There were maybe a dozen suitcases left on the carousel. A woman approached and said, "Excuse me, would you happen to be Devlin Haskell, one of my brother's employees?"

"Yes, that's me, Dev Haskell. Are you Quinnie Gustafson?" She looked to be in her early-forties, although based on the framed photo Tubby had on his desk, she had to be a little older. Either way, she was very attractive. Unlike her brother, Tubby, she was anything but fat. She had a very nice figure in a short skirt, a silk blouse, and stiletto heels with straps and a zipper back. Based on her appearance, I never would have imagined she was related to Tubby, let alone his sister. And then there was the dog.

"Yes, I'm Quinnie, and this is Muffin."

"Very nice to meet you, Quinnie. Muffin, nice to meet you, too," I said, scratching the dog behind the ears. "A labradoodle?"

"Yes, she's perfect."

"Do you have a suitcase?"

She nodded and said, "Yes, I have two bags to pick up."

"I'm sorry I didn't recognize you, but you don't fit the description I was given, and well, your brother didn't mention Muffin."

"That's because my idiot brother, Jerker, hasn't seen me for the past five years. We're not what you'd call close. I'm only here for a memorial to our parents, and some brief business. If I told him about Muffin, he would have told me not to come."

This was going to be interesting. "Excuse me, back up for a second. You referred to him as Jerker?"

"Yes, that's his given name. Why? What do you know him as?"

"Oh, well, Mr. Gustafson."

"That figures. Let me point out my luggage to you," she said and stepped closer to the carousel.

"How was your flight?" I asked as we stepped over to the almost empty carousel.

"The flight was long, the coffee was dreadful, someone's child screamed for the better part of an hour, and there was nothing of interest on any of the entertainment channels."

That pretty much summed it up, and I simply nodded.

"Oh, I believe that Gucci is mine," she said, pointing to a large beige and ebony suitcase with brown leather trim and a green and red stripe down the middle. It had a red tag hanging from the handle. I reached for the suitcase, went to lift it, and it barely moved. I quickly grabbed onto it with both hands and groaned as I pulled it from the carousel. It had to weigh close to a hundred pounds. As I set it on the floor, I noticed a couple examining the suitcase.

"That one's mine too," she said, pointing to a beige suitcase with leather belt straps, almost the last suitcase on the carousel.

Fortunately, it was smaller than the thousand-pound suitcase that damn near threw my back out, and it had wheels. I pulled it off the carousel and said, "Anything else?"

"That's all. I'll take this one," she said, extending the handle on the smaller suitcase with the wheels.

I went to pick up the larger one and quickly decided a cart would be a much better idea. "Let me just get a cart, and we can place both of these on it." I hurried away before she had a chance to reply. The cart cost me three bucks and was worth ten times that. I loaded both suitcases onto the cart.

"It should just take a couple of minutes to get to the car, or I can load the luggage and pick you two up outside. Whatever you prefer."

She frowned and shook her head. "No need to waste time. We'll follow you to the car."

We took the elevator down to the lower level and walked to the bank of elevators for the parking ramp. Luckily, I pushed the button for the proper level, and we were at the car two minutes later. I unlocked the car and loaded the luggage into the trunk. Quinnie let Muffin into the back seat, then settled into the front. She didn't say anything until we had left the airport and crossed over the river into town. I took the first exit and waited for two cars to pass before pulling onto the River Boulevard.

"You mind if I ask you a question?" I said. Tubby's mansion was maybe five miles away.

"No, I don't mind, but let me save you the time. My brother's given name is Jerker. It's Swedish. Used to be popular a hundred years ago. From what I understand, our grandfather, a rather successful bootlegger by trade, encouraged my parents to name him Jerker. He thought it would be funny. Does that answer your question?"

"Well, yeah, I guess it does. And your name, Quinnie?"

"Swedish, almost as rare nowadays as my brother's name. But there was a time. Among many meanings, the terms ill-tempered and independent stand out, and I've attempted to model myself with those two terms in mind."

I nodded and focused on the road. The gates opened as we approached, and I pulled onto the circular drive. I drove up in front of Tubby's mansion and stopped. Fat Freddy stepped out of the house, followed by a dark-haired woman I'd seen before but had never been introduced to. I guessed she must be the woman named Madeline that Tubby had mentioned.

Fat Freddy opened the passenger door and said, "Good morning, Ms. Gustafson. My name is Frederick. I hope you had a pleasant flight. Open the trunk, Devlin, and we'll get the luggage up to the guest room."

I pushed a button, and the trunk opened. A muscle-bound thug in one of the navy-blue sports shirt hurried over to the car. He lifted the luggage out of the trunk using just one hand and carried both suitcases into the house. I reminded myself not to mess with him in the future and to stay on his good side.

"Ms. Gustafson, I'd like to introduce you to Madeline, your brother's housekeeper," Fat Freddy said.

Madeline smiled and nodded at Quinnie and then shot me a look that was anything but pleasant. Yeah, maybe she was the housekeeper, but I seemed to recall her attending to Tubby's more personal needs on a regular basis.

Quinnie nodded, smiled, and then opened the rear passenger door. She took hold of Muffin's leash, and together they headed toward the front door. Fat Freddy looked at Madeline, shook his head, mouthed the 'F' word, and followed.

Once the luggage was out of the car, I pulled ahead, parked, and hurried into the mansion. Madeline, Quinnie, and Muffin were just entering the upstairs hallway and disappeared.

I took about five steps into the entryway before the guy usually reading a comic book said, "That's as far as your ass goes, Haskell. You're supposed to cool your heels right here until the guest from hell decides she wants to go somewhere."

"Happy to do so," I said. I stepped over to the antique bench against the wall and sat down.

Seven

I continued to sit on the bench in the entryway. Occasionally, I heard women's voices from up on the second floor, but they were too far away to understand. After a good half-hour, Madeline came bounding down the stairs. She was red-faced with mascara-coated tears running down her cheeks. She glanced over at me, gave me the finger, and hurried down the hallway toward the back of the house. A few minutes later, Quinnie glanced over the stair railing, glared, and then strutted down the staircase with Muffin on the leash as if she was a movie star.

She carried a black Versace handbag with a brass logo. She glanced around, then stormed over toward me. "I'm ready to go somewhere once you decide to get off your dumb ass and get something accomplished today." She was definitely Tubby's sister.

I quickly stood and said, "Just waiting for you two. Did you have any place in particular in mind?"

"I don't suppose you happen to have had a list given to you."

I reached into my back pocket and handed the folded two-page list to her.

"We'd like to be back here by 4:30, so I can get ready for dinner. Will you be joining us?"

"I don't think so. Give me a minute to get the car, and I'll pull up in front for you."

"That would be nice," she said but in a tone that suggested it was expected.

I flashed a fake smile and quickly headed out the door. "Quinnie's going to be out here in just a minute," I warned the three guys leaning against the brick wall. I hurried over to the Cadillac, climbed in, and backed up until I was parked at the front door. I set the radio on a contemporary station I thought she might like.

There were only two guys on the front stoop by the time I placed the car in park. The third one must have hurried around the side of the house. The front door opened, and Quinnie stepped out with Muffin. One of the guys on the front stoop hurried over and opened both doors.

Muffin hopped in and settled in back. Quinnie climbed in without so much as a thank you nod, promptly turned off the radio, and buckled up. As I drove around the circular drive, I glanced in the rearview mirror. The guy that had held the doors open was giving us the finger.

As we approached the wrought iron gates, she held up the two-page list of places to visit and tore it in half, then tore the two pieces in half again. She tossed the scraps of paper into the back seat. "I'd like to see the Mall of America," she said.

"The shopping center?"

"Exactly, and not to worry, I plan to visit the shops on my own. You can busy yourself drinking coffee, minding Muffin, and gawking at the women walking past."

"Actually, your brother, Mr. Gustafson, suggested it might be a good idea if we visited the Swedish Institute and the History Center."

"Of course he did, and the last time I checked, he wasn't here. So take me to the Mall of America, or I'll tell him you attempted to sexually assault me."

We headed down the River Boulevard, past Phoenix Starr's house. I turned onto the entrance to Highway 5, drove past the airport, and eventually turned onto the two-lane exit for the Mall of America. I pulled into the parking lot a few minutes later. I'd barely pulled into a parking spot when Quinnie was out of the car. She opened the rear door for Muffin and headed for the entrance. I had to run to catch up.

"I'm thinking, if it's okay, I'll just tag along and—"

"Well, I'm thinking that's not okay. You'll just be in my way and put a wet blanket on my entire afternoon. Get some coffee. Sit and stare at women who want nothing to do with you, and I'll find you when I'm ready to leave."

"What's your phone number?" I asked, pulling my phone from my pocket.

"Why do you need that?"

"In case I decide to do a little exploring, and you can't find me, you'll have my number."

She seemed to think about that for a moment and then gave me her number. I punched it in as she said the numbers, and a moment later, I heard what sounded like the theme music from the movie Jaws. She actually smiled, pulled her phone from her handbag, and canceled the call. "Lucky you, I'm adding your name to my contact list."

I held the door for her, and she stepped into the Mall. "I'll find you when I'm ready to leave," she said and handed Muffin's leash to me. I watched her strut down the corridor and take the first left. She was probably right. I'd be a real downer for any woman shopping and feeling garments, trying on clothes, and sorting through racks with no intention of ever buying anything. I was a guy. If I needed jeans or a t-shirt, I got them and left as quickly as I could. We followed the signs to Starbucks, got a medium-sized caffe latte and a cinnamon roll with plenty of icing, and settled in at a table.

I'd finished the latte and shared the cinnamon roll with Muffin over an hour ago. I was drumming my fingers on the planter behind my chair. I'd read two discarded newspapers I found on tables and deleted a bunch of obsolete text messages and worthless emails on my phone. I thought it interesting that there were four other guys at different tables, and they all looked as bored as I was. No doubt waiting for wives, daughters, or girlfriends.

It's a little more than a mile walk around the first level of the Mall. Muffin and I were just getting started when who should walk out of Victoria's Secret but Phoenix Starr.

"Phoenix?" I called.

She turned, flashed a quick smile, and then glanced around to see if anyone else noticed her. "Oh, Dev, umm, what are you doing here? And who is this?"

"Oh, this is Muffin. I'm minding her for a friend. I'm actually heading to the Apple store to pick up a computer. I just came from Sterling's office. He's been there all morning," I lied.

"Oh, well, I'd love to chat, but I'm late for, umm, a meeting, so I better run." Which was exactly what she did, literally hurrying away.

We were maybe halfway through my third lap when my phone rang. "Dev Haskell," was how I answered.

"Yes, I'm ready. Where in God's name are you two?"

I was just passing the Apple store and asked. "Where are you?"

"I'm at the Starbucks where you were going to have coffee."

"That was almost four hours ago. Stay where you are. We're on our way." We began to cut across the center of the Mall headed for Starbucks. I saw her before she saw us. She was seated at a table surrounded by a half-dozen different colored shopping bags from a variety of establishments.

"How'd the shopping go?" I said as we approached, hoping to sound interested.

"Nothing that really interested me," she said.

I decided it was best not to comment. I grabbed four of the bags. She picked up the other two, took the leash, and we headed out the door to the car. I opened the trunk using the fob and dumped the bags in. Muffin hopped in the back seat, and I held the passenger door open for Quinnie. She climbed in and yanked the door closed, almost slamming my fingers against the door frame.

The drive back to Tubby's mansion was quiet until we passed Phoenix Starr's house. I braked slightly and stared at the red sports car parked in the driveway. At first, I thought it might be a Corvette, but then I saw the name Equus on the rear and made a mental note of the number on the license plate.

"Look out. Look out. You idiot. Watch where you're going, for God's sake," Quinnie shouted.

I looked up just in time to yank the steering wheel and move back into our lane. The oncoming car leaned on the horn, and the driver gave me the finger as he passed. "What in God's name were you looking at? We almost had a head-on collision. Are you crazy?"

"Sorry about that. I was just thinking of something. There's your brother's place up ahead. The brick mansion with the brick wall and the wrought iron gates."

"I know that's Jerker's place, and not a moment too soon," she said.

I drove up the circular drive and stopped in front of the entrance to Tubby's mansion. One of the guys hurried over and opened the passenger doors. I pressed the button to open the trunk, and the same muscle-bound guy as earlier hurried over and grabbed all the shopping bags. Quinnie and Muffin headed into the mansion. I parked the car and headed toward the front door.

"Not so fast, dip shit. Let me check you out," Billy said and held out his wand.

"How come you didn't check her out?"

He stared at me for a moment, shook his head, and said, "Are you kidding?"

He waved the wand over me and told me to go in. I stepped inside, was patted down and then took up my position on the antique bench against the wall. I pulled out my phone and sent a text message with the license plate number of the Equus parked at Phoenix Starr's house to myself.

Fat Freddy waddled down the hall maybe forty-five minutes later and said, "Haskell, who let you in?"

"Who let me in? What do you mean? I just wasted the better part of a day in my life waiting for Tub…err, Mr. Gustafson's sister out at the Mall of America. Now I'm here waiting for her next command."

He started to laugh. "Oh, that's great. She didn't want to go to any of the places on the list?"

"No. As a matter of fact, she tore the list up as soon as I showed it to her. I thought she'd be interested in some of the places, but she just wanted to go shopping. God, it was dreadful. At least I had Muffin to keep me company," I said.

"Well, his highness has scheduled a family dinner tonight, just the two of them. So you're free to go. That bomb you drive is parked out in the alley. Your key is under the floor mat. We'll expect to see you back here tomorrow morning at 9:00."

"What if she sleeps in?"

"Then you can just wait. It's not like you have anything important going on. Now get out of here."

"Nice talking to you, Freddy. I can hardly wait to see you tomorrow."

"Just get the hell out of here, Haskell."

"I'm going. I'm going."

Eight

I had to walk down the circular drive, out through the gates, and then down the street to the alley. My car was parked at the far end of the alley. I was thinking I was lucky it hadn't been stolen, but then I looked up on the roof of Tubby's garage and waved at the two guys sitting on the second-story deck.

"That's my car down there. Fat Freddy told me where the key is. Thanks for keeping an eye on it."

"We were hoping someone would steal it," one of the guys said, and they both laughed.

As I drew closer, I noticed the branch from an oak tree hanging over the brick wall. Bird droppings were splattered all over the windshield and the hood. I had the feeling the parking spot beneath the branch may have been intentional. I climbed in and ran the windshield wipers and washer fluid four or five times before the windshield was halfway decent. I drove down the alley and turned toward the River Boulevard. When I passed Phoenix Starr's house, the driveway was empty. I drove along the boulevard until it turned into Shephard Road and then followed that for a couple of blocks to Davern

Street. I took Davern into the Sibley Plaza parking lot. It was almost 5:00, and the parking lot was pretty full. Sterling Kozlow's Mercedes was parked in the same place. As I drove past, I checked the chalk line in my side mirror. Kozlow's Mercedes hadn't moved since I walked past it this morning.

I debated stopping in at the office and decided against it. I headed home, pulled into my driveway, and Morton met me at the gate. I let him into the kitchen, tossed him a biscuit, and grabbed his leash. We took a nice half-hour walk and came home and had dinner. For dessert, Morton gnawed on a rawhide bone. I ate chocolate ice cream out of a half-gallon container.

I drove back down to Sibley Plaza. Sterling Kozlow's car was in exactly the same spot. The front office was dark, but there was light drifting out of Sterling's office. He headed out to his car just before 9:30. I followed him home. About a minute after he pulled into the garage, lights came on in the back of the house in what I presumed was the kitchen. The shades were drawn in a room with lights on up on the second floor. I guessed that was probably Phoenix's bedroom. I parked nearby for maybe twenty minutes and then headed home.

I turned on my laptop and Googled Equus. An image of the red sports car came up immediately. Its official name was Equus Throwback. The description referred to it as a Corvette-based supercar. The pictures, there were fifty-five of a red car exactly like the one that had been parked in Phoenix Starr's driveway, showed an absolutely gorgeous vehicle. It also happened to mention the six-figure price, which started at $130,000 and went up from there. No doubt, my personal check would be acceptable.

My first thought had been the car belonged to someone bidding on a painting job or maybe a guy cutting the grass or something. But a vehicle for that kind of dough opened up the possibility of all sorts of options. It couldn't have been parked in the driveway for more than an hour. Interesting, a lot of things could happen in an hour.

I opened the text message I sent to myself and copied down the license plate number on the Equus that was parked in Phoenix Starr's driveway. Below that, I wrote, 'Call Dennis Glazier,' my pal at the Department of Motor Vehicles. Morton and I headed up to bed just after 11:00.

Nine

I was up well before my alarm went off. I cooked up a breakfast of bacon and scrambled eggs. Morton wandered down just as I finished eating. He looked longingly at the frying pan on the stove. I let him outside, filled his food and water dishes, and he was back inside ten minutes later. I'd placed my breakfast plate next to his food dish, and he licked it clean before he started in on his bowl. I set the breakfast plate in the dishwasher and headed upstairs to dress. The memorial service for Tubby and Quinnie's parents was scheduled for today, so I put on a nice pair of gray slacks and a reasonably clean blue shirt.

Just after 8:00, I placed a call to Dennis Glazier in the Department of Motor Vehicles. I ended up leaving a message. "Hi Denny, Dev Haskell. I got a question for you. Give me a call at your convenience. Thanks."

I refilled Morton's food and water dishes and set them out on the back porch. I let him out into the backyard and then headed down to Sibley Plaza. Sterling's car was the only vehicle parked in front of the office. I could see the chalk line from the day before on the rear tire. I made a mental note of where it was positioned and drove over to Tubby's.

Rather than have my car end up in the alley, again, I parked on the side street across from the mansion and away from any trees. I walked up the circular drive toward the front door. Three guys, all wearing navy-blue sports shirts, were leaning against the front of the house.

Once I was close enough, Billy pulled out the wand and asked, "Did you hitchhike this morning?" All three of them laughed.

"Yeah, I tried, but no one stopped to give me a ride," I said.

"Who can blame them? Okay, assume the position," he said, and I stood in front of him with my arms outstretched. The wand beeped when he went over the car keys and cellphone in my pocket. I pulled them out, held them in my hands, and he repeated the procedure. "Okay, you can go on in."

"Is the memorial service still on for today?"

"Yeah. The memorial is scheduled for noon out at Resurrection Cemetery. After that, people are coming back here for some kind of luncheon."

"Great," I said. "Sounds like I might have a day off."

"I wouldn't count on it. I don't think they're talking to one another, so Evil Woman is going to need a ride out to the service."

One of the guys still leaning against the front of the house said, "They were having some kind of argument last night at dinner. Just the three of them in the dining room, sitting about fifteen feet apart at opposite ends of the table. Evil Woman was feeding her dog filet mignon from her plate. The boss wasn't too happy about that. Everyone kept their distance and let them go after one another."

"What were they arguing about?"

Everyone laughed, and then Billy said, "She called the boss names, even shouted at him. He gave as good as he got. Just for starters, he's not all that thrilled about the dog. You wouldn't have wanted to be sitting at the table. If she wasn't his sister, I think she'd be dead and floating down the river."

"Nah, he'd just bury her under his rose garden," another guy said, and they all laughed again.

"Sounds nice. Okay if I go inside?"

"Yeah, be prepared. She'll probably chew you out for not wearing a tie and shiny shoes." Everyone but me laughed as I headed into the mansion. I was patted down and then assumed my position on the bench.

My phone rang maybe twenty minutes later. The guy who patted me down shot a look at me.

"Oh, I think this is the response to Mr. Gustafson's question," I said and answered. "Dev Haskell."

"Hi, Dev. Denny Glazier, returning your call. Let me guess. You want the name and address of some woman who waved at you last night. Only that wasn't a wave. She was actually giving you the finger."

I immediately thought of Madeline giving me the finger yesterday when she ran down the stairs. "Can you check out this one for me? Minnesota plates," I said and gave him the license plate number for the red Equus Throwback that had been parked in Phoenix Starr's driveway.

"Checking it now and, oh my God. Are you kidding me?"

"What? Who is it?"

"Oh, I didn't mean who, but that's an Equus Throwback. Did you actually see this thing? And it's got Minnesota plates? It's not like there are a lot of them around. I think they run close to a hundred grand."

"Actually, Denny, I checked online last night. They start at a hundred and thirty grand."

"Oh, man. I'd love to take that for a ride."

"You got a name?"

"What? Oh, yeah, sorry about that. That has to be the only Equus in the state. Probably the only one in the five-state area."

"The name?"

"Okay, okay. It's registered to a business called Northern Star Ventures. The principal on the license is someone named Damien Dambella. You ever heard of this guy?

"No, at least it doesn't ring a bell."

"Me either. They're located downtown. You want the address?"

"Yeah, please," I said and pulled out my pocket notebook and a pen.

"Listen, you ever talk to this Damien character, I'll give you names for the next two years if he'd take me for a spin in that beauty."

"I'll be sure to ask him," I lied. "What's the address?"

"Oh, yeah. Here you go. Four hundred Robert Street North."

"Got it, and you said Northern Star Adventures?"

"No, Northern Star Ventures."

"Okay. Got it, thanks, Denny. I'll check out your ride with the guy. Talk to you later," I said and hung up. Ten minutes later, Fat Freddy waddled down the hallway. This morning he was dressed in a black tux with a dark blue cummerbund and bow tie. "You working the dining room after the memorial service, Freddy?"

"You'd better watch yourself, Haskell, if you know what's good for you."

"Sorry. You look stunning."

"Shut the hell up and follow me," he said and headed back down the hall to Tubby's office.

Tubby was seated at his desk with an open file in front of him. He was dressed in a dark suit, starched white shirt, and a tie. It was one of the few times when there wasn't some scantily clad woman giving him a massage. He looked up from the file, studied me, and shook his head. "Unfortunately, it's too late in the day to send you home to get properly attired. Your task this morning is to drive Quinnie out to the memorial service.

It will be held at Resurrection Cemetery. We will be motoring out there in a procession with a police escort. You will be behind my vehicle. Upon penalty of death, you are not to deviate from the procession. If she attempts to give you instructions, you are to ignore her. Do I make myself clear?"

"Yes, sir."

"I hope so, for your sake, Haskell. You will drive her to the graveside and, following the brief ceremony, you will drive her back here for the luncheon. You will be following my vehicle back here. I think it best that you remain outside until the luncheon is finished, at which point you may take her on another sightseeing trip. Any questions? Good. That is all. Frederick, if you would, please."

"Let's go, Haskell," Fat Freddy said.

There was no point in arguing. Hopefully, Quinnie would want to remain up in her room after the luncheon, and I wouldn't have to deal with her. I followed Fat Freddy back down the hall and out the door.

Fat Freddy escorted me to the Mercedes and handed me the fob. "You can cool your heels next to the car, Haskell. We'll be leaving later this morning. You are not to get into the vehicle until it's time to drive to the cemetery. Do you think you can follow those directions?"

"I'm not sure, but I'll try my best."

Fat Freddy just shook his head and waddled back into the mansion.

Ten

Happy Hoffman stepped out of the mansion an hour later and walked over to the Mercedes. I'd been leaning against the rear of the car since Fat Freddy handed me the key. "Hey, Haskell, it's time to line up for the procession out to the cemetery. I'm going to pull in front of the mansion. You're supposed to be right behind me."

"Yeah, I got my instructions from Tubby and Fat Freddy. I'll be driving his sister."

"Good luck with that," he said and headed for the Cadillac Escalade. He backed out of the parking place then circled around the drive and pulled to a stop in front of the mansion.

I did the same thing and pulled in behind him. We waited a good fifteen minutes before Quinnie, Muffin, and Tubby stepped out of the house. Quinnie was carrying a large bouquet of white roses. Red-faced Tubby glared and remained a good ten feet behind his sister and Muffin. He nodded at one of the security guys who hurried past Quinnie and opened the rear passenger door.

She let Muffin into the back seat and said something I couldn't understand. The guy closed the door and pulled the front door open. She climbed in without thanking him or bothering to give me a greeting, buckled up, placed the bouquet on her lap, and stared straight ahead. I could feel the tension in the front seat.

Once Tubby and Fat Freddy climbed into the Escalade, Happy headed down the drive toward the front gates, and we followed. He stopped for a moment at the gate. A police car with lights flashing pulled in front of the Escalade and led the way down the River Boulevard.

"Be sure to keep your eyes on the road this morning," Quinnie growled.

"Yes, ma'am," I replied and nodded. As we came up to Phoenix Starr's house, I spotted the red Equus parked in the driveway again. I kept my eye on the road and wondered if Damien Dambella was the guy driving it. I was aware Quinnie had glanced over, but she didn't say anything.

With the police car leading, it wasn't even a fifteen-minute drive out to Resurrection Cemetery in Mendota Heights. There were a number of cars in the parking area just inside the entrance. As we made our way toward the far corner of the cemetery, the cars pulled out of the parking area and followed.

The squad car stopped at the top of a little hill. Just off to the left was a granite monument about ten feet tall featuring two carved angels holding a banner. The banner had the name Gustafson carved in large capital letters. There was nothing subtle about it.

I watched as one of Tubby's thugs hurried past our car and opened the car doors on the Escalade for Tubby and Fat Freddy. No one came to open the door for Quinnie.

She waited a very long minute, appearing to get madder with every second. Finally, she took hold of the door handle and said, "Oh, God, I can't believe he'd do this, but actually, I'm not surprised."

"Wait a minute. I got this," I said. Before she could say anything, I hurried around to the passenger side and opened the door for her. Quinnie stepped out with the bouquet, actually smiled, and whispered, "Thank you."

I closed the door, then opened the rear door and grabbed Muffin's leash. "You want to carry those roses, or should I?"

"I'll take them and thank you. That's very nice of you."

I extended my arm, and she gave me a look. "Come on, do it," I said. She wrapped her arm around mine. I tugged on Muffin's leash, and we followed Tubby and company up the little hill to the monument. There were three rows of chairs arranged on the far side of the monument. Tubby took a seat in a corner chair and stared straight ahead.

As we walked past Tubby, Quinnie glanced over and smiled at him. She settled into the chair at the opposite end of the row. Muffin and I stood off to the side. Names were attached to the back of the chairs, and once Tubby and Quinnie were seated, the chosen people headed for their assigned seats. The backside of the monument featured the granite carving of a large, open book, no doubt supposed to represent the Bible.

I recognized a number of people, but I didn't actually know any of them. They made up the city's privileged class. Lawyers, politicians, and business bigwigs. They were probably all criminals of a sort. They just were a lot more subtle about it than Tubby. I was pretty sure none of these folks had ever spent time in The Spot bar.

Once everyone was seated, a minister in black and wearing a clerical collar stood and turned to face the group. He thanked everyone for coming and then gave an eight-minute monologue on all the wonderful things the Gustafson family had done for the city over the last hundred and twenty years. He failed to mention the murders, schemes, gambling, bootlegging, and other assorted endeavors.

When he was finished, Quinnie stood, walked to the monument, and placed the bouquet of flowers on top of the granite carving of the open Bible. One had to wonder, with the Gustafson family in mind, exactly what page the Bible would be open to. Perhaps the book wasn't the Bible but a crime novel instead. Who knew?

The minister thanked Quinnie and then led everyone in prayer, although only a couple of people seemed to know it. He finished, made the sign of the cross, and that was it. He walked over to Tubby, shook hands, and hurried to his car. Apparently, he couldn't get away fast enough. People were mingling, shaking hands with Tubby, and chatting. Quinnie got a couple of polite nods, but no one came over to chat.

"I'm ready to get the hell out of here," Quinnie said.

"I've been instructed to follow your brother's vehicle back to the mansion, and even if you want to go, our car is blocked in, so we can't leave. How about you and I talk, and you won't have to stand here looking like you don't know anyone?"

She gave a little laugh and said, "Actually, I really don't know anyone. I might recognize a name, but I left this town when I was eighteen and never looked back."

"Yeah, I get it. I always tell people St. Paul is the world's biggest small town. Everybody knows everyone. A lot of folks end up living a block away from where they grew up. We know three generations of every family. At least that's the way it's been. Unfortunately, things seem to be changing. We've got happy thoughts people on our city council. A mayor with the best of intentions, but they're all in over their heads. The city would rather put in more bike lanes than hire enough cops to fight crime."

"Well, what do you know? You really do have a mind of your own," Quinnie said.

"What?"

"Oh, I've heard some stories. Tell you what. Let's go arm in arm. You bring Muffin, and we'll introduce ourselves to all these high rollers."

"You serious?"

"Oh yes," she said, then linked arms with me, and we headed into the crowd. We introduced ourselves to a couple of city council members, lawyers, and businesspeople. Everyone was pleasant and just a bit standoffish in that St. Paul way. Eventually, the crowd began to thin. Tubby and Fat Freddy headed toward the Escalade. Happy Hoffman gave me a nod, and we finished our conversation with a state senator, whose name I'd already forgotten, and headed to our car. I let Muffin in the backseat and held the door for Quinnie. As she slid in, she said, "Thank you."

Eleven

The police car turned on its flashing lights and led the way back to Tubby's place. This time, a line of fifteen or twenty cars followed. Quinnie seemed a bit more relaxed, and she actually asked a couple of questions. "So, you said you were born and raised here. Where'd you grow up?" She sounded genuinely curious.

"The Ramsey Hill area. My folks bought a house for ten grand back in the 70s. I guess it was four or five apartments at the time. Over the next thirty years, they restored one room at a time, and when they were finished, it was time to start over again. There was always a project going on, but I've got fond memories of the place. I just live a couple of blocks from there now. You live in Los Angeles?"

Quinnie nodded. "Yeah, I went out to Hollywood to seek my fame and fortune. That didn't exactly work, but fortunately, my parents had set up a trust fund. Probably the only sensible thing the old man ever did."

"I take it you don't see your brother very often."

She looked over at me and then shook her head. "No, we weren't that close as kids, and the years have done nothing to change that. I guess you could say we aren't especially fond of one another. From the little I know, I'm not impressed by the fact he stuck with the family business. It ruined my parents' lives, so you'd think he'd do something different. It's one of the many reasons I left. By the same token, he considers me worthless and never misses the opportunity to tell me so. That makes our infrequent meetings more of a mutual agreement."

"I'm sorry to hear that."

We rounded the curve along the River Boulevard and passed Phoenix Starr's house. The driveway was empty. A minute or two later, we pulled onto Tubby's circular drive. The Escalade stopped, and two guys opened the doors for Tubby and Fat Freddy. Once they were out, Happy pulled ahead, and I moved forward so Quinnie and Muffin could get out. One of the guys opened Quinnie's door, and she climbed out. She turned, leaned in, and said, "Thanks for your help today, Haskell."

"My pleasure," I said. Of course, the thug had already slammed the door closed, so I don't think she ever heard me. She took Muffin from the back seat. I pulled ahead and parked next to the Escalade.

"You're supposed to stay out here in case the Evil Woman and the bow-wow want to grab an earlier flight," Happy said.

"Actually, given a chance, she can be kind of nice."

"Yeah, right." He chuckled and headed into the mansion.

The line of cars pulled up one by one. The doors were opened by one of Tubby's smiling thugs. Everyone walked into the mansion. Four thugs acted as valets parking the cars outside the grounds on the side street. I wondered if one of the cars would end up in the alley where my car had been parked yesterday.

I stood around for the next two hours. I rolled the sleeves up on my shirt and caught a little sun for thirty minutes. Eventually, people began to walk out the front door. They'd hand a tag to the valets, and a minute or two later, their car would appear on the circular drive. Always polite, the valets held the door open for the women. I was pretty sure every car had probably been searched for any valuables.

There were still a few guests inside when Quinnie stepped out the front door and headed toward me. "I didn't realize you were still here. I'm going to be a while reviewing some family business with my brother and an attorney. I'm not looking forward to it. Once we're finished, I'm planning on locking myself in the guest room, climbing into a hot bath with a bottle of wine, and then watching TV. If you want to leave, be my guest."

"Are you sure that's okay with Tub…umm, your brother?"

"He doesn't tell me what to do. Well, let me rephrase that. I don't have to listen to what he tells me to do. Maybe swing by around 11:00 tomorrow morning. I'd like to buy you lunch."

"Buy me lunch?"

"Relax, nothing beyond that, and I promise we won't go out to the Mall of America. Besides, I've got an early evening flight. In fact, you pick the place—something low-key. I don't want to have to dress up tomorrow. Oh, and Muffin will be joining us."

"You really don't have to do this, Quinnie."

"Yeah, I do. I've been bitchy ever since I got the word I had to come here. You've been the only nice person I've met. Go on, get out of here, and I'll see you tomorrow."

"Okay, see you at 11:00, and thanks, very much appreciated."

I watched as she walked back into the mansion. I headed over to Happy, who seemed to be in charge of the valets. "Hey, I've just been given the word to leave. Here's the key to the Mercedes," I said and handed the fob to Happy.

"That's okay with the boss and Freddy?"

"She said it was," I lied. "They're going to be working with a lawyer for the rest of the afternoon. I'll be back here tomorrow."

"See you then," Happy said.

Twelve

I walked down the drive and over to my car. I made a U-turn and pulled onto the River Boulevard. Nothing was shaking at Phoenix Starr's house, and I headed to Sibley Plaza. I drove past Kozlow's office. Based on the position of my chalk mark on Sterling's tire, he hadn't driven anywhere. I thought about hanging around and decided it might be a better idea to head to the office.

I parked across the street from my building. Louie's Ford Fiesta wasn't around so I figured he was either in court or interviewing a potential client in the drunk tank. I crossed the street and headed up the stairs. My cellphone started ringing, and I quickly unlocked the office door before I answered. I didn't look at the screen to see who was calling.

"Haskell Investigations," was how I answered.

"Is this Dev Haskell?"

I glanced at the screen and said, "Hi Phoenix, how are you doing?"

"Mmm-mmm, okay, I guess. I just wanted to see if you were in your office. I'm not too far from there and wanted to get you paid for your work so far."

"Actually, I just came from Sterling's office. He hasn't left it since he arrived early this morning."

"And you were there this entire time?"

"Back and forth. I don't want to have him recognize me or my car. I can tell you that just like all the other days, his car hasn't moved an inch."

"Well, I guess that's something. You going to be there for a bit?"

"In the office? Yeah, for a while, at least another hour or so, then I want to get back and keep an eye on Sterling," I lied.

"I can be over there in fifteen minutes."

"Oh, you don't have to do that, Phoenix. Maybe wait until—"

"No, I want to see you," she said and disconnected.

I'd been checking out the apartment building across the street with my binoculars. It wasn't even ten minutes when the blue BMW convertible suddenly pulled to a stop behind my car. I quickly returned the binoculars to the desk drawer then watched as Phoenix applied some lipstick and adjusted her hair in the rearview mirror. She placed the lipstick in her purse, loosened two buttons on her blouse, and stepped out of her car. Her shorts were white, tight, and appeared to be see-through. Even looking down from the second story as she crossed the street, absolutely nothing was left to the imagination. A moment later, I heard the staircase creak ever so slightly. The office door opened, and Phoenix stepped in. I was speechless and stared.

"Mmm, I'll take that look as a compliment. Like what you see?" she said and struck a pose.

"Yeah, I mean, yes, you look lovely. Umm, could I get you some coffee?" I asked, too busy staring at the shorts to know if there even was some.

"Actually, no, it's a little late in the day for coffee. I'd take a glass of wine if you wanted to offer one."

"I'd love to, but we don't have any."

"I might consider stopping in more often if you had some," she said as she took a seat in one of my client chairs.

"I'll keep that in mind."

She bent over and lingered for a long moment, giving me a full view of her ample cleavage in the process. Eventually, she pulled the purse onto her lap. "I wanted to get you paid," she said, bringing me back to reality.

"Oh, don't worry, Phoenix. You don't have to write a check."

"I wasn't planning to," she said as she pulled an envelope from her purse. "Here, hopefully, this will cover you for the first few days. You didn't mention anything about expenses, so I paid you the daily rate plus a little more. I want to make sure you're taken care of," she explained and raised her eyebrows. She reached across the desk and held out the envelope. I reached up to take it, but she hung on and smiled when I pulled on the envelope. "Mmm, sexy," she said, eventually letting go.

I opened the envelope and counted ten crisp, hundred dollar bills. "This is very kind of you, Phoenix. I wish I had more information other than nothing has happened thus far. I'm sorry, I didn't mean that to sound the way it did. I'd like nothing better than to tell you your husband isn't having an affair and that he's just working late."

"There are a lot of things you could tell me that I'd enjoy. I'm not sure Sterling working late is one of them." I must have given her a look because she suddenly said, "Oh, don't take that the wrong way, Dev. It's just that you seem like a really nice guy, and well, I haven't had much of a relationship with my husband for quite some time."

"Maybe, if the only thing I find out is he's been working late, things will get back on track for you two."

"Don't hold your breath," she said and stood. "Anyway, I just wanted to say thanks. I'm glad I met you and glad you're helping me out. It means a lot to me," she said as she leaned forward and gave me a lingering kiss on top of my forehead. My nose was about an inch from her deep cleavage. I couldn't see anything that suggested a bra was in the neighborhood. "Let's stay in touch," she said and sauntered toward the door. I stared at the see-through shorts as she closed the door behind her.

I quickly turned, grabbed the binoculars, and watched out the window as she strutted across the street and climbed into the BMW. She waited for two boys, about twelve, to ride past on their bikes. They both turned to stare at her, seated in the BMW. Once they passed, she waited a moment, accelerated, and disappeared up the street.

Thirteen

Louie pulled in behind my car fifteen minutes later. I was still sitting at my desk staring at the envelope filled with hundred-dollar bills and recalling the shorts Phoenix had been wearing. Louie stumbled into the office. He settled in behind his picnic table desk, breathing heavily, as if he'd just set a personal best after running a mile. It took a couple of minutes before he dialed down and asked, "You seem focused on something. Everything okay?"

"What? Oh, yeah, sorry. Just had a client drop off a payment, and it really caught me by surprise."

Louie sort of wiggled his nose and said, "It wouldn't happen to have been that blonde woman I watched crossing the street the other day, would it?"

"Yeah, as a matter of fact, it was. God bless her. She paid me a thousand bucks in cash."

"That would explain the lipstick on your forehead. A thousand bucks? In cash? You'd better hang on to her."

"You should have seen the way she was dressed. Blouse unbuttoned, tight white see-through shorts."

"Sounds like you should be paying her."

"Not far from the truth. Let me ask you something. You ever hear of a company called Northern Star Ventures?"

Louie seemed to think for a moment and shook his head. "No, not ringing a bell. What is it, some travel company? Getaways up to the wilderness or something?"

"I'm not sure what it is. How about a guy named Damien Dambella?"

"That might be ringing a distant bell, but I can't tell you why. Who is he?"

"I'm not sure, except that he owns a car worth at least a hundred and thirty grand. It's called an Equus Throwback."

"Now that's something I'm sure I've never heard of, Equus Throw up?"

"No, Louie, Equus Throwback. Apparently, they're modeled after classic Corvette's or something."

"Might be better if we discussed this over at The Spot," Louie said.

"I can do one, and then I have to get Morton. He's been on his own all day."

Louie's idea to go over to The Spot was a good one. Between the Gustafson memorial service and Phoenix Starr's cash payment, it had been a pretty crazy day. The first beer tasted so good I had a second. Louie told me the little he knew about Damien Dambella.

"I can't recall specifics, but I think he was involved in some internet investor scam maybe ten or twelve years ago. Everyone ended up losing big time. Well, everyone but Dambella. I think investors were given promissory notes on loans that were tied to property or something. The things were marketed as low-risk, and it turned out they were anything but. I know the feds were involved, and a couple of higher echelon folks went to jail. Dambella somehow dodged the bullet as far as I recall."

"Is he back in that biz?"

"Not that I'm aware of, but then I'd be the last guy to know. What'd you say his company was called?"

"Northern Star Ventures."

"That wasn't the company involved in the scam ten years ago. Now I'm wondering if he was even the head guy. Might be he was just an understudy."

"Well, except that he's riding around town in a car worth over a hundred grand."

"Yeah, maybe. But he could be living in a one-room efficiency so he can make the payments on the car. Check him out, and don't take my word as gospel. He could be delivering pizzas for all I know. What's up with the blonde woman?"

"Phoenix? God bless her. She paid me in cash."

"Yeah, I know that, but you said she was barely dressed."

"I think I said she was wearing white shorts and a blue blouse."

"Tight, see-through white shorts."

"It's nothing. She's an attractive woman who happens to be a new client. She's afraid her husband might be having an affair. I've been checking the guy out, and so far, there's no indication he's doing anything other than working fourteen to sixteen hours a day."

"Self-employed?"

"Yeah, runs an accounting firm. He has a couple of employees. I've never spoken to him."

"You ready for another, Dev?" Mike, the bartender, asked.

"Thanks, Mike, but two is my limit tonight. Louie, you up for another?"

"Since you're buying, why not?"

I pulled the envelope from my back pocket, took out a hundred-dollar bill, and gave it to Mike.

"Where'd you find this?" he said and held it up to the light to make sure it wasn't counterfeit, then headed for the cash register. Once he poured two beers for a couple at the far end of the bar, he was back with Louie's drink and my change. I left a tip and headed home to Morton.

He met me at the back gate, standing on his hind legs with his tail wagging. Poor guy had been on his own all day. We headed inside, and I tossed him a biscuit, gave him a good scratch behind the ears, and we went out to the car.

I stopped and got some take-out tacos along the way, and we pulled into the Sibley Plaza Parking lot. Kozlow's car hadn't moved since the last time I saw it. I parked a couple of spaces behind it and opened up the bag with the tacos. Morton's head was suddenly hanging over my shoulder. I pulled off a piece of taco and gave it to Morton. I took a bite and had to give Morton another piece. It went like that through all three tacos.

"Sorry, pal, that's all there is. If I'd known you like tacos, I would have ordered four."

Kozlow left his office at 9:20. I'll say we followed him home, which we did, although Morton was asleep in the back seat. The taco seemed to have an effect on him, and I drove with the windows down to air out the car. I parked within sight of Phoenix Starr's house for forty minutes, but Sterling Kozlow never left. When I saw the second-floor light come on at the opposite end of the house from what I presumed was Phoenix's bedroom, I headed home. Morton took a ten-minute break in the backyard, and we headed up to bed. Thankfully, he'd apparently gotten all the gas out of his system. I slept soundly and woke up a half-hour before my alarm went off.

Fourteen

I'd finished breakfast and was on my laptop when Morton appeared in the kitchen. I gave him a scratch behind the ears and let him out into the backyard. When he'd finished eating, we drove over to Sibley Plaza. We walked past Kozlow's Mercedes, left a fresh chalk mark on his rear tire, and then drove to the office.

I poured the coffee pot remnants down the drain and made a fresh pot. Louie arrived just as the coffee was ready. Once he was able to talk after climbing the stairs, he asked, "Have you finished up babysitting Gustafson's sister?"

"Not quite. We're actually going to lunch today. It's her idea, and I get to pick the place."

"That almost sounds nice."

"Yeah, she loosened up yesterday after the memorial service. I think she was maybe stressed out over the deal, and, well, she and Tubby don't seem to get along at all. You can imagine how that goes with her staying in his place. I guess he's not all that happy that she brought her dog."

"Maybe she did that just to piss off her brother."

"That might not be far from the truth. She told me she rarely comes back here, which based on the interaction with her brother, I can understand. Both parties are guilty."

"What does she do? You said she lives in L.A."

"According to her, she's on a trust fund her father set up, so apparently, she can do whatever she wants. If she has a job, she's never mentioned it. Might be part of what pisses Tubby off."

"Families, you gotta love it," Louie said and took a sip of his coffee.

I spent the next hour looking for anything online regarding Damien Dambella. Other than the occasional mention as someone in a photo at a golf club or attending some high society soirée, there wasn't much. Still, he seemed to be rubbing shoulders with the privileged class and the bigwigs. In two of the online images, Phoenix Starr and Sterling Kozlow appeared in the same six-person group.

One photo was taken at a political fund-raiser, and the other was a fund-raiser for the public library. The photos appeared to have been taken recently. Even in the upper echelons of the city's residents, it was still, at the end of the day, a small town.

"You going to be around this afternoon?" I asked Louie.

"Don't worry about it. Enjoy your lunch with Tubby's sister. It might be an opportunity to get some inside information."

"This isn't that kind of lunch. We're just going to talk about everything and nothing. It was nice to see her begin to relax once that memorial service was over. She can actually be a pretty nice person."

"I like your story about the minister going on about all the good things the Gustafson's have done for the town. Just incredible, another guy who promotes good deeds and willingly accepts contributions from bad apples. You think he might have suggested Tubby should occasionally turn the other cheek."

"I think he just smiled and held out his hand for the check. Thanks in advance for watching Morton. I'll try to get back as soon as possible."

"Take your time and enjoy the lunch. If we're not here when you get back, you know where we'll be."

"Thanks again," I said and stepped over to Morton. I bent down, gave him a good rub behind the ears, and headed out the door. I drove through the Sibley Plaza parking lot on my way to Tubby's mansion. Kozlow's car was exactly where it had been earlier in the morning. I drove over to Tubby's and pulled up to the front door. The guys lingering around the large front stoop appeared to have a much more relaxed attitude than I'd seen in recent days.

Billy approached as I climbed out of the car. "Haskell. Are you driving the Mercedes today? It's parked in back. No one told us you were coming."

"Relax, Billy, I'm going to lunch with the sister. We'll take my car."

"You are a glutton for punishment. Still going to have to check you out. Assume the position, Haskell."

I spread my legs and held my arms out. Billy ran the wand over me. When he reached my front pocket on the left side, the wand beeped.

"Wallet," I said. He went over the pocket on the left side, and the wand beeped again. "Cell phone and car keys."

"You dumb shit. Why didn't you take them out of your pocket?"

"What are you bitching at me for? I'm trying to make sure that wand works. Trying to keep you on Tubby's good side, and here you are giving me a hard time."

Billy looked like he was about to say something when the front door opened and Quinnie stepped onto the stoop with Muffin. "All ready to go?" she asked just as Billy was about to read me the riot act. She was wearing blue jeans and a faded blue t-shirt that said 'Los Angeles' in letters that used to be white.

"Yes, I am. We'll take my car if that's all right with you."

"Oh, what an experience that will be. Let's go."

I smiled at Billy and said, "See you later." I stepped over to the car, opened the rear door for Muffin and the front door for Quinnie. She got halfway onto the seat, handed me the empty taco bag from last night, then settled in and buckled up.

I thought about giving Billy the bag but decided that might not be the best idea. I folded the bag in half twice and placed it in my back pocket as I made my way to the driver's side. I glanced over at Billy shaking his head.

"So, you survived yesterday?" I asked Quinnie as we headed down the circular drive and out of the mansion grounds.

"Nothing a hot bath, the better part of a bottle of wine, and a movie of no redeeming value couldn't fix. I slept until after 9:00 this morning when Muffin finally woke me."

"Then you must have really needed it. Now, I know you said I'd choose where we go for lunch, but is there anywhere you'd like to go?"

"No, I'm fine with wherever you decide. Like I said, nothing too fancy."

"Okay. I'm thinking of a place called Shamrock's. It's a popular burger joint on this end of town. Usually a live local band on the weekend. St. Patrick's Day is a big deal for them, but then it is for just about every bar in town."

"That sounds just fine. I plan on breaking all my dietary rules today. I might even order a dessert."

"It's just down on West Seventh street. We'll be there in ten minutes."

"Good, I'll just stare out the window and see if I can recognize anything while you drive."

Quinnie made some general comments along the way. Mostly wondering what had happened to businesses that used to occupy certain buildings or the two restaurants now occupying what used to be fire stations in a different time. I parked in the small parking lot behind Shamrock's. The place was very popular on this end of town, and from its original site, it had expanded into three adjacent units over the last thirty years, not to mention opening a fast-food takeout across the street.

We walked in the side door with Muffin. Quinnie looked around and said, "Oh, this is just perfect. Exactly what I needed after yesterday."

We grabbed a high table opposite the bar. Muffin settled in on the floor next to Quinnie. A moment later, a server set menus down in front of us and said, "Can I get you something from the bar?"

"I'll have a glass of your Sauvignon Blanc," Quinnie said.

"Sir?"

"I think a Summit IPA," I said. As I watched the server disappear, I found it interesting that Quinnie didn't ask what the label was on the wine.

"So, my brother told me you're actually a private investigator."

"Yeah, which makes me one of the more boring guys in town."

"I don't know about that. If that's what you do, how come you work for my brother? I would think you're the last kind of person he'd want nosing around."

"I've wondered the same thing from time to time. I'd say the information we impart to one another, knowingly or unknowingly, serves to benefit both of us. That said, a lot of what I do is work for insurance companies, things like that. I'm working a case right now where a woman thinks her husband may be having an affair."

"Does that mean you're staked out in hotels?"

"Actually, just the opposite. Up until now, all I can report is that he works twelve to fourteen hour days and then goes home."

"Interesting. Well, if you ever want someone to keep you company let me know. The less time I spend at my brother's, the happier I'll be."

"I thought you were going back to Los Angeles later today."

"That was my original plan, but some legal issues came up this morning, and I want to stay until they're addressed. Basically, my way of adding pressure."

The server returned with our drinks, set them on the table, and placed a dog biscuit next to Quinnie. "Oh, thank you, how nice," Quinnie said.

"Would you like to order?"

"Maybe give us a minute to check the menu," I said. "I know what I'm going to have, so go ahead and take a look."

"What are you getting?"

"I always get the bourbon bacon chicken sandwich. I love the thing and have no interest in looking at anything else on the menu."

"All right, that's what I'm getting, too."

"They've got great burgers if you're—"

"No, your choice sounds delicious."

I waved the waitress over. We placed our order and added another round of drinks. We chatted for maybe ten minutes before the food and drinks arrived. Quinnie studied the bourbon bacon chicken sandwich for a moment, then cut it in half and took a bite.

"Mmm-mmm, delicious. Great choice," she said, then bent down and gave the dog biscuit to Muffin.

Fifteen

We ate and talked. Quinnie ordered another glass of wine, and I begged off on another beer, saying I had to drive. She took a sip of her fresh wine and asked, "Has my brother ever been arrested?"

I thought for a moment before I said, "On one or two rare occasions, he's been asked to answer questions. To my knowledge, both of those instances occurred in his office. He was never arrested, and in both instances, I believe he added to the investigation."

"I know he's never done jail time. I believe he's been sued a couple of times."

"Correct on both counts," I said. "The lawsuits I'm aware of were more the everyday relationship, or maybe disagreement is a better term, between a tenant and the landlord. I believe, in all three incidents, your brother won, and the other party had to pay court costs."

"It seems like the city is missing a big part of how my brother makes his money."

"That's probably true. Either they're missing it, or they don't want to poke the lion."

She looked at me, took a sip, and nodded. We left a few minutes later. I tried to pay the bill, but she insisted. Once we were back in the car, she said, "Thank you, Dev. That was a great place. I loved the food, and it reminded me of some of the places I went to years ago. You go there often?"

"Oh, from time to time. Usually, I'm a regular for a beer or two across the street from my office. A nice neighborhood place and no food menu. I think they'll do up a frozen pizza on occasion, but that's about it."

"What's the name of the place?"

"It's called The Spot."

"I think I may have heard it mentioned by someone on Jerker's staff."

"Really? I know they're aware I go there, but I've never seen any of them in there. Well, Freddy Zimmerman, but that's only been once or twice."

"You call him Fat Freddy, don't you?"

"Not to his face, but yeah. He and I had a bit of a disagreement some years back. This was before he started working for your brother. I don't think he's ever forgiven me."

"He's a different type of character," she said. "You know, would it be too much to ask if we stopped at The Spot? I'd love to see the place."

"Really? Yeah, sure. I guess we could. I'm not kidding. It's not a fancy club or anything. It's just a great little neighborhood place. People are nice. A lot of folks just stopping in for one on their way out or on their way home."

"It sounds wonderful."

"Yeah, okay. It's just a couple of minutes from here," I said. We circled the block and headed back in the opposite direction. I drove past The Spot and parked behind Louie's car. I hurried around the car, but Quinnie had already let herself out.

"Do you want me to leave Muffin in the car?"

"No, not at all. Bring her along." I glanced up at my office window and then headed to The Spot. It was just after 3:00. Mike was behind the bar. There were four other people in the place, all seated in the same booth playing a card game.

"Hi, Dev," Mike called as I walked in. He studied Quinnie and Muffin for a moment and said, "Has this man been bothering you, ma'am?"

"Yes, he has, but I'm used to it by now, so it's okay."

"Fair enough. Can I get you something?" Mike asked.

"I'd better just have a coffee," I said.

"Sauvignon Blanc?" Quinnie asked.

"Coming right up."

We headed to the far end of the bar and sat where I usually ended up. I settled onto Louie's stool. Mike brought the coffee and wine, and we chatted for a good half hour. Quinnie asked a lot of general questions about what had happened in the city over the last twenty-five years. She never mentioned her brother and I didn't bring him up. Muffin had been patient for most of the time but seemed to have grown anxious in the last five minutes.

"Think she needs to go outside?" I asked.

"Probably. Is there a park nearby?"

"Tell you what. Why don't you sit here, and I'll take her around the block?"

"Are you sure?'

"I do it a couple of times a day with my dog, Morton."

"You have a dog?"

"Oh yeah. A Golden Retriever. As a matter of fact, he's just across the street in my office."

"Oh, he's been there all alone? Why didn't you say something?"

"He's not alone. My officemate Louie is up there. They're probably both napping. Tell you what, would you mind if I called Louie and he brought Morton over? He's in here just about every day. I mean, Morton is, well, Louie is too, come to think of it."

"You sure it will be alright?" she said and glanced down the bar at Mike.

"Yeah, not a problem. Like I said, it's a neighborhood place."

"Okay, give him a call."

"I'll call Louie while we go around the block," I said. I slid off the stool, grabbed the leash, and we headed out the side door. Muffin squatted next to the first tree we passed and did her business.

I phoned Louie once we turned the final corner, and The Spot appeared at the end of the block. "Everything okay?" was how he answered my call.

"Yeah, going fine. Hey, I'm with Tubby's sister Quinnie and her dog, Muffin. We're over at The Spot and wondered if you'd like to bring Morton over and join us."

"On my way," Louie said and disconnected.

We hadn't made it back inside The Spot before Louie and Morton literally ran across the street. We met at the front door. "Perfect timing," I said as Morton and Muffin examined each other. I held the door open for Louie and Morton. "We're at the far end of the bar in our usual place. The blonde woman is Quinnie."

"Nice looking. Never would have pegged her for Gustafson's sister," Louie said and let Muffin and me lead the way. Muffin heeled perfectly as we headed along the bar to where Quinnie was seated. Morton, on the other hand, was straining on his leash, no doubt in anticipation of pork rinds waiting for him. He rounded the corner and appeared momentarily confused when he saw Louie's empty stool.

Louie settled onto his stool and handed me Morton's leash. I handed Muffin's leash to Quinnie.

Quinnie took the leash and said, "Sit," to Muffin, who then dutifully obeyed.

True to form, Morton gave Louie a mournful look.

"Quinnie, this is my officemate, Louie Laufen, attorney at law. Louie, this is Quinnie Gustafson, and Muffin, who apparently is much better trained than Morton."

"Nice to meet you, Quinnie, and you too, Muffin."

"Pleasure to meet you, Louie. I'm hoping you'll be able to set me straight on all the things Dev has been telling me."

"I'm not sure we have that kind of time," Louie said

Mike came over and said, "The usual, Louie?"

"Yeah, please, Mike, and you'd better give me two bags of pork rinds."

"Anything for you two?" Mike asked as he glanced at Quinnie.

"No, thanks, I'm fine," Quinnie said.

Mike pulled two bags of pork rinds from the rack, set them in front of Louie, and headed down the bar. At the sight of the bags, Morton's tail began slapping against the side of the bar.

"These are salted pork rinds," Louie said. "I usually give Morton a handful or two. Would you mind if I gave some to Muffin as well?"

"Not at all, in fact, I'm sure she'd love it."

Mike returned, set Louie's drink in front of him, then hurried down the bar as a couple strolled in. Louie opened a bag of pork rinds and gave a handful to Morton and a handful to Muffin. When he reached down to Muffin, she looked up at Quinnie.

"Go, Muffin," Quinnie said, and she devoured the pork rinds just as quickly as Morton had.

Once it was clear there were no more pork rinds, Muffin and Morton introduced themselves to one another. They ended up with their noses inserted in each other's rear ends. Morton's tail was wagging so hard it kept knocking Muffin to the side.

We chatted for a good hour. Louie served up the second bag of pork rinds and then had to get back to work. Quinnie and I chatted for a few more minutes before we headed out to the car.

"Oh, this has been a wonderful afternoon and exactly what Muffin and I needed. I take her to the dog park at home every afternoon, and she's been isolated since we arrived here, so this was really special."

"You have dinner plans?" I asked.

"No, nothing. I have the sense Jerker has had just about all he can stand of me."

"You're welcome to join us for dinner. I've got a fenced in backyard. They can chase each other around."

"That sounds wonderful. Are you sure we won't be imposing?"

"Absolutely not, come on."

Sixteen

We settled Morton and Muffin into the back seat, and I drove up two blocks to Rooster's. Quinnie gave me a look as I pulled to the curb.

"Just a little treat from this end of town. If you'll keep an eye on our two friends, I'll be back in five minutes."

"At least let me pay for this," Quinnie said.

"Not on your life. Back in five." I hurried out of the car. It was just early enough that there was only one person ahead of me. I ordered two BBQ pork sandwiches with fries and two pork shoulder bones. I was back out in just under five minutes. I climbed in behind the wheel and handed the bag to Quinnie. Morton immediately thrust his head into the front.

"Back off, Morton. You'll get yours once we're home. I'm sorry, Quinnie. I should have asked if you like BBQ."

"You kidding? I love it. We've got some great places in L.A. I'm in them at least a couple of times a month."

"Well, I think you're really going to like Rooster's." I started the car and headed home. I glanced more than once in the rearview mirror. Muffin continued to sit, staring straight ahead. Morton continued to sniff her.

I pulled into the driveway and rolled up to the garage. "Let me just get those two into the backyard, and then I'll open the door for you," I said.

"Oh, relax, I think I can open a car door," she said, then promptly opened the passenger door and slid out of the car.

I hurried out on the driver's side and opened the rear door for Morton and Muffin. I grabbed their leashes, walked them over to the gate, and let them in the backyard. Once I unclipped the leashes, they took off running.

"Oh, Dev. This is so nice of you. This is just what she needed. Look at the two of them." They were running back and forth, Morton chasing Muffin around the yard.

"Come on, let's head inside. We can check on them through the window. I'll get some water out there for them." I took the bag of BBQ from Quinnie and led her up the steps onto the back porch. I unlocked the back door and stepped aside so she could go in first.

"Oh, you're such a gentleman," she said as she stepped into the kitchen. "What a lovely Victorian home. How long have you lived here?" she asked as she looked around the room.

"A lot of years."

"My memory of this area is that it used to be a no-go area."

"Yeah, that's correct. But back in the 70s and maybe the 80s, a bunch of young couples started moving in. I think I told you. My folks were part of that group. I grew up just three blocks from here."

"Are you going to give me a tour of the house?"

"I'd be happy to if you want."

"I'd love it. Really I would," Quinnie said and smiled.

"Okay, let me get the canine couple out there watered, and there's a treat for them in the bag."

"Oh, I don't think I want Muffin eating BBQ. Not a good end result, if you know what I mean."

"Not to worry. I feel the same way. I just got a bone for each of them. It will keep them occupied once they're finished chasing each other around." I filled two water dishes and took them out to the backyard. Morton was still chasing Muffin.

"I've got beer or wine if you're interested."

"Any Sauvignon Blanc?"

"As a matter of fact, yeah, and it's even chilled."

"Why stop at this point?" she laughed.

I opened the bottle and poured her a glass of wine. I grabbed a beer from the refrigerator for myself, and we proceeded with the house tour. I showed her every room. She was interested in my bedroom and sat on the four-poster bed.

"Oh, wow, this is really comfortable. How do you ever manage to get out of bed in the morning?"

"I've learned that bills that need to be paid can be a pretty good incentive. More often than not, I'm up before my alarm goes off."

"Well, I'm sure there's always the overnight guest who has to get to work, too."

"Not of late," I said.

She drained her glass of wine and handed it to me. "If only the walls could talk. I'm sure there are a lot of stories that have happened in this room."

"How about those BBQ sandwiches for dinner?" I changed the subject.

We sat at the kitchen counter and ate Rooster's BBQ sandwiches. Quinnie must have been very hungry because she literally wolfed hers down, along with another glass of wine, while I continued to sip my beer.

I cleared the kitchen counter, which consisted of tossing both takeout trays into the recycling bin and served up two ice cream sandwiches for dessert. "I'm just going to run to the bathroom, back in a minute," I said.

"Need a hand?" she said and giggled. "Mind if I help myself to another glass of wine?"

"Be my guest," I said and went upstairs to the bathroom. Before going back downstairs, I wanted to check on Morton and Muffin. I headed to a back room that looked out over my backyard and garage. There they were, the two of them, together, literally. Morton mounted on Muffin. God, how long had that been going on? I ran downstairs and quietly slipped out the front door. No point in getting Quinnie upset. I ran down the driveway, opened the back gate, and hurried into the backyard. Too late, Morton was in the process of dismounting. The deed was done. Muffin struck a pose suggesting she was finished, at least for the moment.

I debated taking them inside but couldn't come up with a reason to give Quinnie. I figured what's done was done and crossed my fingers, hoping that was the end of it. I quietly went back in the front door and into the kitchen. Quinnie wasn't there. I glanced out the kitchen window, thinking she might have gone into the backyard, but there was no sign of her. Probably upstairs in the bathroom, which gave me a chance to get on my laptop.

I turned it on and quickly Googled the gestation period for a labradoodle, sixty-three days, which meant nine weeks. She'd be back in L.A. for two months by then, and if anything actually happened, she'd hopefully never connect it to Morton.

"Don't tell me you're going to do some work," she said, stepping behind me.

"No, just checking something," I said as I turned. "I was thinking we should probably—Where did you find that?" I said, staring at the unopened fifth of Fireball Cinnamon Whiskey in her hands. The label featured the red image of a devilish figure with a tail, jumping and breathing fire, and for good reason. One of my pals had left the bottle here a couple of years ago on Halloween. I never had the desire to open it.

"I've always wanted to try this stuff. What do you say?" she said and drained her wine glass.

"I was thinking we might have to get you back to your brother's. He's probably wondering where you are and—"

"Believe me, he's just happy he hasn't had to deal with me today. If Jerker never, ever, saw me again, he'd be thrilled," she said and proceeded to screw the cap off the bottle. She filled her empty wine glass above the halfway point, set the bottle on the counter, and put the glass to her lips, daring me to say something. She took a large swallow, gasped, and said, "Oh, wow. You going to join me?"

I thought for a long moment, then opened the cupboard and pulled out a glass. "Just a little bit," I said as she went to fill the glass.

She raised her glass and smiled. "Who knows where this might lead?"

Seventeen

I slowly opened my eyes and glanced at the digital clock on my dresser. It was almost 4:00 in the morning. Morton rubbed his paws against my butt and then licked the back of my neck. He never licks my neck. I started to roll over but had to stop until the throbbing in my head slowed down. I turned to look at Morton. He wasn't there. Smiling, sleeping, naked Quinnie was in his place. I rolled onto my back and closed my eyes. When I opened them again, naked Quinnie was still there.

I slipped out of bed and tiptoed into the bathroom. I splashed cold water on my face and used a washcloth to rub the lipstick off my neck and chest. I stared at the scratch marks on my right shoulder and my left thigh. Oh, God. Tubby Gustafson was going to kill me, literally.

I went back into the bedroom to slip on my clothes, but they were nowhere to be found. I looked out in the hall and saw my socks at the top of the stairs. Halfway down the stairs, I found a pink thong. A pink bra was draped over the newel post at the bottom of the stairs.

The trail of clothing, a blouse, my shirt, t-shirt, and boxers led into the kitchen.

The lights were still on in the kitchen, where two pairs of jeans and our shoes were on the floor. The nearly empty bottle of Fireball whiskey sat on the kitchen counter next to our glasses, along with a spray can of whipped cream. What the hell? I had no memory of any of this.

I glanced out the window to see if Morton and Muffin were still outside. They weren't. I checked the den, looked under the dining room table, and glanced in the front room— no sign of them. I headed up the stairs, attempting to match my steps to the pounding in my head. It didn't work.

I figured I'd have to find them in the daylight and decided it might be better if I crawled into the bed in the guest room. I pushed the door open, and there they were, Morton and Muffin, sound asleep in post-coital exhaustion. God save me.

I crawled back into my bed as quietly as possible. I had just settled in on my side with my back to Quinnie when she suddenly wrapped a leg over my thigh, threw an arm over my shoulder, kissed my neck, and began to snore.

I woke up again a little before 7:00. Thank God I had the sense not to set the alarm last night. Apparently, I was thinking of other things. I snuck out of bed and hurried downstairs to the kitchen. I picked our jeans up off the floor and made my way up the stairs, collecting various items as I went. I pulled the covers up on my side of the bed, smoothed out my pillow, and arranged Quinnie's clothes on the bed.

I stepped out into the hall, dressed, and hurried down to the kitchen. I started a pot of coffee, took two aspirin, settled in on the couch in the den, and fell back asleep.

Morton poking his nose against my back woke me an hour later. I rolled over and stared at the two of them, Morton and Muffin. I got up and let them out into the backyard. I gathered the two water dishes I'd left out there last night, refilled them, and placed them in the kitchen. I filled two bowls with dog food and looked out the window. They were lying next to one another, chewing their bones, ever the happy couple.

At 9:00, I poured a mug of coffee and took it up to Quinnie along with the aspirin bottle. I knocked on my bedroom door a couple of times before I heard a groan. I opened the door and stepped in. Quinnie appeared to be attempting to open her eyes. I set the coffee and aspirin on the bedside table next to her.

"Oh, God, what on earth happened?" she groaned and slowly sat up against the headboard. She suddenly realized she was naked and pulled my pillow over her chest.

"I believe someone suggested we drink Fireball whiskey."

"Oh, my God," she groaned.

"I've got fresh coffee here for you and some aspirin. The bathroom is across the hall. Grab a shower. I'll set out clean towels for you. Morton and Muffin have been fed, and they're outside chewing those bones."

"Umm, where, exactly, did you sleep?"

"Downstairs on a couch," I said, telling a version of the truth. "You were up here, and the dogs were in the guest room."

"Oh, you poor thing. I'm so sorry."

"Don't worry about it," I said. "I'll make you breakfast once you're downstairs. Take as much time as you need and grab a couple of those aspirins. It'll help."

She closed her eyes as I left the bedroom. I set out a clean towel and washcloth in the bathroom. As I headed downstairs, I casually glanced back into the bedroom. Naked Quinnie was standing on the far side of the bed with her back to the door. I focused on what looked like a bite mark on her otherwise perfect rear. Oh, God.

Fifteen minutes later, I heard the shower come on in the bathroom. I poured the last of the Fireball whiskey down the sink, rinsed out the bottle, and placed it in recycling.

Fortunately, I had a half-dozen eggs in the refrigerator and four slices of bread for toast. I debated cooking up hotdogs for sausage and decided against it. I cut up a red pepper, sliced up some Swiss cheese, and mixed them up in the bowl with the eggs.

Quinnie arrived in the kitchen forty-five minutes later. "How's the head?" I asked.

"Still waiting for the aspirin to kick in."

"I'm going to make us some breakfast. Hopefully, that will help. Would you like some toast?"

"I'm not sure."

I opened the refrigerator and took out a jar of grape jelly. "Put this on the toast. The sugar will help that head," I said and placed four slices of bread in the toaster.

Quinnie was quiet until halfway through breakfast when a combination of the aspirin, breakfast, and grape jelly started to kick in. "Well, no offense, but I think I probably have had my fill of Fireball whiskey for the rest of my life."

"Yeah, I didn't mean for things to get so crazy."

"Was there any Fireball left?"

"Less than a shot glass. I poured it down the sink."

"Oh, thank you. If I never saw it again, it would be fine with me. God help me, I really can't remember much except that we were playing some game with shots of whiskey."

"Yeah, only we weren't using shot glasses. I don't know when you went up to bed."

"And you said you slept on a couch?"

"Yeah, in the den. Morton woke me up this morning poking me in the back with his nose," I said, trying to use what few remnants of truth I could recall.

"Okay," she said, not sounding all that sure if she bought my story, but I was going to stick to it.

"When you feel up to it, I'll take you back to your brother's. I'm sure he's wondering where you are."

"Not to worry, Dev. He's just glad he doesn't have to deal with me. If he asks, I'll just tell him you picked me up early this morning to catch a sunrise on the Mississippi, and then we went out to breakfast."

"You think he'll buy that?"

"I don't think he has a choice."

Eighteen

We headed out to the car, leaving a whining Morton in the backyard. Muffin stretched out in the backseat and closed her eyes. She'd obviously had a busy night. Quinnie kept her eyes closed as well, and other than her mumbling, "Oh, God," a couple of times, she never said anything, which was fine with me. I could see no point in mentioning the bite mark on her rear.

I pulled into Tubby's. Two guys leaning against the front of the house watched as we approached. I noticed the navy-blue sports shirts were nowhere in sight. Apparently, they were back to wearing their everyday attire. As we drew closer, they looked at one another, smiled, and laughed.

I pulled to a stop in front of the mansion and started to get out of the car. "Relax, I can let myself out. I plan to be back in bed in about five minutes. Thanks for an enjoyable adventure, at least the part I can remember," Quinnie said.

"Thanks, Quinnie. Safe trip back to L.A. whenever you go. Feel free to call me anytime, as long as you promise there won't be any more Fireball."

"Believe me, once was enough. More Fireball is the last thing I want." She climbed out of the car, pulled Muffin from the back seat, and headed into the mansion. I began to make my way around the drive when one of the security guys came running across the lawn, waving his arm and calling my name.

"Hassle, Hassle. Stop, damn it, stop." I stopped and lowered my window. "Hey, the boss wants a word with you," he said, breathing heavily, just like Louie did after he climbed the stairs to the office.

"Tub…err…Mr. Gustafson?"

"Yeah, Freddy's waiting at the door. He didn't seem too happy."

I glanced past him, and there was Fat Freddy standing at the front door. The guy was right. He didn't look very happy.

"Oh, shit. Are you sure he wants me?"

"You're the guy who just dropped off the Evil Woman, right? I think Freddy is going to be the least of your problems. Just telling you what he said."

I looked over at Fat Freddy again. Just in case I had any doubts, he gave me the finger. My headache immediately increased.

"Okay, I'll turn around and park."

"Good luck, Dude."

I slowly made my way back around the drive and pulled into a parking space next to the Harley Davidson with the XXX sticker that read 'Free Rides.' When I got out of the car, Billy was hurrying toward me with the wand. I set my wallet and keys on the trunk, leaned against the trunk, and assumed the position.

"Just a warning, man," Billy said as he waved the wand over my back. "I don't know what you did, but the boss and his sister are screaming at each other inside. Freddy's ready to kill. I'd be on my best behavior if I were you." He quickly turned me around and waved the wand over my front pockets. "Okay, man, you're good to go. Be careful."

I walked toward Fat Freddy. I didn't run, but I wasn't wasting any time.

"Get your dumb ass in here, Haskell. What the hell were you thinking? You thought it would be a good idea to shack up with his sister? The man is really pissed off. Better get your ass inside and come up with an explanation."

"I didn't shack up with her, Freddy. We caught the sunrise on the river, and it was just easier if she slept at my place. Come on, man. We're both adults, and nothing happened."

I followed Freddy into the entryway. The guy usually seated reading a comic book was standing there with a frightened look on his face. I saw Quinnie just as she disappeared in the hallway upstairs. Red-faced Tubby was there, glaring at me. I held my arms out to be patted down. Tubby growled, "Forget it. They already ran the wand over this idiot. I can only hope he tries something. You, my office, now, " Tubby shouted. With that, he turned and stormed across the entryway and down the hall.

"You heard the man. Get your dumb ass in gear. Come on. Move," Fat Freddy said.

Apparently, I had to be told twice. I hurried down the hall and into Tubby's office. Fat Freddy closed the door behind us once we entered. Tubby was standing at his desk. His face appeared to be slightly less red, but then he shouted, "Just what in the hell did you think you were doing? You idiot."

"I thought I was helping you out, sir. I know it's been stressful having your sister here. Stressful for both of you. I took her to lunch, we saw some sights, and then I took her to my house so her dog, Muffin, could play with Morton. She told me how the trip had been hard on Muffin and that she takes her to a dog park every day but hadn't been able to do that here. We let the two of them chase one another around my backyard. I stopped at Rooster's BBQ and got a bone for each of them. We ate BBQ sandwiches. She wanted to see the sunrise on the river. Instead of driving in here before sunrise and scaring you or your staff, she spent the night at my place, thinking it might give you a break. She was in my room with the door closed, and I slept on the couch in my den."

"Are you telling me you two didn't…"

"No way, sir. First of all, she's not that sort. Second, I have a pretty high opinion of you, sir, and the last thing I would ever do would be to—"

"Enough. Shut. The. Hell. Up," Tubby shouted.

"Okay. It's just that she mentioned the two of you were going over some family business. Said it had been stressful and wanted both of you to be able to take a break. I thought I was helping. We were just like our dogs. We got to know one another," I said, regretting that last part the moment I said it.

Tubby shot me a look after my last comment, and I bit my tongue before I said anything else. "Haskell, if I ever find out that you—"

"I have to be honest, sir. I have no recollection of anything untoward occurring."

He gave me a long look and then said, "Get him out of my sight, Frederick."

Freddy pulled on my arm and led me out into the hall. Once the door closed behind us, he looked at me and said, "Do you have any idea how close you came to being neutered in there?"

"I'm telling you, Freddy, nothing happened."

"You better get in your car and get the hell out of here before he changes his mind, Haskell." He led me to the front door and said, "Just a little advice. It might be a good idea if you kept a low profile until the Evil Woman is out of town, for your own good."

I nodded and hurried out the door. Freddy slammed it closed behind me. One of the guys said, "Well, was she worth it?" Both of them laughed.

I stayed silent and headed for my car. My ears were tuned for the sound of the front door opening. If I heard that happening, I was going to run. I made it to my car, backed out of my parking space, and took the drive at a normal speed. Once outside the gate, I stepped on the gas and got away from Tubby's place as fast as possible. I drove past Phoenix Starr's house. The driveway was empty, but it reminded me to check on Sterling Kozlow.

I headed down to Sibley Plaza. At no surprise, his red Mercedes was parked in its usual place. I debated marking his tire with chalk. My hangover convinced me to head home, get Morton, and go to the office.

Nineteen

The office was empty when we arrived. Louie had left a two-word note on my desk, 'court date.' Actually, that was just fine. I checked my computer for emails, put my feet up on my desk, and closed my eyes.

"Dev? Dev? Honey, are you awake?"

I opened my eyes, and there was Phoenix next to my chair, staring at me. She was wearing a solid white cross halter top and a very short, tight skirt. Her skin appeared even more tan than usual. I stared for a long moment before I realized I wasn't dreaming. I pulled my feet off my desk and jolted forward. "Oh, Phoenix, sorry. I must have dropped off to sleep for a moment."

"Busy night?" she asked, raising her eyebrows and smiling.

"No, not really. I mean, umm, yeah, in a way, actually. I followed Sterling home last night and then spent the night on that park bench across the street from your house."

"What?"

"Yeah, standard investigative procedure. I've been following him home every night around the same time. I wanted to see if he waited until you were asleep, and then maybe he'd sneak out of the house."

She shook her head. "And did he?"

"No, and I was awake until dawn," I lied. "I just had to be sure. You did tell me you have separate rooms, didn't you?"

"Yes, we've had them for a couple of years. They're on opposite ends of the house, actually."

That fit with the few times I did follow him home and watched the lights go on up on the second floor. "Well, I'll keep checking him out. So far, I haven't seen anything that would suggest he's involved with someone."

"That's why I stopped by. I overheard him on the phone this morning, telling someone he'd meet her a little after eight tonight."

"Really? Did he happen to mention where?"

She suddenly straddled my right leg, standing on either side of my thigh. She looked down at me and smiled. I could actually feel the warmth from her shapely legs. I tried to back up, but my chair was up against my desk. "He did. He's meeting her at a bar called Scuttlebutts. Do you know where that is?"

"Yeah, I think so. It's over on the west side." Actually, I knew where it was. I'd even been there a few times. It was more than just a bar. It used to be a strip club. Now it was more of a pickup place, with a band playing most nights. "And you're sure he was talking to a woman?"

"Well, he called her honey and said he couldn't wait to see her. That doesn't sound like something he'd say to some guy."

"You're right about that. You said he mentioned he'd be there a little after eight."

"Yeah, that's what he said."

"I'll be there ahead of him and check it out. You know, Phoenix, I'm sorry to hear this. I was really hoping there was nothing going on. Maybe he's just meeting with a client."

"Sterling wouldn't meet with a client in a bar. Believe me."

"All right. I'll check it out and keep you posted. If there is something to this, I'm going to try to follow them, so don't phone me. I'll call you either way first thing in the morning."

She smiled at that, kicked my legs further apart, and stepped between them. She placed her hands on my shoulders, leaned down close to me, and said, "Oh, Dev, you have been so wonderful. I just want to thank you." She leaned forward and kissed me on the lips, staying there for just a second or two longer than necessary. My heart was racing as she stood and smiled. "Thank you. I'll be waiting for your phone call."

I watched as she strutted out of the office. I pulled the binoculars from the desk drawer and watched as she crossed the street and climbed into her BMW. A moment later, she disappeared up the street. I sat there and wondered what the hell had just happened.

I took Morton home and let him out in the backyard. He seemed to be searching for something, and it dawned on me he was probably looking for Muffin. He did find one of the bones and settled down to gnaw on that. We had finished up all the BBQ from Rooster's last night, so I put a pizza in the oven, set the timer, and headed upstairs.

I grabbed a quick shower, put on some clean jeans and a fairly clean shirt. I noticed a business card next to my alarm clock and picked it up. It was Quinnie's. Just her name, phone number, and email address. I turned the card over and read her note. *'Thanks, I remember everything!'*

Oh, God. Hopefully, she wasn't going to tell Tubby. I debated calling her and decided that would probably be the dumbest thing I could do. I heard the timer on the stove going off and hurried downstairs.

I let Morton inside, watched about fifteen minutes of news before I couldn't stand anymore, and turned it off. I wrapped up the remaining pizza and placed it in the refrigerator, washed the plate, filled Morton's water dish, and drove over to the west side.

Scuttlebutts had been a strip club for close to ten years. For the past five or six years, it has served as a pick-up joint. Just a little after 7:00, the lot was maybe half-full. I didn't want to take the chance Sterling Kozlow might recognize my car, so I parked in the far corner of the lot. If memory served, things didn't really start here until sometime after 8:00.

I walked inside and made a beeline for the bar. It was a large oval affair, and I settled onto a stool on the far side. A wall was to my back, and I was looking out across the bar to an area with tables, a dance floor, and a stage. Just now, a couple of guys were arranging amplifiers and a set of drums on the stage. Obviously, they were the band for tonight.

"What can I get you?" the bartender asked. Her dark hair was pulled back in a ponytail. She had dark brown eyes, a nice figure, and her name tag read Katie.

"Hi, Katie. I think I'll start out with sparkling water and a twist of lemon."

She didn't even blink, just said, "Back in a minute," and grabbed a glass from behind the bar. It was more like thirty seconds when she set the glass down in front of me. "You want to start a tab?"

"Yeah, I think so."

"I'll need a credit card," she said.

I dug a debit card out of my wallet and handed it to her. She ran the card and set the receipt in a glass she placed in front of me. I spent the next ninety minutes watching as the crowd gradually grew. There were a lot of people, but none of them looked anything like Sterling Kozlow. In fact, just looking around, I had the sense he would feel very out of place in here. I pegged the average age at late twenties, maybe early thirties. Sterling could have fathered just about all the people in here.

The stools around the bar were all taken. At the moment, I was eyeing a couple of women seated across from me. I thought one of them may have given me a look, but a minute later, they'd both turned around to face the stage and the dance floor, so obviously, they weren't that interested. It was almost 9:30 when I waved the bartender over.

"Another sparkling water?" she asked.

"No, I'd like to settle up," I said and handed her my credit card.

"Already got you in the system," she said. "Back in just a moment."

It was actually a couple of minutes, but she returned with my receipt. "Just need you to sign at the bottom," she said.

I glanced at the receipt, six sparkling waters at six-fifty each, which added up to thirty-nine bucks. I added a five-dollar tip, signed the receipt, and said, "Thanks."

"Come back again," she said.

I smiled, nodded, and headed for the door. I studied the crowd but didn't see anyone who resembled Sterling Kozlow. Just on the off-chance, I checked the men's room. It was empty, and I headed out the door. The parking lot was now full, and I walked back toward my car. I was almost there when I stopped and looked two rows over at a red Mercedes. From where I stood, it looked to be the same model as Kozlow's.

I cut through a row of cars and read the license number. It was definitely Kozlow's car. In case I had any doubts, there were two chalk marks on the rear tire.

I walked over and glanced inside. Kozlow was in the front seat. He was wearing a gray suit and leaning over the console. The driver's window was covered in blood, and I could see a hole in the window. Sterling Kozlow, with a hole in the back of his head, was deader than a doornail. I pulled out my phone and called 911.

Twenty

The first squad car arrived about three minutes after my call. I was still on the line with the 911 dispatcher when I heard the siren. The squad car pulled into the parking lot about fifteen seconds later. I stepped into the middle of the lane and waved. The squad car headed toward me.

"Police are here, just pulling into the parking lot," I said to the dispatcher.

"Do you want me to stay on the line?" she said.

"No, they're just stopping now." The squad car pulled to a stop, and an officer opened the driver's door. He left his flashers on and stood behind the open door, talking into his radio. He didn't look familiar, which didn't mean anything other than he probably didn't know me. I heard another siren in the distance.

I held my phone up in my right hand so he could see all I held was a cellphone as I slowly walked toward him.

"You called this in?"

"Yes, I did. My name is Dev Haskell. I'm a private investigator. Lieutenant Aaron LaZelle in homicide is a

Surprise Surprise! ♦ 125

friend of mine. I spotted the body in the red Mercedes. The victim was shot. The car doors are locked."

As he said something into the radio attached to his left shoulder, another squad car pulled into the parking lot. The siren was cut off, and a moment later, they turned off their flashing lights. Both doors on the second squad car opened, and two officers climbed out. They closed the car doors and walked over to the first cop.

One of them looked at me and said, "Haskell?"

Officer Pete Wagner. "Hey, Pete, sorry to screw up a quiet night. Shooting victim in the red Mercedes."

"Haskell's okay. I know him," Wagner said, and all three officers hurried over. I didn't know the other officer who rode with Wagner. He slipped on a pair of latex gloves, looked in through the passenger window on the Mercedes, and then tried the locked passenger door.

"Put a call in. We're going to need crime scene, the medical examiner, and BCA. We'll want to close off this area." The officer pulled out a small flashlight and shined it over the area where he was standing, then got down on his knees and shined it beneath the Mercedes.

The first officer to arrive walked back to his car, turned off the flashing lights, and opened the trunk.

Wagner looked at me and said, "What can you tell us?"

"Not much. I've actually been investigating that guy. His name is Sterling Kozlow. He's an accountant and has an office over in Sibley Plaza. His wife suspected him of having an affair, so I was checking that out."

"And was he? Having an affair?"

"I didn't find anything that indicated that. The guy worked twelve to fourteen-hour days in his office. He never left the office during the day, as far as I could determine. Once he did leave, he went straight home, never stopped anywhere. The wife told me this morning she heard him on the phone telling a woman he'd meet her here just after 8:00. I got here at 7:00, waited inside for almost two and a half hours, figured he was a no show. I walked out to my car, saw the Mercedes, realized it was Kozlow's once I saw the license plate. I looked in the window, and there he was. So I called 911."

"You touch anything?"

"I tried to open the passenger door. It was locked. You're liable to find my prints on the door handle."

"You have any idea who he was supposed to meet?"

"No idea."

"Wife's name?"

"Phoenix Starr, two 'r's' in that last name. They live on the River Boulevard. I've got the address written down at my office."

"Contact information?"

"For the wife? Umm, yeah, I've got her phone number. Hang on." I turned my cell on, went to recent calls, and gave him the phone number for Phoenix.

"You mind hanging around for a bit?" Wagner asked in a tone that suggested, like it or not, that's what I would be doing.

"No, not a problem. Is it all right with you if I grab a seat in my car?"

"Where is it?"

"Just two rows over, in the corner of the parking lot. It's that black Ford Crown Victoria Police Interceptor," I said and pointed in the direction of my car.

"Where in the hell did you get that thing?"

"Are you kidding? I got it at your police auction maybe eighteen months ago. I really like it."

"Yeah, okay, grab a seat over there," he said, shaking his head. "You talk to anyone inside?"

"About this? No, I called 911 from out here. Your guy who was first on the scene was here in just a couple of minutes. I stayed on the line with the dispatcher until that first squad car pulled into the lot." As I spoke, another car pulled into the lot and parked. It was unmarked, but I could see where the flashing lights were on the dash and the grill. The tires didn't have any sort of white wall. In short, it was unmarked but obviously a police car.

"Oh, shit, here we go," Wagner said as he turned and looked at the vehicle that had just pulled up. The driver's door opened, and Detective Norris Manning stepped out from behind the wheel.

"Oh shit. You aren't kidding. Manning will have me fingered for this the second he sees me. God, can the night get any worse?"

"Grab a seat in your car and let me see if I can't run interference for you, Haskell. Thanks for calling this in."

"What else could I do?"

"You'd be surprised at the number of folks who would have just left and never thought to report it."

"Unfortunately, I wouldn't be surprised. The world just keeps getting crazier. If you want me, I'll be in my car, Pete."

Twenty-one

There were now a half-dozen squad cars in the parking lot and out on the street. A BCA (Bureau of Criminal Apprehension) van and a medical examiner's vehicle with the back doors open were parked near Kozlow's Mercedes. It was after midnight, and the parking lot was even emptier than when I had first arrived. I found it interesting that no one leaving Scuttlebutts had any interest in hanging around, which was probably wise on their part.

I was still sitting in my car. More than once, I thought about asking Pete Wagner if I could go home, but the thought of alerting Detective Norris Manning to my presence made me perfectly content to wait in my car and hope I never had to deal with him.

Apparently, I dozed off. Someone knocking on the passenger door window caused me to suddenly jerk awake. I glanced over. My nightmare was about to begin. Detective Norris Manning knocked again and said, "Hey, open up, Haskell." He indicated the locked door.

Against my better judgment, I unlocked the door. Manning slid into the passenger seat, looked over at me, and smiled. I just shook my head. His smile seemed to suggest he had just solved the case. All he had to do was take me down to the station, tie me to a torture rack, and question me nonstop for seventy-two hours.

"Gee, thanks for letting me in, Haskell. This can't be the first time you've slept in this parking lot."

"How can I help you, detective?"

"The word out there is that you knew our victim."

"I told everything I know to Officer Wagner."

"How nice. Why don't you tell me what you told Officer Wagner?"

I took a deep breath and repeated my conversation with Wagner.

"So you're in a relationship with Mr. Kozlow's wife?"

"No, Manning, I'm not in a relationship with her. She's a client of mine. She suspected her husband of having an extra-marital affair, and she hired me to see if there was any credibility to her suspicions."

"And what did you find out?"

"What I learned was the guy works very long hours in his accounting firm. He's in there early every morning. He works all day and goes home sometime after 9:00 at night. Once home, he remains there until the following morning. He leaves for work at roughly 7:00. Thus far, that's all he's done every day I've checked him out."

"And yet you met him here, in a bar, this evening at 8:00?"

No surprise he'd have the facts wrong. "Actually, I did not meet Mr. Kozlow. I was not scheduled to meet him. I have personally never met Mr. Kozlow. I was here because his wife thought he was meeting a woman here, at Scuttlebutts, at 8:00 this evening. I arrived just after 7:00 in the hopes of seeing him meeting with the aforementioned woman. He never showed. I walked out of the bar and headed toward my car at 9:30. I noticed the Mercedes in the parking lot looked very similar to Kozlow's car. Upon closer examination, I found that the license plate was Kozlow's. I looked in the vehicle, saw the body, and immediately phoned 911. I waited for the first squad car, which arrived maybe three minutes after my 911 phone call."

"So what you're telling me is you had no interaction with Mr. Kozlow this evening."

"That is correct, sir."

"And you've had no interaction with him previously."

"That is correct, sir. Other than watching him from a distance. But we've never spoken. I've never phoned him or received a phone call from him. As far as I know, he never even knew I existed."

"Interesting, how is it, do you think, that he had your business card in his suit coat pocket?"

"What?"

Manning pulled an evidence bag out of his jacket pocket. What was definitely my business card was in the bag. Manning looked over my shoulder and nodded. As

I turned, the driver's door opened, and a deep voice said, "If you would please step out of the car, sir."

"Oh, come on. You guys gotta be kidding. I didn't do this. I never gave Kozlow my card. I don't know how in the hell he got it."

"Sir, please, if you would step out of the car now."

I looked over at Manning. "Did you set this up?"

"Sir, please. I'm not going to ask again," the officer said.

"Okay, okay. I'm coming out." I pulled the key from the ignition and stepped out of my car.

Manning climbed out on the passenger side and said, "Careful, he's probably carrying."

"Oh, God. I'm not carrying, but check me out, so Manning doesn't try something stupid," I said. I spread my feet and arms and leaned against my car.

The officer duly patted me down. Manning began to read me my rights. When he finished, he said. "Do you understand?"

I shook my head and said, "Jesus Christ, of course, I understand. What I understand is that I'm being set up once again by you, Detective Manning." I raised my arms, placed my wrists together, and turned to the officer who had just patted me down. "I'm sure you'll want to cuff me."

"Yes, if you'd turn around please, sir," the officer said and then gently pulled my arms behind my back one at a time and slapped the cuffs on me. He walked me over to a squad car and placed me in the back seat. We drove down to the police station, and I was placed in a holding cell. There was no point in saying anything. The poor cop was just following idiot Manning's instructions.

It was just after 7:00 in the morning when the door opened on the holding cell. An officer said, "Mr. Haskell, if you would come with me, please."

I followed him down a hall to a bank of elevators. "Aren't you going to handcuff me?" I asked.

"I don't think that's necessary, well, unless you want me to, and then I would be happy to oblige if it means that much to you."

"No, believe me, I can live without it."

We rode the elevator up to the third floor, and he led me into an interview room. "If you'll grab a seat, someone will be with you shortly. Can I get you a coffee or something?"

"Yeah, a coffee would be nice, black, and thanks," I said.

"Not a problem. Back in a minute."

It was more like ten minutes, but he did bring me a coffee, and surprise, surprise, it was halfway decent. After a couple of sips, the door opened, and my pal Aaron LaZelle stepped in. "How's it going, Dev?"

"Are you kidding, Aaron? Really? How's it going? That idiot Manning has me arrested for murder. I'm the guy who called 911 to begin with. How's it going? I'm going to sue Manning's ass. That's how it's going. Kozlow's body would still be in his car in that parking lot if I hadn't called 911."

"Had you been drinking?"

"Yeah, after all, it's a bar. I pounded down six drinks, but I was okay to drive, Aaron. You see, I was drinking sparkling water with a twist of lemon the entire damn night. And if idiot Manning had bothered to check the damn security tape, he would have seen me sitting on the same stool at the bar from 7:00 until 9:30. Meaning, whenever Kozlow was shot in the parking lot, I was inside sitting at the bar. But you know, I get it. Manning doesn't have to deal in facts. He's had an in for me for years. God only knows why. But I'll tell you what, this time I'm not letting it pass. I've got a long history with that dickhead, and this time, I'm not backing off. I'm gonna sue his ass."

"Look, Dev, I know he was a little out of hand, and—"

"A little out of hand? What if I wigged out and had a heart attack? Or fought with an officer, and they shot me? Your department would be paying me millions. But don't worry, I'm not going to do that. I'm just going to sue, and all I want is Manning off the force and any pension benefits denied. Now, I've got a business to run, and I need to get back to my car, so I can get home and let Morton out. Then I'm going to have to go see my client and tell her that her husband has been murdered."

"Actually, two detectives are talking with her now."

"Oh, please, don't tell me one of them is Manning."

Aaron shook his head. "No, he's been placed on desk duty."

"Desk duty? Aaron, you should have him scrubbing out every toilet in the entire building. Honest to God. That son of a bitch is a loaded gun just walking around. He's an absolute nut job. You gotta do something. I mean, the press that police are getting across the country isn't bad enough? You've got this dumb shit out there hassling innocent people who reported a murder to 911. You need to dump him and fast before you have a real mess on your hands."

"How 'bout I get you out of here and give you a lift over to your car."

"Yeah, sure. That would be great, much appreciated. But I'm warning you, man, you got a loose cannon there, and he's primed to create a real disaster."

"Come on, let's get your personal items, and I'll drive you to your car."

I collected my wallet, car keys, cell phone, and belt. Aaron led me out to his car in the parking lot. I didn't say anything on the five-minute drive over to Scuttlebutts until he pulled alongside my vehicle.

"Thanks, Aaron. Look, I have a right to be pissed off, and enough said on that front. I'm just really worried about the problems Manning is going to cause or has caused. And I'm just the one guy you know about. You don't have to say anything, and, umm, let's maybe grab dinner one night soon. Oh, and here," I said and pulled my drink receipt from last night out of my wallet.

"Like I told you, I was just drinking sparkling water. The first glass was at 7:12. The last glass was at 9:18. I never got off the barstool. The bartender was a dark-haired woman named Katie. If he was doing his job, Manning would have checked this out. I told him about it, but— Anyway, thanks for the lift," I said and climbed out of the car.

Aaron waited until I climbed out before he took off. We'd known one another since we were kids. I knew he was furious. The question was, would he do anything about it?

Once home, Morton met me at the front door. I hurried inside and let him out into the backyard, then checked the house for any deposit. God bless him. The place was clean.

Twenty-two

While Morton was outside, I hurried upstairs, shaved, took a shower, and slipped into sweatpants and a t-shirt. I filled Morton's food and water dishes and let him in. I made bacon and eggs for breakfast with extra bacon for Morton. Once I had the kitchen cleaned, I changed into nice slacks and a shirt from the dry cleaners and drove over to Phoenix Starr's house.

I pulled into her driveway. Apparently, the police were finished, at least for the moment, because mine was the only car there. There was no sign of the red Equus. I walked to the door and rang the doorbell. Phoenix answered the door a moment later. Surprisingly, she looked just fine, actually gorgeous. She was dressed in a tight fitting gray workout suit with a bare midriff. The 'GYMSHARK' logo on the workout suit was just below her left breast. The outfit was so tight absolutely nothing was left to the imagination. "Oh, Dev, I'm sorry I didn't call. I was on my treadmill. How did you find out?"

I'd been staring and quickly looked up. "I was there last night. I—"

"Did you see who did this? Oh, where are my manners? I'm sorry, please, come in, come in."

I stepped inside, and she closed the door behind me. She wrapped her arms around me and held me close for a long moment. I picked up the lovely scent of her perfume. She kissed my face a couple of times as she gradually let go and asked, "Can I get you something to drink?"

Since it was just after 10:00, I shook my head and said, "No thanks. I just want to say I'm so sorry, Phoenix. What can I do to help?"

She took hold of both my hands and said, "Just don't leave me alone. I need to have you here. Need to have your support."

"Sure, I'll do whatever you need. Let's sit down. The police were here earlier?"

"Yes," she said as I followed her through the living room and into a smaller room with a large flat screen mounted above the fireplace. A movie was playing on the flat screen, but the sound was turned off. "Yes, they were here very early. They had a lot of questions, and I don't know if I was any help. I think they're probably at the office right now, Sterling's office. I signed a form they had so they could go through the files and things. Sterling kept a spare key in the kitchen, and I gave that to them."

She took a seat on the corner of a leather couch. Her treadmill was behind the couch. I sat in a leather recliner just opposite her. "Did the police have any idea who may have been responsible?" I asked.

Phoenix bit her lower lip and shook her head. "No, I told them about that phone call I overheard yesterday morning. But I don't know who he was talking to. You were there. Did you see her?"

"No, I waited inside the bar for Sterling. I was there for almost two and a half hours. I finally left, and that's when I saw his car and the…I mean, with him inside, and I called the police."

"I'm sure they'll have more information as time goes on," Phoenix said.

"Maybe they can trace that phone call from yesterday morning, just for starters," I said.

"She probably used a burner phone."

I nodded, thinking *that was a strange comment coming from Phoenix, but then this was a very strange situation.* "Do you have someone coming over? Family members, friends? Is there anything I can get you?"

"Do you know how to make margaritas?"

"Margaritas, yeah, but I would advise you not to have one, at least not now. You're going to get news people knocking on your door and calling. Once this is on the news, if it isn't already, neighbors will be calling. Maybe clients of Sterling's or people from the firm. Do you have any friends or family you should get in touch with?"

She seemed to think for a long moment, then picked up a remote and turned off the TV. Her cellphone was on the end table next to her. She grabbed it, swiped her finger across the screen, and said, "Hang on, I want to change my message." She tapped her finger on the screen a couple of times and then said, "Hi, this is Phoenix. I'm unable to take your call right now. Please leave a message, and I'll get back to you just as soon as possible. Thank you."

She smiled, set the phone back on the end table, and said, "That should eliminate anyone I don't feel like talking to. You know, Dev, now that things have suddenly changed, I'm hoping we might get to know one another a little better," she raised her eyebrows. "I really appreciate all the work you've done, and I wish there was some special way I could thank you for coming over this morning."

"Don't worry about it, Phoenix. It's the least I can do. I should probably get out of your hair. I'm sure you'll have all sorts of arrangements to deal with over the coming days. If you need—"

"Actually, Sterling had everything planned out. He wanted to be cremated. I've already arranged for a memorial service, but that's dependent on when his body will be released. Once that's over, I'll take his ashes up to the lake place and distribute them. Of course, there's bound to be some things at the firm, but he has a very efficient staff, both just as boring as he was," she giggled.

I nodded and said, "Well, you've got my number. Call me if you need anything. You still have my card, don't you?"

"I'd never lose it, Dev."

"All right, then I'll get out of your hair."

"I might need someone to keep me company tonight. My first night alone and everything."

"Let me know if I can be of any help," I said and stood from the recliner.

Phoenix was on her feet, took my hand, and walked me to the door. Just before she opened it, she wrapped her arms around me, straddled my knee, and planted a hot kiss on my lips. I couldn't remember the last time I'd had to fight a woman to pull away. "Mmm," she said. "Thank you. I meant what I said. I could use some company later tonight."

"Let's see how you're doing," I said and opened the front door.

"I'm looking forward to it," she purred and then pinched my butt as I stepped out of the house.

I didn't know what to say, so I just smiled, gave a little wave, and hurried to my car. She'd definitely gone off the deep end.

I drove past Sterling Kozlow's office. There was an unmarked car parked where Sterling's Mercedes normally would have been. I drove home, picked up Morton, and we headed down to the office. I kept thinking about Phoenix. I never saw a tear or heard any comment suggesting she was in distress. She didn't seem the least bit upset. As a matter of fact, I had the distinct impression she was coming on to me. But then, everyone reacts differently, and there's always a great deal of shock in a murder situation like this.

Morton and I headed up to the office. Louie wasn't in. I got onto my computer and looked online to see what information was out there on the Kozlow murder. All I found were local news reports of a murder in the Scuttlebutts parking lot, sometime between 8:00 and 9:00 last night. Sterling Kozlow's name wasn't mentioned, and the reports ended with the standard, 'Police are asking anyone with any information to contact them.'

It was still early, and I expected the Kozlow murder to be a lead story by evening. My phone rang just after the noon hour. I expected it to be Phoenix, but instead, it was Quinnie calling.

"Hi, Quinnie," I answered.

"Mr. Haskell, I'm calling to see if you're busy."

"Busy? Well, I'm always working or doing something. What's up?"

"Muffin and I could use a break. Would you happen to know of a dog park we might go to?"

"I can think of a couple. You have a time in mind?"

"Not really, but the sooner, the better. I've been reviewing a contract for the better part of the morning, and I just need to let my mind relax for a bit."

"We could be there in maybe thirty minutes."

"Oh, no, you don't have to do that. I can borrow a car from my grumpy brother, and we'll find our way."

"It's not a problem. Besides, Morton loved being with Muffin," I said, not going into any detail.

"Are you at your office?"

"Yes, we are."

"A half-hour would be perfect. Why don't you text me when you leave, and we'll be waiting for you outside the gate? That will save you having to be searched within an inch of your life and dealing with this bunch of morons around here."

"You sure that's okay?" I asked.

"It's okay with me, and that's all that counts," she said and laughed.

"All right, keep an eye out for that text," I said and disconnected.

I finished up on the computer over the next ten minutes. I left Louie a note saying we were out for an hour or two. I clipped the leash onto Morton, and we headed down to the car. We stopped at Rooster's, and I got two pork shoulder bones. I sent Quinnie a text message, and we drove over to Tubby's.

I took a slightly indirect route and drove past Phoenix's house. The red Equus was in the driveway. I wasn't sure if that was good or bad, but at least she wasn't alone. I saw Quinnie and Muffin a minute later standing outside the gate of Tubby's mansion. Fortunately, none of Tubby's staff were with her.

Twenty-three

I pulled to a stop right in front of Quinnie and Muffin. Quinnie opened the back door, and Muffin jumped in. As Quinnie hurried into the front seat, she said, "Oh, Dev, I can't thank you enough for letting us interrupt your day. Honest to God, talk about a stick shoved up his—well, let's just say my brother, Jerker, is not an easy man to work with."

I thought it best not to comment on that. "Well, focus on our gala event. I know a dog park along the Mississippi. Plenty of room for them to run and investigate, and it's fenced in. We can let them off their leashes, and they can run to their hearts' content."

We pulled into the parking area ten minutes later. I had watched Morton in the rearview mirror, but other than normal nonsense, he seemed to behave, so with any luck, Muffin's in-heat session was finished. Since it was the middle of the afternoon, we were the only ones at the dog park. We let both dogs off their leashes, and they took off.

"Oh, Dev, I can't thank you enough. This is so nice of you. Muffin really needed this. Thanks for providing my one dose of sanity today."

"Glad to be able to do it. Wait here for a moment. I have something in the car." I was back a minute later. Morton and Muffin were chasing one another down at the far end of the field. "I picked up a couple of bones on the way over, so whenever you want to leave, these will be an incentive for Muffin and Morton to join us."

"Oh, that's so nice of you. You didn't have to do that."

"Not a problem. It's been great meeting you and Muffin, and I've really enjoyed your company. I'm a little surprised your brother has such a lovely sister."

"Oh, don't get me started. The fund our father set up increases payment every five years. This is the fifth year, and payments are set to increase. It should be a simple task but leave it to my brother to make things more difficult."

"Maybe he's just looking out for what's best for the both of you."

She glanced at me and said, "Nice thought, but don't kid yourself. Despite the distance we've placed between us, there's something else bothering him. I've no idea what it might be, but he seems consumed by it. Would you happen to know?"

"No, I have no idea, honest. He's always involved in a half-dozen different business deals," I said.

"Hmm, no idea, even though you work in his marketing firm," she said and then laughed.

"Are you suggesting you didn't buy that line?"

"Oh, honest to God. Vintage Jerker. He thinks he can pull the wool over my eyes, but I've got news for him. A marketing firm, I can only imagine."

"Did he give you a hard time about not coming home the other night?"

"You mean the night when you got me intoxicated and took advantage of me?"

I gave her a surprised look.

"Not to worry, Dev. I told him we were up early to watch the sunrise on the river, and by the way, I enjoyed myself, so thank you very much. That said, I think I can honestly say I will never, ever have another glass of Fireball whiskey. Not a reflection on you, but I paid the price over the course of the next twenty-four hours."

"You're preaching to the choir and thank you very much. Obviously, I enjoyed myself as well," I said.

We watched the dogs run after one another for the next twenty minutes. When they finally settled down, I gave a whistle. Morton looked up, and I waved the two bones. They were both immediately on their feet and racing towards us. I handed each of them a bone. They settled down about ten feet away from us and began gnawing.

"Do you want to leave?" Quinnie said.

"No, not really. It's lovely weather. The case I'm working on had a bit of an upset, so that's done. I'm in no hurry. We're on your schedule."

"Oh, sorry to hear about your case. What happened?"

I gave her the short version.

"He was murdered? In his car?"

"Yeah, it will probably be on the 6:00 news tonight. As far as I know, the police don't have any suspects. The one person of interest they did have turned out to not be involved," I said, not bothering to mention that person had been me.

"Was my brother involved?"

"What? Oh no, not at all. I've no idea what the cause was or who pulled the trigger. Who knows, in today's world, it could be as simple as road rage or looking at someone the wrong way. The world has gone crazy."

We chatted for another fifteen minutes, and I said, "Say, would you be up for a glass of wine at The Spot? Only one and no strings attached."

"I'd love it. Would it be okay if we brought our friends in?" she asked and nodded toward Muffin and Morton, focused on their bones.

"Yeah, that won't be a problem."

We got the dogs in the backseat and headed over to The Spot. Louie's Ford Fiesta was nowhere to be seen, so I figured he was probably still in court. We headed down to the end of the bar and Louie's stool. Morton and Muffin carried their bones.

At no surprise, Quinnie ordered a Sauvignon Blanc, and I ordered an IPA. We chatted some more about nothing in particular, and after another round of drinks, I drove back to Tubby's. This time, I pulled onto the circular drive and stopped in front of the mansion. The two guys at the door must have noticed Quinnie because one of them hurried over and opened the door for her.

"Thanks, Dev. Very much appreciated," she said and gave me a quick kiss on the cheek. She got Muffin out from the back seat. Muffin carried her bone. Quinnie gave me a wave, and they headed into the mansion. I drove around the drive and out through the gates before Tubby or Fat Freddy could ruin my evening.

I swung past Phoenix's house. The red Equus had been replaced by an unmarked police car. Not necessarily unusual, but I thought it best not to intrude. We headed home, and I ate a dish of leftover pasta in front of the 6:00 news.

The news broadcast led with a four-minute segment on Sterling Kozlow. He'd been involved in a number of organizations helping the underprivileged and basically sounded like a very nice guy. Interestingly, no mention was made of Phoenix, other than the line, 'Sterling Kozlow is survived by a spouse.'

I drifted off to sleep on the couch. My phone woke me. I glanced at the screen. Phoenix was calling me just after 9:00.

"Hi, Phoenix, everything okay?"

"Hello, Dev. I'm feeling very alone and frightened. Do you think you might be able to come over and keep me company for a bit?" I didn't respond for a moment. "Hello, Dev, are you there?"

"Oh, yeah, Phoenix. I guess I could come over for a bit. Has anyone been over to see you today?"

"Oh, some neighbors stopped by, and a client of Sterling's checked in. The police were here earlier."

"Everything okay?"

"With the police? Yes, they just had some follow-up questions. They wanted to know about Sterling's employees. Just standard stuff."

"I can be over in a bit. Let me just take care of some things on this end. I'm working on a file," I lied.

"Oh, I'm sorry if I interrupted your work. God, you're just like Sterling, always working."

"Well, like I said before, a not-so-funny thing happens if I can't pay the bills. I'll see you in a little bit."

"Thanks, Dev. I can't wait."

Twenty-four

I let Morton out into the backyard. I got the coffee ready for the morning and set the kitchen counter for breakfast. I enticed Morton back in the house with a biscuit and turned the staircase light on, so he could find his way up to bed if I was late getting back.

I pulled into Phoenix's driveway, locked my car, and headed toward her front door. Phoenix opened the door before I was halfway there. She pushed the screen door open and struck a pose, standing there with the entry light shining behind her. She was wearing a long-sleeve black lace robe that draped down to her ankles. A black satin belt was tied around her waist, although the lace robe was completely see-through, so it's not like she wasn't exposing herself. At least she had on a black G-string. She stood there with her right hand on her hip and her left arm extended over her head, resting on the door frame.

"I've been waiting, handsome," she said and stepped to the side so I could enter.

My mind was jumping back and forth between two thoughts. *Her husband had just been murdered, and she was upset.* My second thought was, *God, what a fantastic body*.

"How are you getting on, Phoenix?" I asked. As I stepped into the house she didn't move an inch and I couldn't help but brush against her. I added a third thought to my sequence, *Shut up, you idiot*.

"I think I'll be better now that you're here, Dev. I felt so alone all day. I've been out of control ever since the police were here with the news this morning. I just can't believe this has happened to me," she said and took a step closer. She ran her hand lightly up and down my arm, then took hold of my hand and led me into the kitchen.

I tried my best not to stare at her figure as she sashayed ahead of me, but I wasn't very successful.

"I'm going to have another glass of wine," she said. "Can I get you a glass, or maybe you'd like something else? I've probably got just about anything you'd like," she offered, striking a pose.

I stared for a moment and reminded myself not to ask for any Fireball. "Maybe just a beer, if you have any."

She smiled and opened up the refrigerator. "Let's see, a stout, an IPA, a Lager—"

"The IPA would be just fine."

She pulled a bottle from the bottom shelf, set it on the counter, and closed the refrigerator. She stepped over, opened a cabinet, took out a glass emblazoned with an IPA logo, and set it next to the beer bottle. Next to the

IPA glass, she set her wine glass with the remnants of red wine in the bottom and lipstick around the edge.

"I'll let you do the honors," she said, sliding the beer bottle and glass along with a bottle opener across the marble counter toward me. While I poured the IPA into the glass, she refilled her wine glass from a bottle of Titus Cabernet, Napa Reserve. I wasn't familiar with the label and made a mental note to check it out.

"I want to thank you again for coming over, Dev. I've just been beside myself the entire day."

"I'm glad you called, Phoenix. Happy to help you. It's a tough situation losing someone."

"Well, then here's to you for helping me out," she said and raised her glass. We clinked glasses in a toast. "Let's go into the den and get comfortable." She topped up her wine glass again and grabbed the bottle.

"Good idea," I said and followed her into the den, all the while staring at her figure through the lace robe that left nothing to the imagination.

"You grab a seat on the couch there, Dev. I'm just going to put on some relaxing music."

I settled onto the leather couch as Phoenix picked up the remote off the end table. She clicked a couple of times, brought up a site, and hit play. Lovely soft music suddenly filled the room. She lowered the sound and then picked up a second remote, dimmed the lights, and turned on the gas fireplace.

"There, that should help get us in the mood."

"It's lovely," I said as she settled onto the couch and faced me. She wasn't on top of me, but she was close, and the truth was, I didn't mind. "You've got a lovely room here, Phoenix. Absolutely gorgeous."

"Yeah, it's very nice. Just wait until we're up in my bedroom," she said, making it sound like just a passing comment. "I really want to thank you for coming over tonight, Dev. I just didn't want to be alone. And thank you so much for your work investigating Sterling. I guess now we'll never know." She shook her head, gave a shrug, and took a sip of wine.

"Maybe that's for the best," I said.

"Do you think the woman he was supposed to meet might have been the person that shot him?" she asked.

"I don't know. I mean, it could be entirely possible. Maybe even the most logical thought. But until we find out who that is, or was, we'll never really know."

"The police told me they have his cell phone, and they'll be going over calls that were made and received. I hope they find something."

"That would be the best thing that could happen. Do you know if Sterling had a security system in his office? You know, filming people who came in."

"I really don't know. I was only in there a handful of times over the past years. I'm not sure how long he had his office there. We'd been married almost five years. The firm has been there ever since I've known him."

"How did you meet?"

"Funny story. We met in a liquor store. I was buying a bottle of wine. Sterling was in line behind me. Of course, they go to ring me up, and my card is declined. The bottle was seven dollars and change, but I only had six one-dollar bills. Believe me, I was completely embarrassed, literally red-faced. God bless Sterling. He stepped up and paid the extra two dollars. I thanked him, and he gave me his card and said, if there was anything he could do to help me, I should give him a call. So that's what I did. I gave him a call, invited him to my apartment for dinner, and the rest is history, as they say."

"That's a really nice story."

"Yeah, it is. Unfortunately, that was probably the high point. After dating for six weeks, we got married. He suddenly became more focused on the business and numbers than he was on me. Then I started thinking, maybe there's someone else."

"Other than that phone call the other morning, what else made you think that?"

"Oh, nothing in particular. I mean, he didn't come home and run to the shower because he smelled like perfume. I don't ever recall lipstick on him. I just had this sense, you know. Phone calls he'd get and step into another room to talk for just a minute or two. Going through things online in his bedroom once he came home from the office. He's got an office up in his room. I'd pop my head in to say good night or something, and he'd immediately shut down the computer so I wouldn't see what he was looking at. Honestly, I didn't care if it was porn or something. I mean, if it was porn, I would love that. Hell, I'd probably want to watch it with him," she said and raised her eyebrows.

"Did he take any business trips?"

"No, never. Occasionally he'd have a meeting in someone's office. But more often, at least as far as I know, the clients came to see Sterling."

"What about his employees?"

"Well, he had three. One of them, an accountant named Jeremy Robins, left maybe a month or a month and a half ago." She suddenly extended her right leg, wiggled her toe against my thigh, and raised those eyebrows again.

"Do you know why he left your husbands firm?"

"Yeah, nothing bad. They have a little girl, maybe two years old. His wife is expecting another child, and Jeremy got a job with some company. They've got a lovely house on Goodrich Avenue, been working on restoring it for the past four or five years, at least as long as I've known them. The new company would pay him more, and the insurance was a lot better than what Sterling provided, and it was a large enough company that there was a path for future growth. Sterling told him to take the job, said he would if he was Jeremy."

"So there weren't any problems you're aware of?"

"No, in fact, just the opposite. Jeremy left on really good terms. He told Sterling weeks before that he would be looking for a new position. He told him about the pregnancy and then promised to stay for four weeks instead of just two once he got the new offer. Sterling told him not to worry about it. Tax season is their busy time, and that's well over. Not that you'd know with the hours Sterling kept."

"So, no problem with Sterling. Jeremy didn't screw up an account or anything?"

"No, it was just like I told you." She reached down, grabbed the wine bottle from the floor, and refilled her glass. "Can I talk you into another beer?"

My glass was almost empty, so I drained it and said, "Yeah, that sounds like a good idea. Why don't I just get it, and you can stay here in front of the fire?"

"I think that sounds perfect. But hurry back. I'm missing you already."

I hurried into the kitchen and pulled another IPA out of the refrigerator. The refrigerator had a half-dozen food takeout trays stacked on the shelves— everything from Subway sandwiches to Thai cuisine. I didn't see anything resembling fresh fruit or vegetables. Two bottles of white wine were on the bottom shelf of the door.

I opened my bottle of IPA and hurried back into the den. I couldn't be sure, but I think the lights were just a little lower. Phoenix was stretched out on the couch, and I headed for the recliner.

"Oh no, join me back here on the couch, Dev. It really helps me. I feel better already just chatting with you." She sat back up and moved her legs so I could sit down. Once I sat down, she stretched her legs out, resting them against my thigh. Her toenails were done in a French pedicure design, matching her fingernails.

"So, enough about Sterling. You need to tell me about yourself. And maybe you could even turn and face me. Honest to God, Dev. You've never seen a woman's body before?" she said and gave me a playful kick.

Twenty-five

We chatted through her bottle of wine, and she had me open another for her. I had one more beer. A clock on the fireplace mantel eventually chimed, signaling it was midnight.

"Well, I suppose I should get out of your way and let you get to bed. You're going to have some busy days ahead of you," I said.

"I can tell you, I'm not looking forward to them."

"Yeah, it will be hard, Phoenix. But you'll do it. If I can be of any help, let me know."

"Well, actually, if you wouldn't mind helping me up to my bedroom. I'm more than a little nervous about being alone in the house tonight."

"Upstairs? Yeah, I guess I can. Maybe you should leave the hall light on when you go to bed, and—"

"I'll still be alone." She reached down, grabbed the wine bottle, and refilled her glass. "Oh, God," she groaned as she stood and staggered a half-step. She picked up the remote and turned off the fireplace, then the music and the lights. She held out her hand for me.

Surprise Surprise! ♦ 159

We walked up the staircase hand in hand and down to the end of the hallway.

"This is my room," she said, pushing the door open and leading me into her bedroom. At no surprise, the room was lovely, with a king-size bed and a massive red upholstered headboard. There was an upholstered bench at the foot of the bed with a pair of jeans and a blouse lying on it. A makeup table with bottles and creams was off in the corner. A large double chest of drawers with a mirror the length of the chest sat against the opposite wall. Three large cream-colored candles were flickering away on top of the chest of drawers, illuminating the room. A door led into a walk-in closet, and a bathroom was on the far end of the closet. What appeared to be more candlelight flickered from the bathroom.

"Would it be too much to ask if you'd lie down with me, Dev? I'm still out of sorts."

"No…umm…yeah, I can do that. Once you fall asleep, I can let myself out."

"If you want to. Or, you could just spend the night. I'm not sure I'll even sleep," she said and took another sip of wine. "Who knows, you might enjoy it."

She set her wine glass on the bedside table, pulled the covers back on the bed, and fluffed up two of the three pillows. She picked up a remote from the bedside table, dimmed the lights, and then clicked a sound system. Suddenly, the noise of waves on the shore filled the room.

"Don't forget to take off your shoes," she said as stared directly at me, and undid the black satin belt around her waist. She let her black lace robe drop to the floor and stood there for a moment, completely naked and smiling, then climbed into the bed.

I made an audible gulp and climbed in on the opposite side of the bed.

"Dev, please, I just need to be held, please," she pleaded.

I moved across the bed toward her, slipped my arm around her shoulder, and she rolled over alongside me. "Mmm, this is so much better. It's been so long," she said. A moment later, she rolled on top and kissed me.

I woke up around 4:30, wondering how in the hell I let this happen. Phoenix was asleep with her back to me, snoring softly. The sound of waves on the shore was no more. I slipped out from beneath the covers and began to search for my clothes. I had a vague memory of Phoenix tossing my socks and boxers off the end of the bed. As I slid out of bed, I stepped on my jeans, and next to them was my shirt. My socks, boxers, and t-shirt were scattered across the floor at the end of the bed.

I gathered my clothes up and tiptoed toward the door. I slowly turned the doorknob, pulled the door open. I stepped out into the hall, closing the door as quietly as possible. I quickly dressed then realized I'd forgotten my shoes in the bedroom. I quietly reentered the bedroom. One of my shoes peeked out from beneath the bed. I reached down and pulled. Out came both shoes resting on a metal cookie sheet. The sheet was loaded with a variety of battery-operated appliances, two furry tails, and clamps for various organs. I pushed the cookie sheet back under the bed. Phoenix snored a couple of times. I remained frozen, in hopes she wouldn't wake.

After a long moment, I carried my shoes out of the bedroom. I checked to make sure my wallet and car keys were in my pocket. I tiptoed down the hall, hurried downstairs, and out the front door, and drove home disgusted with myself.

Twenty-six

Morton wandered down to the kitchen a little after 7:00. I gave him a good scratch behind the ears and said, "Sorry I wasn't here last night, Morton. Things just seemed to get out of hand." I went to let him out the back door, and that's when I noticed that the door was unlocked. I always lock the door.

I looked at the outside doorknob and the key cylinder. There was no apparent sign of anyone tampering, but I always lock the door. I replayed my previous evening movements. I'd been asleep on the couch when Phoenix called. I'd gotten up, let Morton out, and got the coffee ready for this morning. That must have been it. When I got Morton back in the house, I gave him a biscuit, turned on the light going upstairs, and apparently neglected to lock the back door.

But that didn't sound like me. Between Quinnie and Phoenix, I've done some stupid things, but I always lock the door. My laptop was right where I left it. Nothing seemed to be missing. I went upstairs and checked my dresser drawer. A couple of family heirloom rings were still there, along with a pair of diamond earrings that had been left so long ago I'd forgotten the woman's name.

I opened the bedside table, and the pistol I kept was still there, apparently untouched. Strange, I still had a hard time getting my head around the fact that I may have left my back door unlocked.

Morton and I finished breakfast, and after checking the back door two more times to make sure it was locked, we headed down to the office. The coffee pot had been left on, and I poured the remnants down the sink and made a fresh pot.

Louie came into the office a little after 9:00. Once he'd recovered from his climb up the stairs, he said, "So, how was your evening? You do anything?"

"No, nothing worth talking about, just fell asleep on the couch." He gave me a look like he didn't believe me. "What are you looking at?" I said.

"Somehow, it just doesn't sound right. You didn't end up with Tubby's sister again, did you?"

"No, not that she wouldn't have been fun. Once you get her away from her brother, she's really very nice. But no, I didn't see her. She mentioned yesterday that they're in the process of going over some family stuff, a trust fund among other things. I know it's hard to believe, but apparently, Tubby's not playing nice."

"So she's still in town."

"Yeah, at least for a couple more days from the way she sounded. Fortunately, or well, unfortunately, my recent investigation into the accountant, Sterling Kozlow, ended when someone killed him. So, if Tubby's sister Quinnie needs a break, I can pick her up and take her someplace."

"God, things really are bad if she's setting her sights on you for an interesting time." Louie's phone suddenly rang, and he answered.

I turned on my laptop, and suddenly the wine Phoenix was drinking last night, Titus Cabernet Napa Reserve, popped into my head. I googled it. A picture of the bottles Phoenix was drinking popped up immediately, not bad, eighty-nine bucks a bottle. It struck me as funny in a way. She met Sterling Kozlow because she didn't have the cash to cover a seven-dollar bottle of wine, and now she's drinking almost two bottles that, with the tax, are more than ninety bucks apiece. Not Bad.

As long as I was on Google, I looked up Damien Dambella. Nothing new came up. On the offhand chance, I called Aaron LaZelle and ended up leaving a message. "Yeah, Aaron, Dev calling. Give me a call back when you have a minute. Thanks."

"Something shaking?" Louie asked as he hung up his phone.

"What?"

"You were just calling LaZelle. You checking into the Kozlow murder?"

"Actually, no, but I'd be interested if they had anything. I think the autopsy is scheduled for later today. I just had a question about someone else. Oh, as a matter of fact, it's Damien Dambella. You were telling me about him the other night at The Spot."

"Well, I didn't tell you much, and I was basically repeating fourth-hand information, so don't take it as gospel."

"Not to worry, I won't. I just had a couple of questions for Aaron. More like putting me in touch with someone who could check to see if there's anything on Dambella. Aaron doesn't have the time. With the murder rate in this town right now, I'm surprised he can make it home to sleep."

"Don't limit it to here. It's all over the country."

"It's crazy. I was just thinking—"

My phone rang, saving Louie from my lecture. "Haskell Investigations," I said.

"Hi, Dev, Aaron, calling back. What's up?"

"Oh, thanks for getting back to me so fast."

"Have you calmed down yet?" Aaron asked

"Yeah, I have. I'm not going to report Manning or sue his dumb ass, which I have every right to do. But I'm calm. I still meant what I said, Aaron. He's going to pull some shit on someone who is not going to back off, and the department is going to be screwed. I'm just like you. I really don't want to see that happen."

"That's why he's on desk duty for the foreseeable future."

"Which is exactly what you don't need right now because you're shorthanded, to begin with, and people are going nuts out there on the street."

"Tell me about it. Look, he's dealing with some serious problems with his son. The kid has some issues. He's disappeared again. I've got to cut him some slack."

"Anything I can do to help?"

"Yeah, you could find the kid and get him back to his father. They'll stick him in treatment, again. Maybe this time it'll work."

"What's the kid's name?"

"No, I don't want you looking for him. Thanks, all the same, but I think it would just add to the problem. Not a reflection on you, but you know how it is. So, you called, and I'm guessing it wasn't a dinner invite. What's up?"

"I wanted some background on a guy. There might be a record, maybe not. Seems to be a high roller, in with all the upper class in town. I just wondered if you might have anything on him or if you could put me in touch with someone I could talk to. I know you're really jammed."

"Yeah, it's crazy. Thanks for backing off on Manning. Much appreciated. Who's this guy you're looking at?"

"Name is Damien Dambella. I think he runs a firm called Northern Star Ventures. Drives a fancy sports car called an Equus Throwback."

"Equus Throwback? I've never heard of it."

"I think his car is the only one in about a five-state area. Money doesn't seem to be an issue. The thing starts at a hundred and thirty grand and goes up from there."

"Oh, man. Does that price include the chauffeur?"

"No, but then, if you have to ask, you can't afford it."

"Yeah, you got that right. I'll look into the name and get back to you. Thanks again for backing off on Manning."

"Yeah. If I can help with that situation, let me know," I said, and we disconnected.

I googled the name Jeremy Robins, the guy who left Sterling Kozlow's office a few months back. I came up with a dozen different names, a movie producer, a musician, guys all over the country. But one of them, oddly enough, listed St. Paul as the town he was from, and I remembered Phoenix telling me he and his wife were in the process of restoring a home on Goodrich Avenue.

I looked up the address in the reverse directory. There was a landline listed. I called and got a recording with a pleasant-sounding woman's voice saying she and Jeremy, "Are unable to take your call at the moment. If you would please leave a message with your number, we'll get back to you just as soon as we can."

"Hello, my name is Devlin Haskell. I'm calling for Jeremy. I believe I have the right number. This is in regard to the sudden passing of Sterling Kozlow." I left my number, hung up, and crossed my fingers. I added the number and Jeremy's name to the contact list on my phone.

Twenty-seven

It was getting toward the end of the day. Louie headed over to The Spot. I took Morton for a walk before we joined him. We followed our usual path. Morton sniffed every other fence gate, got close and personal with the two fire hydrants, and gave a friendly bark to a half-dozen other dogs along the way. Finally, we joined Louie in The Spot.

"A Summit IPA?" Mike asked as I headed down the bar. Morton had the leash pulled taut as he pulled me toward Louie's usual stool.

"Yeah, and better pour another round for Louie," I said.

Louie had a handful of pork rinds for Morton by the time we came around the end of the bar. "Great to see you, Morton. I've been waiting. No doubt, Dev held you up." Morton hurried over and inhaled the pork rinds in a nanosecond.

"How'd your day go, Louie?" I asked just as Mike set our drinks on the bar. Louie drained what was left in his glass and slid the empty across the bar to Mike. "It's suddenly getting better," he said as he pulled the fresh drink in front of him. "What's shaking with your Kozlow woman?"

"Oh, you mean Phoenix Starr."

"Yeah, I forgot that was her name. It seems to fit her appearance a lot better."

"Yeah, she's something, all right. I spoke with her yesterday. She's a bit depressed, which is only natural. I think the autopsy on Sterling was scheduled for this afternoon. Unless they find something unusual, I'm guessing they've either already released the body, or they'll release it tomorrow."

"If it's just the bullet, they'll release. Anyone looking like a suspect out there?"

"Yes and no. As far as I know, there's nothing much to go on. Maybe they'll get fingerprints or a hair sample or something from the car. There was this phone call where he supposedly set up a meeting with some woman, but—"

"The meeting was going to be at that bar with that goofy name?" Louie said.

"Yeah, Scuttlebutts. He was shot in their parking lot. I know the cops have his cellphone. Phoenix told them about the phone conversation she overheard where the meeting was mentioned. Hopefully, they can trace the call, and it will lead them to the murderer. But who knows? As for Phoenix, she's had this whole thing suddenly inserted in her life, and you know, it takes some time."

"It takes a lot of time, and that's under normal circumstances. Something like this, hell, it could be years. You know if she's doing a funeral?"

"She mentioned a memorial service. I don't think anything is scheduled, but it's still early in the process. Apparently, his will stated he was to be cremated and that his ashes were to be scattered at a lake place they have up north somewhere. That's about all I know."

"Crazy world," Louie said.

We both took sips from our respective drinks. My cellphone rang just as I set my glass down. I glanced at the screen, Jeremy Robins.

"Oh, good. Hey, I've gotta take this, Louie. Can you keep an eye on Morton for a minute?"

"Just in time for more pork rinds," Louie said, emptying the bag into his hand. Morton was so focused on the pork rinds he didn't even know I'd stepped outside.

"Hello, Jeremy. This is Dev Haskell. Thank you for returning my call."

"Not a problem. I have to tell you, I was a little surprised to get your call. Do you work for the newspaper?"

"The newspaper? No, actually, I'm a private investigator. I was working on a case involving Mr. Kozlow when this occurred. I wonder if it would be possible to meet with you. I'm just trying to get as much background information as possible and share it with the police. At this point, they don't appear to have much to go on, and anything would help."

"I'll be happy to meet with you, but just so you know, I'm no longer employed at Sterling Kozlow Finance. I haven't been for a number of months."

"Yes, I'm aware of that, and I'm aware that you left under very good circumstances. You gave Kozlow notice weeks in advance that you were looking. I believe you offered to stay for four weeks after you were hired at the new company."

"That's all correct, so any information I have is going to be dated. Sterling phoned me about a month ago with a question regarding one of his clients. We had what was a two or three-minute conversation. That was the last time I spoke with him."

"Most of my involvement would be along the lines of the man's overall personality. He appears to have had a very good reputation. Just trying to get a picture of the guy."

"Well, we can meet. I'm due out of town the day after tomorrow. Things are going to be crazy tomorrow, the usual last-minute nonsense. Would you have time to meet this evening?"

"Yeah, I'd be happy to do that. You name a place and time, and I'll be there."

"Why not come over here? We can meet in the kitchen. My wife is expecting, and she's in that exhaustion stage right now. She'll be in bed by 7:00 tonight, and I'd like to be here just in case our little girl gets up or needs something."

"That's not a problem. You live on Goodrich, right?"

"Yes, six-thirty-four. Blue house with white trim, a tower in front, and a dressed stone facing on the first floor."

"If I'm there at 7:30, would that work for you?"

"That would be perfect. I'm not sure how much I can tell you, but I'm happy to talk. It's an absolute shame what's happened to Sterling. I really have no words for it. The man certainly didn't deserve something like this."

"I couldn't agree more, Jeremy. Hopefully, the police will be able to find who was responsible. I'll see you in about ninety minutes, and thank you in advance for your time," I said.

I stepped back into the bar. Morton was curled up on the floor in front of Louie's stool. Louie had just finished talking to Mike. "Everything go okay?" Louie asked.

"Yeah, I've got to meet a guy in an hour and a half. No big deal. Mike, is Louie being difficult to deal with again?"

"He was headed in that direction, but I put a stop to it," Mike said, laughed, and headed down the bar as a couple stepped in the front door.

We chatted for another forty-five minutes, and then Morton and I headed home. I let him into the backyard, ran upstairs and pulled on a different shirt. I let Morton in, double-checked that the door was locked, and headed to Jeremy Robins' house. I picked up a bottle of wine on the way, not a Titus Cabernet.

Twenty-eight

At no surprise, Jeremy's description of the house was spot-on accurate. Although he'd failed to mention the wrought iron fence around the front yard and the five 4X4 posts supporting the roof over the front porch. Dusk was just settling in, and I parked two doors up and walked back to the house.

As I opened the front gate, a voice called out, "Dev Haskell?"

I saw him sitting on a porch swing on the side of the porch, partially covered by what looked like a trimmed lilac tree. "Yes, Jeremy?"

"Up here on the porch. It's such a nice night outside. I thought it would be better if we sat out here. I've got a monitor on up in our daughter's room, just in case she starts crying. Fortunately, she's a pretty good sleeper," he said as I climbed the four steps up to the porch.

"Wow, quite the place you have here. How long have you been here?"

"We bought it six years ago, scrimped and saved every penny we had. Got a loan from both sets of parents to make the down payment. Now, based on the way housing prices have gone in the past six years, it's worth almost twice what we paid, and that's with stuff like this going on," he said and indicated the posts supporting the porch roof.

"I get it. I grew up about four blocks over on Holly Avenue. My folks did the same thing when we were kids. I live over on Selby now, same thing, always a major project to do. But I like it. Oh, here, a bottle of wine," I said, handing him the paper bag. "I appreciate you taking the time to meet with me. Your wife is doing okay?"

"Oh, yeah, she's fine. She's just in this stage where she's literally exhausted. I come home, she naps, I fix dinner, she eats, and she goes to bed. Doesn't wake up until the alarm goes off in the morning. Her next phase, closer to delivery time, will be full energy, scrubbing, cleaning, and giving me direction, which apparently I need."

"As long as she and the baby are healthy, that's all you want."

"So right. You sound like you have kids."

"No, but I've dealt with enough and couples, friends, growing a family. It's a lot of work."

"So what can you tell me about Sterling's murder? God, I heard it on the news, and I thought that couldn't be right. Sterling?"

"You're not alone in thinking that. From the little I've learned, he was a really nice guy. Worked hard, did a lot of volunteer things. Just a good all-around guy."

Robins seemed to think for a few seconds and asked, "So you're involved in the police investigation?"

"No, at least not directly. I was looking at Sterling for another reason. I suppose it doesn't matter now, but his wife hired me. She was afraid he was having an extramarital affair and—"

"Sterling? You gotta be kidding me. The guy adored her, not that he got much in return. At least from what I could tell. That said, it would be contrary to the man's personality. The guy I knew would never do that."

"Did he ever allude to an interest in another woman?"

Robins shook his head. "No, never. The guy was the original straight arrow. I really can't see it."

"There were rumors he was supposed to meet some woman at the bar where he was murdered. In fact, I was in the place, waiting to see if he'd show up. He never did. Unfortunately, I was the guy that found him shot in his car and called the police."

"Yeah, that whole thing struck me as crazy. Him meeting someone in a bar? That's not the Sterling I knew. If he had anything to drink, he'd limit it to maybe a glass of white wine. Although he was more than happy to pick up the tab for his staff drinking, he always kept himself in line. And what was the name of the place where he was killed?"

"Scuttlebutts."

"Yeah, that right there is just not the guy I knew."

"Did you ever meet his wife?"

"Oh, yeah, Phoenix. Talk about opposites attract. I think we met her twice. Fortunately, Maddie, that's my wife, was with me, so Phoenix more or less stayed in line. But the other guy on staff, Marshal Jones, he said he had some stories, not that he ever told them to me, but he alluded to things.

"What kind of things?"

"Oh, you know, Phoenix doing things you'd expect someone who was trying to pick you up might do. Posing, maybe she'd have an extra button or two undone at an all-staff dinner with our spouses. Maddie and I had dinner at their house once, and only one time in four years, she came into the office. I think I saw Phoenix four or maybe five times in four years. She's very attractive, but she has this aura about her that suggests there's always the chance for trouble close by, so you best keep your distance."

I nodded and completely understood what he was saying. "Sterling seemed to work long hours," I said.

"Yeah. He was there when we arrived in the morning. On a few occasions, I drove past the place in the evening, and I could still see his car parked out front after 8:00 at night. The man was a real workhorse. That's also why he owns that mansion over on the River Boulevard. The guy works his ass off. It's his life, or, well, it was his life."

"Do you know if his wife was employed?"

He shook his head. "Not that I'm aware of. He never talked about her. I think her big activity was decorating the place. You can imagine what it was like when they got married. First marriage for Sterling, I'm not sure about the wife, but if you told me she'd been married a half-dozen times, it wouldn't surprise me. Don't get me wrong, she was always nice, polite, and all that. But Maddie warned me after we had dinner at their house, there's something there, and she's not afraid to use all her charms to get whatever she wants."

"Sterling never said anything along that line?"

Robins shook his head. "No, like I said, that wasn't his style. He was an old-fashioned gentleman, a really nice guy. If she was flirting around, I'm not sure he would have even been able to pick up on it."

"The name Damien Dambella mean anything to you?"

Robins exhaled and said, "So that's really why you're here?"

"What do you mean?"

"Dambella, he's one of, no, let me rephrase that, he's the major reason I left the firm."

"He was a client of Sterling Kozlow Financial?"

"As far as I know, he still is. The guy's as crooked as they come. I'll give him this much, he's good at hiding it. His primary company is called Northern Star Ventures. That's the account that's listed on the books. The problem is that guy has all these little things going on that contribute a ton of money to the organization. One look at the books, by the way, he has at least two sets, but one look at the books, and I figured it would just be a matter of time before I was hauled in and jailed for being a participant. I'd lose my license, serve time, and a thug like Dambella, he'd probably pull a few strings, walk away, and start all over again."

"So why would Sterling keep him as a client?"

"That's the million-dollar question, literally. I didn't get it. I was very clear with Sterling about what I'd found, none of it good. It's the main reason I left. Well, that, and I got a better job offer, with a future instead of jail time, and I'm working for an honest organization instead of catering to a sleaze bag like Dambella. Not that Sterling wasn't honest. It just did not make any sense that he handled the Dambella account."

"I had no idea. Are you familiar with his car?"

"Dambella's? You mean that red sporty thing he drives around town in? Yeah, it's officially leased to Northern Star Ventures, but he has some ghost operation pay the bill, and he writes it off as an investment. I mean, the guy is just, well, he's not good news. I warned Sterling. God, I really did. Now look what's happened."

"Did you ever go to his office?"

"Oh yeah, don't get me started. His office is supposedly in a building downtown on Robert Street. It's a scam. He writes off the rent and creates a bunch of phony invoices related to the place. I went down there twice. The second time, I paid a maintenance guy five bucks to look inside. The place was empty, always has been. I mean, not so much as a stick of furniture, no employees.

He's got something like fifteen or twenty names supposedly working there at all times. He writes off their salaries, has a ton of fake receipts for the cost of doing business, and absolutely nothing is happening there."

"Is that what he wanted you to do?"

"No, he just wanted me to file his papers to make the whole thing appear legit. I was never invited down to the office. I just went there because the records and receipts I was looking at weren't making sense. A fleet of cars but no fuel or repair charges? Daily lunches and dinners at restaurants that are closed, but apparently, Dambella owns the places. A bunch of employees that don't exist. It's a big-time scam just waiting to be discovered.

"God, he's got a place on the river bluff, just off of Randolph and Shephard Road. A house about a hundred and fifty years old or even more. The joint looks haunted if you ask me. Always a couple of thugs hanging around. I was going to stop, knock on the door, and ask him some questions. I took one look at those goons and kept driving. I don't want my family or myself exposed to that stuff or someone like Dambella."

"What did Sterling say when you told him about this?"

"He just smiled, told me thanks, and wished me luck in my job search."

"He didn't tell you, you were fired?"

"No, I told him that, because of my suspicions regarding Dambella, I was going to be looking for another position. He wasn't mad. In fact, he was very understanding. He wished me luck, and you know how that worked out for him."

"If I talk to Marshal Jones at Kozlow Finance, would you mind if I mentioned you?"

"No, not at all. We've been meaning to get together but just haven't had the time. Now, I guess this will serve as the impetus. Tell him I said hi and want to meet for a beer some night."

We chatted for a few more minutes. I thanked Jeremy Robins for his time. He thanked me for the wine and told me to call if I had any other questions.

Twenty-nine

It was dark as I made the way back to my car. I drove over to Summit Avenue and went down Ramsey Hill onto 35E, eventually I drove past The Spot. Louie's car was gone, so he must have headed home. I drove down Randolph and ended up on Stewart Street.

There it was, the structure Jeremy Robins had referred to as a haunted house. Actually, that appeared to be a pretty accurate description. The house was a large three-story red-brick Victorian structure with a mansard roof. A long porch ran across the front of the house. A four-story tower with a peaked roof was centered on the house. I slowed down to get a closer look.

Based on Robins' description, I was sure it was Dambella's place. In case I had any doubts, there were two guys sitting on the front porch. Both men had the look of someone you wouldn't want to cross. As if that wasn't enough, up on the fourth floor of the tower was a round window. Some guy was seated in a chair, looking out the window. Just now, he was in the process of bringing a pair of binoculars up to his eyes, apparently checking me out as I drove past. I looked back to the road and increased my speed, hopefully without anyone noticing.

I knew the place had to have a history. Obviously, Dambella didn't build it. Robins had said it had to be at least a hundred and fifty years old. I'd seen enough for the night and had a number of questions bouncing around my thick skull after talking with Jeremy Robins, so I decided to head home.

I took a round-about route just to make sure no one from Dambella's followed me. I parked in the driveway ten minutes later. Morton met me at the front door with an anxious look. I let him out into the backyard. Thankfully, the back door was still locked. I turned on my laptop and googled Dambella's address on Stewart Street.

It turned out the house had originally been built by the brewmaster for the Banholzer Brewery Company, and, among other things, it was reputed to have an entrance in the basement to a series of caves where beer from the brewery had been stored. The cave opened up onto the Mississippi River plain below the bluff. This was not unusual for the time, and there were a number of breweries in the area in the late 1800s that did exactly that, stored beer in the caves with access to the river below.

The Banholzer Brewery went out of business in 1904, and at some point, the caves were apparently sealed. My first thought was, *What a perfect location for a series of illegal enterprises.*

I let Morton back into the house, checked my phone, and was thankful there wasn't a message from Phoenix Starr. I shared a cold pizza with Morton. I checked online to see if Sterling Kozlow's body had been released. It turned out it hadn't been. I was in bed before 11:00.

I drove past Phoenix Starr's house the next morning on the way to the office. Low and behold, a red Equus Throwback was parked in her driveway. I thought the odds were probably pretty slim that Damien Dambella had recently arrived with an early morning breakfast. Lucky him.

We were down at the office a good half-hour before Louie. After sipping his coffee for a bit, he said, "You seem to be awfully busy on the computer this morning. Usually, you're looking through the binoculars at the apartment across the street. What's up?"

I filled him in on last night's meeting with Jeremy Robins. Then told him about Dambella's house and the history behind it.

"Yeah, the brewery caves were a big deal in the late 1800s. I think just about all of them have been sealed up, more of a dangerous hazard, and there was a problem with kids throwing wild parties in them back in the 60s and 70s. The neighbors finally had enough of it, and the city closed them down."

"Yeah, except this Banholzer cave supposedly had an entrance to it from the basement of the house. If that still exists and Dambella has the house, I mean, he could be doing anything down there. Cooking up drugs, holding hostages, running some sex club—"

"You might be getting a little bit ahead of yourself, Dev. First of all, it would be against at least a half-dozen city codes to have the structure connected to the cave."

"Oh, yeah, how could I forget about the city code? Certainly, that would be a concern to someone like Damien Dambella. You think some scammer like him gives a damn about the city code? He probably looks at the code just so he can figure out ways to get around it."

"So, you think he's running some drug operation under his house?"

"Well, yeah, when you say it like that, it sounds a little crazy, but his place is like Tubby's, well, except he doesn't have a brick wall running around the property. But Tubby has guys watching the front and the back twenty-four hours a day, seven days a week. It looks like Dambella is the same. Or, how about this? What if Dambella is actually a competitor of Tubby's?"

"If he was in the same line of work as Tubby, wouldn't the cops know about him?" Louie asked.

"Well, yeah, probably, and Aaron LaZelle didn't mention anything about him when I asked. So maybe Dambella is still operating under the radar."

"Yeah, sure, Dev, he's doing that in his cave. In fact, that's why he's down there because it's under the radar," Louie said, then chuckled and shook his head.

"Well, go ahead and laugh all you want, but I think I may be on to something here. Maybe Sterling Kozlow somehow got wind of it. Maybe he finally figured the money just wasn't adding up, and he was duty-bound to report it. The next thing you know, someone blows his brains out while he's parked in his car at Scuttlebutts."

"Let me know when you find something a little more concrete than just conjecture. Look, Dev, you may be right. Hell, I'd be surprised if you're not on to something here. It's just that, right now, you're talking in, well, guesses and assumptions. But there's nothing concrete."

"That's what I'm going to find out, Louie. I think this Dambella was involved in Kozlow's murder, and I'm going to nail his ass."

Thirty

When I met with him, Jeremy Robins had mentioned the name Marshal Jones. I decided I would pay him a visit rather than call. With any luck, he was still at Kozlow Financial, and they'd be open. I put Morton in the back seat, and we drove over to Sibley Plaza. I half-expected to see Sterling Kozlow's red Mercedes parked in front of the office. Instead, there was a gray SUV in its place. A round sticker was on the rear window that read, 'My Child is an Honor Student.' I didn't see anything that resembled an unmarked police car in the parking lot.

I pulled in next to the SUV, lowered the windows to let fresh air in for Morton, and for the first time, actually entered Kozlow Financial. A woman at the front desk looked up from her computer and smiled. I noticed there was a framed picture of Sterling Kozlow resting behind her on a credenza. I wondered if it had always been there or if it had been a recent addition.

"Good morning. How may I help you?" she said with a smile.

"Hi, and good morning to you. I'd like to see Marshal Jones if he's available."

"Do you have an appointment?" she asked and pulled what looked like a desk calendar over in front of her.

"Actually, no, I don't, but a friend thought it might help to chat with him. My name is Devlin Haskell."

"Let me check to see if he has time to see you. The last couple of days have been rather crazy."

"Yeah, I can't imagine. My condolences. I didn't know Mr. Kozlow personally, but everything I've heard suggests he was a real gentleman."

She nodded, picked up the phone, and punched in three numbers. After a moment, she said, "Yes, Marshal, I have a gentleman named Devlin Haskell out here. He'd like to speak with you if you have a moment. He doesn't have an appointment, but a friend recommended you to him."

"No. All right. Yes, I will. Thank you." She hung up the phone and looked up at me. "He has some time. If you'll head down the hall, Marshal's office is the second door on the right."

"Thank you. I can go down now?"

"Yes, sir, second door on the right."

I walked past Sterling Kozlow's office. The door was closed, but his name was on the door, and for a brief moment, I recalled the evenings I sat out in the parking lot while he worked late and then followed him home.

The second door was labeled 'Marshal Jones.' I knocked on the door and began to open it just as a voice called, "Please come in."

The desk was positioned in front of the far wall. The credenza behind the desk had six different framed photos of what appeared to be family. A wife and four boys, maybe a twelve-year span across the photos. Marshal Jones stood as I entered. His blue shirt had been starched, but the sleeves were rolled up to his elbows, and it looked to be day two or possibly three in the shirt.

He was an average-sized guy with thinning dark hair. He carried an extra ten or twenty pounds and had a dark mole on his right cheekbone. His brown eyes sparkled as he held out his hand and said, "Hi, I'm Marshal Jones. How can I help you?"

I extended my hand, and we shook. "Dev Haskell, Mr. Jones. Nice to meet you. I got your name from Jeremy Robins. He says hi, and I'm supposed to tell you he'd love to get together with you for a beer sometime soon."

"That guy. We miss him around here. Now more than ever. Have a seat, and please, call me Marshal. I've had enough of the formal stuff over the last couple of days."

"Yeah, I can believe it. Actually, that's why I'm here."

Any sense of joy seemed to disappear from his face. "Are you with the police?"

I shook my head. "No, I'm not. I'm a private investigator. I was looking into something involving Mr. Kozlow. I'm actually the guy who found him shot the other night and called the police."

Jones seemed to think for a moment and said, "What do you mean looking into something involving Mr. Kozlow?"

"I was hired to check some things out. Personal, nothing business-related."

"It wasn't a question regarding a client?"

"No, it was not regarding a client, and to be honest, I never found one scrap of evidence that would have added any credibility to the suspicions my client had."

"I'm going to guess your client was a woman named Phoenix Starr, who is married, or rather was up until three days ago, to Sterling."

"Very perceptive."

"Not really," Marshal said and shook his head. "Marrying that woman was probably the worst move Sterling could have ever made. Unfortunately, he was such a straight shooter he never would have dreamed of initiating anything like a divorce. If there's anything positive about this entire situation, it's that he got that woman out of his life. Although, one hell of a way to do it."

"You're not a big fan of Miss Starr?"

"That's an understatement. She almost caused my wife to divorce me, and I didn't even do anything. We were at a company get-together, Christmas as a matter of fact. This was two years ago. Starr kept coming on to me. My wife thought I was encouraging her. God, I was just trying to be polite, you know, laugh it off. She was the boss's wife, after all. What the hell was I supposed to do?"

"What do you mean coming on to you?"

"You know, striking the sexy poses, winking, she blew me a couple of kisses. That got the wife riled up, and then Phoenix comes over and whispers in my ear, 'I want to ride you and eat you alive.'"

"She actually whispered that?"

"Yeah, the boss's wife, if you can believe it. Everyone was watching. My wife was embarrassed and ready to murder me. Thank God, the woman whispered when she said it. Otherwise, I would have been out on the street that night. It ended up costing me close to two grand in a number of dinners and a getaway weekend the wife and I took down to New Orleans."

"You say anything to Mr. Kozlow about this?"

"No, I didn't. Maybe I should have, but I was afraid he'd take it the wrong way and blame me for encouraging her or something. The last thing I need is that kind of trouble. I've got four kids. Our oldest will be heading to college in a year. Not the best time in life to have me out there, looking for a job."

"Did Phoenix ever try anything like that again?"

"No, but I never gave her the chance. We were only out with her one other time, last year's Christmas Party.

I drank water the entire night, and the wife played interference with a look on her face you wouldn't want to cross."

"Have you ever done any work for Northern Star Ventures?"

He shook his head. "Man, you can sure pick 'em. No, no one works with them except Mr. Kozlow. I'm not sure what's going to happen to that account now. I know I'm not going to touch it. In fact, Jeremy Robins told me about them on his way out the door. He didn't just tell me. He basically warned me and based on what he said, I don't want to go anywhere near those people."

"You know anything about Damien Dambella?"

"No, and I don't want to. I know he's the CEO of Northern Star Ventures, and my knowledge ends there."

"Anything else you can tell me?"

He shook his head. "I don't know why Mr. Kozlow was murdered. Maybe it was just a carjacking gone wrong. I just hope they get whoever did it."

"I guess I don't have any more questions. Thanks for your time, Marshal. I appreciate you talking to me."

"Good luck. I wish I could have been more help. If you talk to Sterling's wife, please don't mention my name."

Thirty-one

I thanked the woman at the front desk on my way out and climbed into the car. Morton was stretched out in the backseat. He opened one eye, saw it was me, and went back to sleep. I pulled out of the Sibley Plaza parking lot and headed toward the River Boulevard.

We drove past Phoenix Starr's place. The red Equus Throwback was parked in her driveway. I didn't leave a chalk mark on one of the tires, so it was impossible to know if it had been there since the last time I saw it or if it had just returned. Either way, Damien Dambella seemed to be rather involved. We were almost back at the office when my phone rang. By the time I parked and turned off the car, the ringing had stopped. I checked my recent call list. Quinnie.

I returned her call.

"Oh, Dev, thank God."

"Hi, Quinnie. Sorry I missed your call a moment ago. I was driving. What's up?"

"Would you have it in your heart to provide some sanity for Muffin and me? I just survived a major league explosion by Jerker, and I need some fresh air. If you can't, no pressure. We'll just head out the door, start walking west, and never look back."

"Don't do that. Listen, we're in the car, and Morton is just waking from his nap. A nice chase around the dog park might be just the thing for him, and I'd like to see you."

"Oh, if you don't mind, we would love it."

"We'll see you in ten minutes."

"We'll be waiting outside the gate just like before and thank you so much."

"How about I pick up a couple of bones at Rooster's? I have to pass right by there."

"Are you sure?"

"Not a problem. Add five minutes to my arrival time. See you then."

I stopped at Rooster's for the bones then headed up Randolph to the River Boulevard. No sign of a red Equus in Phoenix Starr's driveway as we drove past. Morton began pacing in the backseat as we approached Tubby's mansion. Quinnie and Muffin were just where she said they'd be, leaning against the wall outside of Tubby's gate.

I'd barely pulled to a stop before Quinnie had the back door open and Muffin hopped into the back seat. She and Morton greeted one another in true canine fashion. Quinnie hurried around to the passenger door and slid in.

"Oh, Dev, I can't thank you enough. Just get us out of here," she said as she buckled up. I stepped on the gas.

I checked the rearview mirror a couple of times, but no one was following. Given earlier remarks from Tubby's crew, I figured they were just as glad to see her leave as she was to get out of there.

"Bit of a stressful morning?" I asked.

"You could say that," she said and didn't make another sound until we pulled into the parking lot at the dog park. As soon as I stopped, she hurried out of the car and opened the rear door. Muffin and Morton jumped out and charged into the park, taking turns chasing one another back and forth.

I followed Quinnie and was just about to say something when she let out a loud scream and then another. I quickly looked around, thought about getting the pistol in my glove compartment, and wondered what in the hell was wrong. We were the only people there. Well, a car with an older woman had just pulled in, but at the sound of the scream, the woman made a quick U-turn and drove off.

"What is it? What's wrong?" I said, looking around and not seeing anything. Morton and Muffin had stopped running and were staring at Quinnie.

"Oh, God, I'm sorry. I just needed to scream and relieve some stress. Jerker is being a complete and total ass. God, how appropriate. Surprise, surprise."

"You want to talk about it?"

"No," she said and let out another scream. "There, okay. I'm feeling much better now."

"You sure you're okay? You had all three of us going there for a minute."

"Yes. I'm fine. God, we're all ready to sign things, get everything finished, and Jerker comes up with a half-dozen items not quite to his liking. He must have stayed up all night just to think them up. He's such a major pain in the ass. No wonder he's got all these guys around the place. Anyone who has ever had to deal with him probably wants to kill him."

That may not have been too far from the truth, but I thought it best not to comment. "Well, it looks like Muffin and Morton are enjoying themselves."

She shot me a look that seemed to suggest I was an idiot. She eventually walked down toward the dogs. She picked up a couple of sticks along the way and threw them to the dogs for a good fifteen minutes until both of them laid down next to one another. I waited until Quinnie headed back toward me before I pulled the bag of bones out of the car.

"Would it be all right if I gave them the bones?" I asked once she was back.

"Could we just let them lounge for a bit? I'm finally starting to relax. Sorry if I was a bit on the crazy side earlier."

"So not a problem. Believe me. I've had to deal with your brother for years. I get it. By the way, he'd probably say the same thing about me."

"I honestly don't know how you can stand him."

"I hesitate to use the term relationship, but we somehow manage to, if not get along, at least to interact occasionally."

"I don't know how you do it," she said. She put her finger to her lips and gave a whistle. Muffin looked up and then stood and trotted toward us. Morton followed closely behind.

"You mind if we just let them gnaw on the bones for a bit?"

"That's fine with me. Here, you hand them out, and I'm going to grab a seat on the hood of the car." I handed her the bag. She gave them each a bone. A minute later, she joined me on the hood of the car.

"God, I don't think I've sat like this since I was about fifteen."

"Yet another benefit to hanging out with a guy who's childish."

"Oh, actually, you're anything but. What's happening with your case that ended so abruptly?"

"Nothing really. But it's led me to another aspect of investigation. Just talking to folks, getting some general information. You know how life is. You think you've got a handle on things, and suddenly it turns out not to be the way you thought."

"Mmm-mmm, sounds like you're describing dealing with my brother."

"Funny you should say that. A name keeps coming up with the folks I've talked to, and I'm wondering if your brother might have some information."

"Information of any sort is not something my brother willingly gives out."

"Mmm-mmm, don't I know. Say, could I talk you into a late lunch? My treat."

"You certainly could, and you wouldn't have to talk me into it. Would it be all right if we went back to that same place?"

"You mean Shamrock's? Yeah, that would be fine with me."

"I'd kill for another one of those bourbon bacon chicken sandwiches."

We ended up in the back room, which was just fine. Morton and Muffin were stretched out on the floor, focused on their bones. We were focused on lunch. Quinnie had two glasses of wine, and I had a beer. We chatted for another half-hour after we finished eating.

Quinnie finally said, "You know, Dev. Just in case I haven't told you, thanks. I really mean it. I needed this break today."

"Hey, my pleasure. It's nice to talk to someone with their head on straight."

"I was just about over the edge when I phoned you. Thanks, much appreciated," she said and leaned over and gave me a peck on the cheek.

We loaded the dogs into the backseat and headed back to Tubby's. Still no red Equus in the driveway at Phoenix's house. As we drove past, I wondered if Sterling Kozlow's body had been released yet.

"You want me to let you off outside the gate," I asked as we approached Tubby's Mansion.

"No, that's okay. You can just drive in and drop us at the door. I plan on hiding in the guest room for the rest of the day."

Thirty-two

We drove into Tubby's and I stopped in front of the mansion. One of the guys hurried over to open the door for Quinnie as I pulled to a stop. He held the door as she got out. Quinnie opened the rear door for Muffin and then leaned in and said, "Thanks, Dev. This really helped."

"My pleasure. You hang in there, now."

I watched as she turned and headed into the mansion. Fat Freddy suddenly scurried out the door and brushed past her. "Haskell, wait a minute. You're wanted in the office. Park that thing and get your dumb ass inside."

Quinnie looked like she was about to say something but then shook her head in disgust and stepped inside. Fat Freddy waited with his arms crossed while I parked. I lowered the window for Morton and took my time climbing out.

Billy was standing behind the car waiting. I assumed the position. He waved the metal detecting wand over me and said, "All right, man, you're good to go."

"About damn time," Fat Freddy growled as I approached.

"Just trying to follow directions around here, Freddy. Does the boss need some more advice from me?"

"Don't kid yourself. Advice from you would be the last thing he'd want. Let's go. He's waiting in his office."

I followed Freddy inside, got patted down again, and then had to hurry to catch up to Fat Freddy waddling down the hall. "You got any idea what this is about?" I called as I caught up to him.

Freddy shook his head. "Against everyone's advice, he apparently wants to talk to you."

I figured a meeting with Tubby could go a couple of different ways. None of them amounted to anything beneficial to me. Freddy knocked on the office door as he opened it and stepped inside. "I've got Haskell here as you requested, sir," he said.

Tubby was seated behind his desk wearing a strappy white t-shirt. One of the Asian women I'd seen climbing in the taxi to the airport just a week ago was apparently back in town. She was standing behind him, massaging his dimpled, hairy shoulders. Surprisingly, she was dressed, meaning she was wearing a pink skintight top and high-waisted yoga shorts. "Thank you, Frederick. If I need your help, I'll send for you. Haskell, please, come join me."

Fat Freddy stood there for a moment with a shocked look on his face. "See you later. This is my big chance," I whispered as I hurried past Freddy and headed toward Tubby and the woman. Who knew? Maybe I was going to get a back rub.

An almost empty glass with a slice of lime floating in it rested on Tubby's desk. His suit coat and shirt were draped over one of the client chairs in front of his desk. "Take a seat," he said and nodded at the empty chair. For a split second, I thought about sitting on his coat, then quickly settled into the empty chair.

"That will be all for now, Chen," Tubby said. The woman gave him a final rub then stopped massaging his shoulders. She bowed slightly, grabbed the drink glass, and exited the office through a rear door hidden in the paneling. "Care for a beverage, Haskell?"

"Oh, very kind of you to offer, but no, thank you, sir. I've a busy afternoon ahead."

"Do tell," he said, sounding like he didn't believe a word. He studied me for a long moment, slowly tapping an index finger on his desk. Finally, he said, "You seem to be spending an inordinate amount of time with my sister. How is that working out?"

"Just exercising our dogs together, sir, and then we grabbed a late lunch today. She's a very nice person. Her dog, Muffin, is very well trained."

"Interesting. I'm not sure I've seen that particular side of her yet. But that's neither here nor there. It's not the reason I wanted to speak to you. I've heard some rumors that you've been asking questions regarding a local individual by the name of Damien Dambella. I wonder if I might be able to help."

There it was, Dambella. *How in the hell did Tubby know? And what's up with Tubby pretending to be nice?*

"Yes, sir. Just asking some general questions. I ran into his name in an earlier investigation. I was unaware of who he was. I still don't know a great deal about the man. He apparently heads up a business called Northern Star Ventures. Other than the name, I don't really know anything about the organization. Are you familiar with them or Mr. Dambella?"

"Am I familiar? Yes, at least on a certain level. Dambella is, how should I say it? He's a unique business individual. Successful on one level, finance, but there's a path of destruction and damage in his effort to make it to the top."

"Does he live down on Stewart Street?" I asked.

"He does. A historic home, actually on the bluff overlooking the river."

"I'll have to check the place out," I said, not wanting to tell him I already had.

"Just be careful, Haskell. More going on there than meets the eye. The man lives on the edge. His operation, Northern Star Ventures, is literally a house of cards, always has been."

"I stopped in at his office on Robert Street the other day," I lied. "From what I could see, he doesn't office there anymore. Do you know where he's moved to?"

"Haskell, I fear you're already in over your head. A word of advice, if I may. No good will come from getting up close and personal with the likes of Damien Dambella. Watch out. He's a ticking time bomb and under a good degree of pressure. I'd hate to see something happen to Quinnie because of you. I would not be very happy about that."

"Thank you, sir. I'll keep that in mind."

"See that you do, Haskell. That would be very wise, just so you understand." He paused for a long moment, studying me, and I wondered if he could hear my heart pounding. "Thank you for taking Quinnie off my hands. Just remember I don't want her having to deal with Dambella and his bunch of idiots. Now please, continue with your busy afternoon, and mind yourself," Tubby said.

"Thank you, sir. Always a pleasure," I said and hurried toward the door. As I opened the door, Fat Freddy stumbled a step or two into the office. Obviously, he'd been standing in the hall with his ear up against the door.

"Oh, umm, let's go, Haskell. I'll see him out, sir," Freddy called to Tubby.

I glanced back to look at Tubby, but he was facing in the opposite direction, watching the massage woman return with a fresh beverage, a smile, and now attired in just the high-waisted yoga shorts.

"Mr. Gustafson told me to ask you about a guy named Damien Dambella," I lied as I followed Fat Freddy down the hall.

Freddy shot me a look. "Dambella? That jerk? What about him?"

"What exactly does he do?"

"Let's just say he's out of your league, Haskell."

"Just about everyone is. What is he? Some kind of financial guy?"

"That's how he presents himself. But I don't think Mr. 'G' is very impressed. Dambella's what you'd call connected. He rubs shoulders with people on the city council, politicians, business bigwigs, the high and mighty. They seek him out, not the other way around."

"You ever been to his office?"

"If you're thinking of going there, Haskell, let me save you the time. It's just something he uses as an expense write-off. You check around, you'll probably find whoever owns that building, Dambella has some kind of angle he uses that allows him to write the place off, and he never pays anything."

"So, does Mr. Gustafson deal with him?"

"Have you been listening?" Freddy said as he opened the front door, and we stepped outside. "Deal with him? The only way we deal with him is we keep an eye on him. Mr. 'G' views him as the dark side of competition. And before you say anything, yeah, I know, we're involved in some unique enterprises. Dambella is another matter entirely. Just in case you didn't hear it in your meeting, watch out if you're looking into him. It can get ugly. He's one of the reasons we have people out here," Freddy said and waved his finger toward the three guys standing in front of the mansion.

"Been a pleasure chatting with you, Haskell, just kidding. Watch yourself. Oh, and we'd all like to thank you for getting the evil woman out of here. Don't know how you can stand her. Hopefully, she's headed back to the sunshine state in the next day or two."

"The sunshine state? That's Florida. She told me she lives in L.A.," I said.

"Whatever, just as long as she leaves town."

I extended my hand.

"Have you washed that yet today?" Freddy said and headed back into the mansion.

Thirty-three

Morton was sound asleep when I climbed back into the car. Usually, he opened an eye just to see who was there. This time, he just took a deep breath, pushed the bone closer to his chin, and attempted to snuggle deeper into the backseat.

I backed out of the parking place and drove onto the street. I went past Phoenix Starr's place, and low and behold, there was the red Equus parked in front of the three-stall garage. I thought for a second about continuing down to the office, turned at the corner, drove around the block, and pulled into Phoenix's driveway. I parked at an angle, not really blocking the Equus but making it necessary that Dambella would have to do a couple of back and forth movements if he was going to leave.

When I climbed out of the car, I couldn't help but remember Phoenix striking that pose at the front door the other night in her black lace robe. I only wished I could forget how the night ended up.

I glanced at the tinted windows on the Equus, hoping to see inside as I passed, but they were so dark all I saw was a reflection of myself. I followed the winding path to the front door, stepped onto the stoop, and rang the doorbell. Nothing happened. I rang the doorbell two more times. The fourth time I held my finger against the doorbell for a good twenty seconds. I could hear the thing ringing from inside the house, not that it made any difference. No one ever answered.

As I walked back to my car, I glanced up at Phoenix's bedroom window just in time to see the curtain fall back into place. That probably meant Phoenix and Dambella were enjoying each other's company upstairs in her bedroom. I wondered if she was wearing the black lace robe.

I climbed back in the car and drove down to the office. Morton woke up and stretched just as I pulled to the curb and parked. We headed up the stairs to the office. Louie was seated at his desk, leaning back in his chair with his hands folded across his massive stomach, snoring. The smell of burning coffee filled the air.

I stepped over to the coffee pot and turned it off. There was barely enough coffee left to cover the bottom of the pot. Morton hunkered down on his bed and began to gnaw on his bone.

I settled in at my desk, turned on my laptop, and Googled the address 400 Robert Street, the building where Dambella's fake office was. The building was apparently owned by an organization named Robert Street Enterprise. I was pretty sure that would turn out to be the name of a shell company run by Dambella. It struck me as interesting that Tubby viewed Dambella as competition. I began to think of ways I might use that to my advantage, none of which made any sense.

Louie snored himself awake twenty minutes later. He groaned, stretched, and said, "Oh, you been back long?"

"Not even a half-hour. Apparently, you've had a busy day."

"Just resting my eyes for a moment. Say, are you getting along okay with Tubby Gustafson? You haven't mentioned him lately, and Fat Freddy hasn't been by to force you into his Cadillac Escalade."

"Yeah, funny you should ask. As a matter of fact, I probably had the nicest five-minute conversation with Tubby ever just forty-five minutes ago. Why do you ask?"

"Someone was here checking out the office earlier. Two guys, actually. They knocked on the door and stepped in. Said they were looking for you. Actually, they asked if I was you. They did not look like the kind of people you'd want coming to pay a visit. It was probably a good thing you weren't here. You got a new client out there, or did some woman convince you she was single?"

"No, nothing like that has been going on."

"I watched them drive away. They had a black jeep-looking thing with yellow and red flames painted on the hood and a spare tire mounted on the back."

"And they asked for me?"

"Yeah. They were both big guys. One had a crew cut. The other had dark hair that was slicked back and shaved on the sides."

"Did they say what they wanted?"

"No, and given the first impression, I wasn't going to ask. They didn't bother to leave a card or a note. You might want to watch yourself out there. You sure you're not dating anyone new? Maybe this was a boyfriend or a husband someone forgot to mention."

"No activity in that department. Unless it's some guy Phoenix Starr was maybe seeing. But I haven't seen her in the last couple of days, which reminds me. I want to check and see if they've released Sterling Kozlow's body."

"Who you going to call about that?"

"I'll see if Aaron knows anything, and if I can't get him, I'll give Phoenix a call. It will be interesting to see if she even answers." I dialed Aaron LaZelle and ended up leaving a message.

"Hi, Aaron. Dev calling. Just wondered if Sterling Kozlow's body has been released yet. If you could let me know, either way, thanks."

I phoned Phoenix next. After three rings, I was dumped into her voice mail. "Hi, Phoenix. Dev Haskell, checking up on you. Hope everything is going okay. If there's anything I can do to help, please give me a call. Has Sterling's body been released from the morgue yet? Take care. I look forward to talking with you."

I puttered around the office for another hour, took Morton for a walk, and we met Louie at The Spot. He fed Morton a handful of pork rinds, and we chatted for maybe an hour. We headed home, and I pulled into the driveway. I let Morton into the backyard and went to insert my key into the lock, only the back door was unlocked.

This time, I was absolutely positive the door had been locked when we'd left. I'd even checked it twice just to be sure. I stepped into the kitchen and looked around. Everything appeared to be in place. I hurried up to my bedroom and opened the dresser drawer with the family heirloom rings and the pair of diamond earrings. Everything was just the way it had been the last time I checked.

I pulled the drawer open on the bedside table. My pistol was just where it should be. I went back down to the kitchen and began going through drawers. When I came up empty-handed, I moved into the front room, then the dining room, and finally the den.

That's where I found the pistol.

I have a coffee table next to the couch. It's a big old heavy thing with 4x4 legs, a bottom shelf, and a drawer. The drawer usually holds a corkscrew, paper napkins, and cardboard coasters I pocketed from a bar. Along with all that, tonight, it also had a small, pocket-sized semi-automatic pistol with black handgrips. The handgrip was labeled with the name 'Browning' across the top, as in Browning pistols. It definitely wasn't mine, and I guessed the weapon was a .25 ACP. I guessed it was likely the same weapon used to shoot Sterling Kozlow. In other words, I was being set up for Sterling Kozlow's murder.

I called Aaron LaZelle's office number and ended up leaving a message. I called his private line and crossed my fingers.

"Dev? Everything all right?" was how he answered after the third ring.

"Not really. Oh, and thanks for taking my call. I got home tonight, and my back door was unlocked." I gave him the general details and finished up with, "I've got a strong guess this is the weapon used to kill Sterling Kozlow. Someone, I've no idea who, but someone is trying to set me up for that."

"Let me make a call, and we'll get someone over there shortly. I'm heading over now. You got some dessert for me?"

"Dessert? Umm, yeah, maybe some chocolate chips or something, I think, maybe."

"God, why did I even ask? I'll pick something up. Stay away from the piece and wherever you found it. We'll be dusting for prints."

"Much appreciated, Aaron. I'll see you when you get here."

"Glad you called," he said and disconnected.

Thirty-four

Aaron LaZelle was at the door twenty minutes later holding a grocery bag. As I opened the door, another car pulled up to the curb. It was one of those unmarked cars that were easily recognized as a cop car from a half-mile away. That was bad enough, but when Detective Norris Manning stepped out from behind the wheel, I looked at Aaron.

"Are you kidding me? Manning? The guy will take my fingerprints, handcuff me, and lock me up. I'll be lucky if he doesn't shoot me for trying to escape in my own house. Come on, Aaron. This isn't going to work."

"Will you just calm down? We're both here on our own personal time. Look, he knows he made a mistake the other day. But he's damn good at getting prints and investigating a crime scene, so suck it up and give him some room. His job isn't to make you happy. He's here to try to find out who set you up. So be nice. Besides, I brought you frozen yogurt."

"Frozen yogurt? Do I look like I want something healthy? God, the hits just keep on coming."

"First of all, its sea salt caramel flavor, the best. Second, put a 'F'ing smile on or I'll call some rookie in and let him learn how to gather prints. He'll no doubt screw it up, and it will be a waste of time, but it's a learning process. Your choice."

Message delivered. I heard Manning step onto the front porch. I looked over Aaron's shoulder and smiled. "Oh, Detective Manning. Hey, thanks for coming on such short notice. Come in, come in. I found this gun in the drawer of my coffee table. Someone apparently picked the lock on my back door and got in. It's the second time in the last few days the lock has been picked. I thought maybe I forgot to lock the door the other day, but I double-checked it before I left today. I came home, and it was unlocked. I've got some family heirloom rings upstairs. They weren't touched. I've never seen this pistol before tonight. I'm willing to bet it's the weapon that was used to kill Sterling Kozlow over at Scuttlebutts."

"Let's take a look at where you found the weapon. Just point it out. Don't touch anything," Manning said. I waited for him to tell me what I'd done wrong, but it never happened.

He photographed and then dusted the coffee table, the drawer, and the pistol. The pistol was now in an evidence bag. Manning was currently dusting the back door for fingerprints. He'd already warned us that the chances of getting any prints on whoever broke in were slim to none.

While we were waiting for Manning to finish up, I sat at the kitchen counter watching Aaron as he filled three dishes with sea salt caramel frozen yogurt. I had to admit the stuff looked just like ice cream. Had he not told me it was yogurt, I would never have known.

Manning finished up and hauled his print kit and the pistol out to his car then came back in. We sat down at the kitchen counter and ate the first couple of spoonfuls of frozen yogurt in silence.

I was pleasantly surprised and said, "Okay. I was wrong. This doesn't taste like some low cal health food thing I'm being forced to eat. Actually, it's pretty damn good."

"I have to say, it's really good," Manning said.

"Who knew the two of you would ever agree on something," Aaron said.

Manning shook his head, seemed to think for a moment, and then said, "Haskell, sorry about locking you up the other evening. As logical as it seemed at the time, I may have made a mistake."

I was about to read him the riot act, but Aaron shot me a look. "Yeah, well, umm, thank you. Let's put it behind us. Thanks again for coming over tonight and dusting for prints. I wish I could tell you who was setting me up, but I honestly have no idea."

"What about your friend, Gustafson? You do anything lately to piss him off?" Manning asked, maybe suggesting guilt by association.

"No, in fact, just the opposite. I've been serving as a break between him and his sister. The two of them don't get along all that well."

"Small wonder," Manning said as he scraped the remnants of the frozen yogurt from his dish.

"It appears to be a complicated relationship. Going back to when they were kids."

"She live around here?" Aaron asked.

"No, left town just as soon as she could. At eighteen years old, she went out to Hollywood to make her fortune. Fortunately, her folks set up a trust fund, so she's got something she can fall back on."

"Does that mean the brother has a trust fund as well?" Manning asked.

"I know for certain that he does because they've been arguing over something or maybe a number of things related to the fund for the past few days. She was hoping to fly back to California three or four days ago. Anyway, not my problem."

"All that money, and they still can't get along," Manning said.

I nodded. "A funeral director told me once he usually sees people under unfortunate circumstances. If there's ever a problem, it's almost always related to money."

"Or you have someone you love suddenly go off the deep end," Manning said. "We're dealing with that now. My wife is beside herself, and there seems to be nothing we can do."

"This a child?" I asked, knowing he was referring to his son.

He stared at his dish and slowly nodded. "You'd think, with all my years on the force, all the contacts, I could do something. Find him somewhere, but it just doesn't work that way."

"What's his name?"

"Cullen, after Betty's father. He was a good kid, did the usual stupid things kids do, but then maybe a year ago, he just took a ninety-degree turn and went off the road. We had him in treatment. He left. Put him back in, and once he finished, he was back on the drugs literally the same day, just as messed up as when he went in."

"How long has he been missing?"

"Twenty-six days and counting."

"Any idea where he is now?"

Manning shook his head. "No, if I knew, I'd go get him. I'd lock him up if I had to. We get the occasional report, but by the time we get it, it's old news. Someone spots him on the street, once or twice in a shelter, but nothing ever current. Many's the night I've gotten off work and cruised the streets and shelters looking for him, but I've never found him."

"You happen to have a picture of him?" I asked.

He looked at me for a moment and then nodded. He reached into his pocket and pulled out a small stack of what looked like business cards and handed one to me. There was a picture of a nice-looking kid wearing a t-shirt. He had long hair and a failed attempt at growing a beard. I flipped the card over. It read, *'Cullen Manning. Age 17. Please call if you see him. Anytime day or night.'* A phone number followed.

"I'll keep an eye out for him. You never know. Like you, on occasion, I'm in not the best of areas. I'll call you if I see him."

"Yeah, thanks, Haskell. Like it says, call anytime, day or night. Umm, I should probably head out, get this evidence entered and into forensics. I'm going to use your name on it, L.T. Hopefully, that will speed things up."

"Yeah, good idea. Thanks for coming out. Let me walk you to the door. Any problems, give me a call, and I'll yank whatever chains I have to," Aaron said as he slid off his stool.

I stood as Manning wiped his hands on a napkin and placed it in his empty bowl.

"Thanks, Detective, really appreciate it. I see or hear anything on Cullen, I'll call you immediately."

Manning nodded and flashed a quick smile then followed Aaron to the front door. I waited while they chatted for a moment. Once Aaron closed the front door after Manning, I opened the back door and let Morton in the house. He hurried past me and got a head scratch from Aaron.

"Hey, Dev, thanks for offering to help find Manning's son. We've got the entire department looking for him, but no one has found a trace."

"Maybe he left town?"

"That would be one of the better options. He's been missing long enough now that death is quickly becoming the more likely scenario."

"I really feel for the guy, and there's nothing he can do."

"Yeah, it's sad. I worry if, or maybe when, the boy is found, if he's dead, it's liable to cause a breakdown for both him and his wife."

"She's not doing well?"

Aaron shook his head. "Isolated, depressed, on meds, seeing a therapist, and each day probably getting just a little worse."

"Jesus, it makes this deal with the pistol seem like small potatoes. Other than breaking into my house and trying to set me up for a murder, I got nothing to bitch about."

"Plus, I was able to introduce you to sea salt caramel frozen yogurt."

"Actually, it was pretty good. I'm a fan."

"Good. I've got an early day tomorrow, so if it's all right with you, I'll leave you under Morton's trusted care."

"He's more than capable," I said and walked Aaron to the door. I thanked him for coming, thanked him for getting Manning involved, and promised to talk tomorrow. I went back to the kitchen, rinsed off two of the bowls, and placed them in the dishwasher. I refilled my bowl with another helping of frozen yogurt.

Thirty-five

I woke up three or four times during the night and went downstairs to check the back door to make sure it was locked. I still woke up almost an hour before my alarm went off, tired but nonetheless awake. We had breakfast and left the house at 7:30. I stopped at two different homeless shelters that served breakfast but didn't see anyone resembling Cullen Manning.

Louie arrived in the office just before 9:00. Over a cup of coffee, I brought him up to date on the pistol planted in my coffee table and my evening with Aaron and Manning.

"Wow, you actually got on with Manning?"

"The guy is feeling a good deal of pain. His seventeen-year-old son got into drugs and has been living on the street for almost four weeks. You can imagine how well that's playing on the home front. Apparently, his wife is totally depressed, no surprise. The way he talked, it sounded like any spare time he has is spent looking for the son and coming up empty-handed. That's got to take a toll after a while. I can't imagine."

"That might help explain his decision to lock you up the other night."

"Well, yeah, that, plus the fact that he hates my ass to begin with. But, after talking last night and seeing the guy with the wind knocked out of his sails, I really felt for him. Hopefully, that works both ways, and they can get an ID on whoever left that gun in my coffee table. Someone was trying awfully damn hard to set me up. I don't think they're going to stop just because we got wind of this attempt."

"You might want to invest ten bucks and get a chain lock to secure that back door. Maybe an alarm system would be an even better idea."

"I'll be doing that shortly."

Morton and I went to the hardware store and purchased two brass door chain locks. It took all of ten minutes to install them. I hooked the chain up on the back door. The front door chain was for nights before I went to bed. We climbed back in the car, and I drove past Phoenix Starr's home. No red Equus in the driveway and no way to know if Phoenix was home. I drove around the block, pulled over, and phoned Phoenix.

I ended up leaving a message. "Hi, Phoenix, Dev Haskell here. I'm just touching base. Call me if you need help with anything. Has Sterling's body been released yet? Give me a call when you have the time. Bye," I said and disconnected.

I thought I'd get a jump on things and called Quinnie. I got dumped into her voice mail. "Hi, Quinnie, Dev

Haskell, checking in. Hey, I'm thinking of taking a walk along the riverbank. Wondered if you and Muffin wanted to join us. No time scheduled. Give me a call if you feel like it. All the best, Dev."

We headed back to the office, and I phoned Aaron. At no surprise I left a message with Aaron too. "Hi Aaron, Dev calling. Just checking in to see if you have any news on the forensics examination of that gun removed from my coffee table last night. I just left a message with Phoenix Starr asking if her husband's body has been released. If I hear anything, I'll let you know."

I put Morton back in the car, and we drove down to Stewart Street and went past Dambella's house. A blue BMW convertible was parked in the driveway behind the house. I figured the odds of the car belonging to someone other than Phoenix Starr were close to zero. I drove past the house at a normal speed and headed back to the office. Quinnie phoned maybe a half-hour later. "Hi Dev, returning your call. Sorry you had to leave a message."

"Not a problem. Just checking in. I was wondering if you and Muffin wanted to take a walk today. No pressure if you've got something else going on."

"I'm just out of a meeting and going to have a quick sandwich. I could be ready in thirty minutes if that fits your schedule."

"That works. Pick you up outside the front gate?"

"We'll be there, and no stopping to get a bone or a treat. You've done more than enough."

"Okay, see you in a half-hour," I said, and we disconnected.

We pulled up outside Tubby's mansion and picked up Quinnie and Muffin thirty minutes later. Quinnie was a hundred percent more positive than yesterday.

"Hi, Dev," she called as she opened the rear door, and Muffin jumped into the back seat next to Morton. "How's it going?"

"Sounds like this morning's meeting may have gone a little better than yesterday," I said.

"Yeah, actually, it went pretty well."

"Good, you earned it. I was afraid you were going to run out of patience with your brother."

"I probably would have if you hadn't been around to offer an occasional dose of sanity. There's a pretty good chance we may wind things up tomorrow."

"Tomorrow? Really, that's great. It's been a long haul."

"You don't have to tell me. So, back to the dog park today?"

"Actually, no. I was thinking we'd just do a quiet walk along the river shore. It's a gorgeous sunny day. We'll have to keep the dogs leashed so they don't take off into the woods chasing squirrels, or worse, a skunk. But it'll be a nice walk. Sound okay?"

"It sounds perfect. Thank you in advance."

We drove back down the River Boulevard. We passed Phoenix Starr's place, no car present, so she was apparently still shacked up at Dambella's. The Boulevard turns into Shepard Road, and we stayed on that for four miles and then turned onto James Avenue and pulled into the parking lot for the Waterford Bay apartments.

The Waterford Bay apartment building was a new structure with outdoor swimming pools, fire pits, a boat launch, and walking and biking trails along the Mississippi River. I parked in the lot. We clipped the leashes on the dogs and made our way to the walking paths heading upriver.

After about five minutes, the walking paths began to bend back toward the apartment complex. "Ready for an adventure in the wild?"

"Yeah, let's do it," Quinnie said.

We stepped off the path and headed to the river shore. We walked along the shore, heading upriver. After about a half-mile, I could see the rooftop of Dambella's house located on the bluff. We ignored the sign with the red letters that read, 'PRIVATE PROPERTY.'

"You see that rooftop up there on the bluff? That was the home of the brewmaster of a local brewery. Apparently, they stored the beer in a cave somewhere around here, which wasn't uncommon."

"Are they still doing that?" Quinnie asked.

"No, the place went out of business a hundred and twenty years ago. The house looks like it's haunted. Some guy lives in there now," I said, not bothering to mention Dambella's name.

I scanned the base of the bluff, looking for a cave entrance but didn't see anything. We rounded a bend, and suddenly, there was a small inlet with a wooden dock. A large white boat was chained to the dock. What looked like a garage was up against the river bluff, and an asphalt drive led down to the water. I wondered if the garage led to Dambella's cave.

"That looks like a nice speedboat," I said.

Quinnie gave me a look and shook her head. "Actually, Dev, that's not a speed boat. It's what's called a swift trawler. The cockpit probably has a pair of hinged transom gates with fold-down bench seats, plus a ladder to access the fly that folds flush against the aft end of the wheelhouse structure. There's also a broad side deck to starboard with shelter from the elements and a surprisingly generous skipper's door for easy seamanship."

I stopped and just stared.

"What? I'm into boats. You're into whatever? Beer? Maybe thongs? I don't know."

"Do you have a boat out in California?"

"No, but I've got a lot of friends who do, and I love them."

"So, you're familiar with that one," I said, nodding at the boat chained to the dock.

"Oh, yeah. One of my friends has one just like that. It's always a fun time, and God bless them because I can enjoy the thing and don't have to make the payments."

We suddenly heard the sound of an engine and looked up the asphalt drive at a blue all-terrain utility vehicle heading toward us. A tan, muscular-looking guy in a t-shirt and shorts drove down the drive past us and stopped at the dock. He turned the engine off and climbed off the vehicle.

"Hey, you guys know this is private property?" he called. He sounded nice enough. There were two boxes of wine bottles resting on the back rack of the utility vehicle. He grabbed one and stepped onto the dock, walked alongside the boat, and set the box down on the dock.

"Yeah, we saw the sign, but we're going upriver. Did we miss something? Is there another path to take to go further?"

"Well, there is, but it's along the road on top of the bluff, and then you have to walk almost another half-mile before you can make it back to the water."

"Is that even legal?"

He laughed. "You're not the first guy to ask that. It's from some law back in the 1880s that was grandfathered in. Rather than pay for court expenses to have it overturned, people just ignore it, and, as long as there isn't a fence you can't get around, everyone just comes and goes. I don't have a problem, but the boss can get ticked off about it."

"Looks like you're getting ready to go on a cruise," I said as we kept walking.

"Yeah, a little later this afternoon. I'll take the boss and a woman downriver. They have dinner and some nice conversation, and we're back by about 8:00. The river gets pretty busy in the afternoons between boats and barges. You really have to watch where you're going."

I glanced at the name of the boat stenciled on the back. 'Northern Star.' No doubt Dambella's boat, and I wondered if the woman was Phoenix Starr.

"You have a saloon and two berths arranged below?" Quinnie asked.

"Yeah, as a matter of fact, we do. You familiar with the vessel?"

"Friends have one out on the west coast. They dock in Santa Barbara. We've had a lot of fun times on it," she said.

"Yeah, I really like it. The river can be a bit confining, and the commercial traffic can be a pain. Santa Barbara sounds nice."

"Oh, it is."

"You store this boat in that garage during the winter?" I asked.

"Yeah, It's actually a boathouse. That's its primary function. We take the snowmobiles out in late fall and put the boat in. We just have to back the trailer in. Once spring comes around, and after the flood season, we pull the boat out and put it in the water. We're fortunate to have that boathouse there, although it got caught up in the spring floods about six years ago. That did some damage, but what are you going to do?"

"Nice chatting with you. Have a nice cruise and stay safe tonight," I said.

"Thanks," he said. He bent down, hoisted the second box of wine up, and carried it onto the deck.

Thirty-six

We continued upriver and walked for another half-mile along the shore until we could see a portion of the 35E bridge running across the Mississippi. We sat on a large boulder and watched a couple of boats head upriver. One of them pulled into the dock across the river at the Pool and Yacht club. Six barges came down the river, two abreast. They were pushed by a tugboat, and given how high they were riding, I figured they were probably empty. They seemed to be approaching slowly, but once they were abreast of us, it was obvious they were moving faster than it appeared. Just the sheer size of a river barge, let alone six of the things chained together, would give one pause. "You about ready to head back?" I asked.

Quinnie nodded and said, "Yeah. This was a great idea, Dev. I'm trying to remember if I was ever down here along the river as a kid. I think I was, but I just can't recall."

We headed back downriver. Just as we approached the inlet where the boat was docked, the door to the boathouse rose, and a guy stepped out. He was chatting with the person we'd spoken to earlier. He was large, muscular, and had dark hair that was slicked back. The sides of his head were shaved. I remembered Louie describing two thugs looking for me at the office. This guy fit the description of one of them.

Fortunately, he seemed to be engaged with the guy on the all-terrain vehicle and didn't appear to notice Quinnie and me. We continued back to the walking paths and the parking lot at the Waterford Bay Apartments. We let the dogs in the backseat and climbed in front.

"Oh, what a perfect break. Thanks so much, Dev. I'd love to do that tomorrow if you have the time," Quinnie said.

"I'll make the time. It was really nice. Who knew you were a boat aficionado?"

"Hardly. I've just had a nice time on my friend's boat and looking at that one today reminded me of all the fun. To tell you the truth, I'm looking forward to getting back to the coast—nothing against you, Dev. You've been beyond wonderful. In fact, if you're ever out that way, look me up. The door is always open to you."

"Thanks, I may just take you up on that."

I drove out of the parking lot and waited for the light to change. I pulled onto Shephard Road and headed in the direction of Tubby's. It couldn't have been more than a minute when I glanced in the rearview mirror and saw the black jeep with yellow and red flames painted over the hood. That pretty much confirmed my suspicions of the guy with slicked-back hair chatting up the man on the all-terrain vehicle. He was definitely one of the guys Louie described who were looking for me in the office the other day.

The jeep held back and appeared to be content just to follow. That was fine with me. The opportunity for them to cause a problem reduced with every turn of the wheels as we headed to Tubby's. I wondered if they had any idea where we were going.

No cars were in Phoenix Starr's driveway, and a minute or two later, I slowed and pulled into the safety of Tubby's mansion.

"Oh, Dev. Thanks again for a wonderful afternoon. Check out our friends," Quinnie laughed.

I turned and looked in the back seat. Both Morton and Muffin were curled up in the backseat, sound asleep. Quinnie leaned over and gave me a friendly kiss on the cheek just as one of Tubby's thugs opened her door.

"Thanks again, Dev. I really enjoyed it."

"Thank you for coming and bringing Muffin with you," I said.

Quinnie slid out and opened the rear door for Muffin. Morton opened his eyes but made no effort to move. Once Muffin was out, Quinnie closed the door, and Morton stretched out across the back seat. She waved goodbye and headed into the mansion. I checked the rearview mirror for anything that looked like the jeep with the flames. Then I sat there for a long minute, hoping Fat Freddy or someone would tell me I was supposed to go inside.

Nothing happened, and I eventually followed the circular drive out of the mansion grounds. I didn't see the jeep anywhere. Not that it stopped me from taking a route back to the office that would have been difficult to follow even on the best of days. I parked in front of The Spot, thinking the foot traffic coming in and out might be enough to dampen any desire to tamper with my car.

I woke Morton, and we hurried across the street and up to the office. Amazingly, Louie was awake and actually appeared to be working.

"Hi, Dev. How's it going?" he asked, not looking up from his keyboard.

"It's going okay, Louie."

"You had a couple of phone calls come in. I think the callers left a message."

"Thanks, I'll check it out," I said and hurried over to my desk. I actually had three messages. The first message was from Phoenix Starr.

"Hey, baby, sorry I missed your call. I was tied up." I wondered if she meant literally? "Sterling's body will be released at noon. I've contacted O'Halloran Funeral Home. They'll pick him up and take him to their facility on Snelling Avenue. Chat later, have to run," she said and disconnected.

The next call was from Detective Manning. "Haskell, the results are in from forensics. They were unable to pick up fingerprints or DNA from the pistol. There was a long blonde hair pinched behind a handgrip. Unfortunately, no match to anything in our database.

Ballistics is test firing the weapon as we speak. We were unable to recover the round that killed Mr. Kozlow. A record will be established, but we've nothing to compare the round to at this stage."

The third call was from Aaron. He told me Kozlow's body was going to be released at noon and reiterated the information Manning had given me.

I hung up and said, "You thinking about anything for lunch, Louie?"

"I'll be just fine with whatever you decide," Louie said and kept typing. I was going to take Morton for a walk, but he was sound asleep. "Back in fifteen minutes," I said.

Louie answered with a grunt. I walked up to Rooster's, got two BBQ sandwiches to go, and went back to the office. Fortunately, it was a quiet afternoon. I was living in fear of getting a call from Phoenix, but it never happened. I had a beer with Louie at The Spot. Morton and I headed home for a quiet night after the one beer.

Thirty-seven

We'd been in the office for a couple of hours the following morning. Louie had a court appearance at 10:00, so he was gone. I'd just finished checking the apartment across the street with my binoculars when my phone rang. "Haskell Investigations."

"Woo-hoo-hoo," Quinnie yelled into the phone. "We're done, finished, signed, sealed, and delivered."

"Really, you were able to come to an agreement?"

"Yes, if you can believe it. I've got a flight scheduled for late this afternoon. Would you be available for a final walk this morning? I'd like to take you to lunch afterward."

"You bet. That would be perfect. You don't have to buy lunch. We can just—"

"I insist on buying lunch. That's not open for discussion. How 'bout we do the same walk as yesterday. I can see the boat, and we can sit for a bit on that rock and watch the river traffic."

"You ready to go now?" I asked.

"We can be. We'll meet you outside by the gates."

"We're heading to the car now. See you in ten minutes."

I locked the office door behind us, and we hurried out to the car. Morton must have picked up on the fact that something was happening because he was pacing back and forth in the back seat. About the time he began to slow down, he recognized the route to Tubby's, and that got him pacing in anticipation.

No cars in the driveway when we passed Phoenix Starr's house. Quinnie and Muffin were waiting outside of Tubby's gate. Morton barked a welcome as we pulled to a stop. Quinnie let Muffin in the back and slid into the front seat. "Ooo, I'm so excited. I finally get to go home."

"Well, congratulations to you for hanging in there. Everything work out okay?"

"Oh, the usual, it ended up we both gave a little. I'm just glad it's over, and I won't have to deal with my brother for another five years. Oh, thank God. Yippee!"

"Man, you deserve the iron cross for hanging in there this long."

"Oh, Dev, if it wasn't for you and the dose of sanity you provided every day, I don't know what I would have done. He literally had me worn down."

"One of the many things he's good at."

"Oh, please. Okay, enough about what a marvelous malcontent Jerker is. We're going to do the same route this morning, right?"

"Yes, we'll walk upriver. You can see the boat chained to the dock and be thankful you live on the west coast and not here. Now, what time is your flight?"

"6:00, so I should be out at the airport no later than 4:00. That will give me the better part of two hours to twiddle my thumbs and look at people walking past my departure gate."

"You may just want to raise a glass of wine once you take off."

"It may be more than one glass."

We pulled into the Waterford Bay parking lot and parked in the same place we had yesterday. Morton and Muffin appeared to be all geared up with their tails banging against the side of the car. Just like yesterday, we followed the walking paths and then stepped off and walked along the shore. I immediately picked up on the fact that Quinnie appeared to be braless. Things were shaping up to be a wonderful walk.

The boat was chained to the dock. No sign of the guy we'd talked to yesterday. Since no one was around, we walked up on the dock and examined the swift trawler, Northern Star. I told Quinnie how proud I was of myself for remembering that the boat was actually a swift trawler. She just rolled her eyes and pointed out various items on the Northern Star. The information went in one ear and out the other.

We walked upriver until we came to the rock. We sat down, Quinnie actually moved closer to me, and we held hands while we watched the river traffic. We made our way back downriver, past the Northern Star, and let the dogs into the back of the car.

Once we settled into the front seat, Quinnie leaned over and gave me a kiss on the cheek. Then she adjusted her position, placed a hand on either cheek, and kissed me on the lips. "You know, I've never seen your bedroom, at least that I can remember."

"Well, fortunately, I've removed every trace of Fireball Cinnamon whiskey from the house."

"Gee, whatever will we do there?" she said and ran her tongue over her upper lip.

It was nothing less than a miracle that I wasn't pulled over for speeding on the city streets. I passed a half-dozen cars, and at one point, Quinnie said, "Dev, it would be nice if we arrived in one piece. If you're that anxious, pull over, and we'll take care of things here." Quinnie rubbing my upper thigh as I drove did nothing to calm me down.

I pulled into the driveway, and we hurried into the house. I tossed biscuits to Morton and Muffin, grabbed Quinnie's hand, and we ran up the stairs. I closed the bedroom door, tossed my t-shirt onto the top of the dresser, and dropped my jeans.

I knew she'd been braless and was able to make note of the fact that Quinnie was devoid of any undergarments. She apparently had made plans in advance. God bless her.

It had been ninety minutes of extreme passion for both of us. At the moment, we were both lying on our backs, gazing at the ceiling and catching our breath. Morton barked downstairs, and my first thought was he was just going to have to wait. Quinnie rolled over on her side, gave me a passionate kiss on the cheek, and snuggled closer.

"I think I'm going to sleep all the way home on my flight. This was just wonder-"

My first thought was that Morton was pushing against the bedroom door, only there was no way he knew how to turn the doorknob. The door suddenly flew open, and two muscular guys sauntered in with guns drawn.

"Sorry to interrupt. Actually, no, we're really not. Mmm-mmm, you're looking rather delicious, lady. Too bad you wasted your talent with this piece of shit," the guy with the slicked-back hair that was shaved on the side of his head said.

As Quinnie pulled a bedsheet up, I rolled over and reached for the drawer on the bedside table. The other idiot took a step forward and kicked my hand away from the drawer.

"Ahh, God, get the hell out here while you still can. You don't know who you're screwing with here."

"You mean your worthless ass and Gustafson's slutty sister. Yeah, I think we got a pretty good idea of who we're dealing with. You both have an appointment with our boss, and right now, you're running late. Honey, get your perfect ass out of bed and get dressed. Dumb shit, you just stay put for a moment."

Quinnie looked at me, absolute fear in her eyes.

"It's going to be okay," I said. "Do as they say, get dressed."

"Or don't. It's up to you, babydoll. Happy to have your naked body in the car."

Quinnie stared for a moment and then slid out of bed. She held the sheet against her figure and reached for her jeans. The other idiot picked her top off the floor and tossed it at her. She turned her back, pulled on her jeans, then picked her top up and pulled it on, all the while facing away from the two of them.

"Thanks for the show," Slicked Back said, and they both laughed. "Now, you dumb shit, get dressed. You so much as even think about trying something, and I'll blow out what little brains you have left." That caused both of them to laugh again.

I rolled out of bed, keeping my hands extended so both of them could see I wasn't doing anything contrary to their instructions. The other idiot dropped my t-shirt onto my jeans on the floor, then he kicked the pile in my direction. I pulled the jeans on, pulled my t-shirt on over my head, and reached for my pair of socks.

"Leave it, Haskell. You'll be happier barefoot. Come on, both of you, move your asses downstairs."

I nodded at Quinnie, and she walked out of the room. I followed right behind her and bumped into the idiot reaching to grab her rear as she passed by. Slicked Back suddenly had the barrel of his pistol up against the back of my head. "Oh, please, don't give me a reason to kill you. It would be so easy and would absolutely make my day."

I nodded and followed Quinnie down the stairs. Morton and Muffin, our so-called watchdogs, heard us and trotted out of the kitchen. Morton approached Slicked Back with his tail wagging and got petted. So much for being a watchdog.

The other idiot pulled a couple of plastic restraints from his pocket and said, "Hands behind your back, Haskell."

"Oh, come on, guys. You don't have to—"

Slicked Back raised his pistol, immediately sending me the message. I quickly turned and placed my hands behind my back. I held them side by side, with my thumbs and forefingers next to one another. Idiot quickly wrapped a restraint around my wrists. I held my hands in the same position as he cinched the restraint tight.

"You too, hot number," Idiot said.

He wrapped the restraint around her wrists, pulled it tight, and then patted her on the rear. "Mmm, considering that was recently used, it's still nice," he said and laughed.

"Move your ass out to the kitchen," Slicked Back said to me. "You too, honey, let's go."

We headed out to the kitchen. Morton's tail was still wagging, and he was all excited because it looked like everyone was going to go for a walk. Muffin appeared to wonder what was going on, although she followed us into the kitchen.

"Put the dogs in the jeep, then come back in, and we'll load these two in Haskell's bomb. Where are your car keys, Haskell?" Slicked Back asked.

"Right there on the counter," I said and indicated the keys sitting about two feet from him.

Idiot undid the door chain and opened the back door, took hold of the collar on Morton and Muffin, and led them out the door. He was back in the kitchen a minute later. "You first, Haskell, out the door. Watch her. She does anything, slap her hard. She'll probably like that," Slicked Back said and followed me out the door.

Thirty-eight

Under normal circumstances, I might have found the ride somewhat enjoyable. I was on my back. Lying on the floor of my car between the front and back seats. Quinnie was on top of me. She looked scared to death.

"Dev, I'm really frightened," she whispered just as Slicked Back sped around a corner, and we shifted slightly to the side.

"Don't worry about this, Quinnie. I got it figured out. We're going to be okay."

"Are you sure?"

I nodded, and she rested her head on my chest. Lying on the floor, I really couldn't tell for sure where we were going, but I had a pretty good idea. Sure enough, just a few minutes later, the car turned onto a residential street, made a right-hand turn, and then slowed and made a left turn. I glanced out the window above my head just long enough to catch a glimpse of a three-story red-brick structure with a four-story tower. Damien Dambella's place.

We made two right turns and stopped for a moment. I heard a noise, and a few seconds later, we pulled into the garage. I heard the same noise again and realized it was the garage door closing. The car door suddenly opened, and someone I hadn't seen before reached in, dragged Quinnie off of me, and stood her just outside the car.

The same guy reached in again, grabbed my ankles, and dragged me out of the car. He stopped just before I was going to fall and probably crack my head on the concrete floor. He shoved his massive hands under my arms and stood me up in one large swoop.

A door opened on a back wall, and a guy stepped out dressed in expensive-looking slacks and a starched white shirt. The top button was undone on the shirt, and he wore a loosened blue patterned tie. I recognized him from his online pictures. No other than Damien Dambella.

"Well, well, well," Dambella said as he approached, smiling. "Ms. Gustafson and Mr. Haskell. How nice of you to join us."

"Dambella, I'm not sure what you thought you could accomplish with this, but let me tell you, it ain't gonna work. It would be a wise move to let Ms. Gustafson go. You can keep me. I got nothing scheduled for the rest of the day and—"

"You were right," Dambella said to Slicked Back. "He's a dumb shit."

"We'll be phoning Mr. Gustafson in a bit. For right now, maybe put them down in the tasting room. Ms. Gustafson, I'm sure your brother warned you about interacting with the lower strata of society. Bad choice wasting your time with Haskell, here."

"Hey, Dambella, guess what? The cops got your number, and just in case they take their time, Tubby Gustafson has been looking for a reason to shut you down. You've just given him the best reason ever. If I were you, I'd think long and hard about releasing us and letting us downplay this tragic mistake you've made while you still have a chance."

"Funny, Haskell. I think when the police search your house and find a certain item, all bets are off. As for Gustafson, he's always had a short fuse where you're concerned. Finding out you tied up and raped his sister, no, we'll be the heroes when we deliver you to him."

"Lots of luck. She hasn't been tied up. She hasn't been raped. You guys are dead in the water before you're even out of the gate."

"We'll see who ends up dead, Haskell. Get him out of my sight. Put them both down in the tasting room, and we'll get things ready," Dambella said.

Slicked Back yanked my arm, and I followed him into the house. Idiot, with a hand on Quinnie's rear, followed us. We walked down a hallway that had to be in the back of the house. We passed a door that was slightly open, and I could smell something delicious.

There was a door at the end of the hall. Slicked Back opened it, and we stepped onto a landing with maybe eight steps heading down to another landing. The temperature was immediately cooler, and there was a damp smell to the area. We walked down to the landing, took three steps to the right, and went down eight more steps to another landing that led to eight more steps.

Apparently, we were at the bottom. Slicked Back opened the door, and we stepped onto a brick path in a large cave. The cave beneath Dambella's house. The brewery cave. The walls were painted with spray-painted graffiti and all sorts of names and designs. Halfway up the wall was a black and white image of a woman's face with big red lips. Marilyn Monroe graffiti from the 50s.

"Quit gawking, dumb shit," Slicked Back said and pulled on my arm. We followed the brick path to another door and stepped into a small room. What looked like a bar was at the far end of the room. Four dusty tables with chairs stacked on top of them were positioned around the room.

"Make yourself comfortable, dumb shit," Slicked Back said and laughed. Idiot led Quinnie into the room. He took a chair off one of the tables, set it on the concrete floor, and guided Quinnie by the arms so she could sit down.

Slicked Back nodded at me. Idiot pulled another chair off the table, and then instead of helping me sit down, he just pushed me onto the chair. I landed on the chair, and it started to tip backward. I jerked forward and just barely stopped the thing from tipping.

The door opened, and suddenly Phoenix's blonde head peeked into the room. "Everything okay?"

"Just fine," Slicked Back said.

"Phoenix?" I stammered.

She shook her head. "Oh, Dev, you had your chance, and you blew it, big time, thankfully. The last thing I needed was another boring man in my life. Too bad, it could have been fun." She glanced over at Quinnie. "Let me know how things work out," she said, laughed and disappeared.

"Enjoy your time together," Slicked Back said as he and Idiot headed for the door. They closed it behind them, and I heard what sounded like a lock clicking.

Thirty-nine

Quinnie asked, "You know that woman?"

"Well, she was a client. Had me investigating her husband until he was murdered the other night. I had my suspicions, but—"

"Dev? What are we going to do? What are we going to do?" Quinnie said.

"I got this," I said just as the door opened, and Idiot let Morton and Muffin into the room. He shut the door, and I heard the lock click again. Morton's tail was wagging, and his tongue was hanging out. This was just another adventure to him. Muffin appeared to be more reserved and looked around, studying Quinnie and me.

I turned the palms of my hands toward one another and then moved my left hand down against the right until I could extend my fingers on my right hand. The restraint felt looser, and after a half-minute of rubbing my hands back and forth, my right hand suddenly slipped free of the restraint.

"Oh, God, that feels better," I said, pulling my arms forward and wiggling my fingers back and forth.

"What the—How did you do that, Dev?"

I was on my feet, heading toward the bar. I stepped behind it and looked for a knife or something to cut Quinnie's restraint. I didn't find anything, but there was an empty beer bottle sitting on a shelf. I held the bottle by the neck and slammed it against the concrete floor. It damn near bounced out of my hand. I held on tighter and, this time, really slammed it on the floor. It broke just at the end of the neck.

I carefully brushed the glass shards away from my bare feet, grabbed the jagged bottleneck, and hurried over to Quinnie.

It took longer than I expected, but I was finally able to cut through her restraint.

"That feels so much better," she said, rubbing her wrists. I hurried over to the door and tried the doorknob. It was definitely locked. I looked around the place. The door appeared to be the only way in and out.

We heard voices outside the room, and I managed to sit down in the chair just before the door opened.

Idiot looked in. "Having fun?"

I noticed the restraint I'd slipped off was on the floor in front of me. I slowly extended my barefoot and placed it on top of the restraint.

Idiot glanced over his shoulder and then stepped into the room, closing the door. He stood in front of Quinnie with his back to me and ran an index finger up and down the side of her face. She shook her head in an effort to keep him away but kept her arms behind her back. He reached down and rubbed a hand over her breast.

"Oh, you know what really turns me on," she said.

"Tell me, honey," he said.

"This," she said and kicked him squarely between the legs.

Idiot doubled up and groaned. She was suddenly on her feet, grabbed the back of his head, and kneed him right on the nose. He went backward and curled into a fetal position on the floor. I was on my feet, grabbing my chair and raising it over my head.

"Oh no, don't—" I slammed the chair just as hard as I could into his head. He went out like a light. I rolled him over and pulled the pistol from the back of his belt. I aimed the pistol, ready to shoot.

"Don't, Dev, don't. They'll hear it."

A pool of blood was gathering around his head. His skull actually appeared to be slightly crushed. I felt his neck for a pulse. I found it, but it was very faint. I checked his pockets, pulled out his cellphone, and then pulled the belt from his jeans.

"Let's get the hell out of here," I said. I attached the belt to Morton's collar and used it as a leash. Morton's tail was wagging. Apparently, this was just another fun adventure.

Quinnie said, "Heel, Muffin, heel," and Muffin sort of came to attention and attached herself to Quinnie's leg. I opened the door slightly and looked around. I didn't see anyone.

We headed out the door, clicking the lock as we left in the event Idiot somehow tried to get out. We went in the opposite direction from the staircase leading back into the house. The cave was lit by a series of lights somehow hanging eight feet up. There was a socket every three or four feet and a light bulb in every other socket. Approximately fifty feet down the path, there was another string of lights and two more after that.

We hurried through the cave, rounded a bend, and what appeared to be an opening into daylight was up ahead. But just as we saw it, we heard shouting, and a moment later, an engine started up. I looked around for an escape route, but there wasn't one. There was a small opening no more than 18 inches high at the base of the wall of the cave.

"Quick, Quinnie, get in there," I said, pointing to the opening.

"What? Are you—" The engine suddenly grew louder, coming in our direction.

"Get in there, now," I said and pushed her toward the opening.

She began to crawl in and suddenly screamed. A rat scurried over her shoulder and disappeared into the darkness of the cave. Morton lunged at it, but I held him back. I pushed Morton and Muffin into the opening after Quinnie and then slipped in.

"Oh, this is so gross, so gross," Quinnie said and started sobbing.

I held the pistol out, ready to shoot anyone who approached. Seconds later, the blue all-terrain vehicle raced past and disappeared around the bend. I could still hear the engine, but the sound was growing distant.

Forty

It felt like hours that we'd been huddled in the rat's nest. In reality, it was probably closer to ten or fifteen minutes. I heard distant shots fired and then the sound of an engine. No doubt the all-terrain vehicle. Sure enough, the sound grew louder as it raced past us. Phoenix Starr was riding on the back, holding onto Damien Dambella for dear life. They sped past, headed toward the distant spot of daylight.

I waited a few more minutes and was just about to crawl out when footsteps and heavy breathing approached. Slicked Back jogged past wearing a backpack and carrying two more backpacks, one in either hand. I couldn't see anyone coming behind him, and I rolled out of our hiding place.

I debated just shooting him but instead politely called out, "Stop right there, you worthless fuck."

He slowed to a stop but didn't turn around. He dropped the bag in his right hand, seemed to think for a moment, and slowly began to turn around. I crouched and placed a two-handed grip on the pistol.

"Don't," I shouted, just as he fired. I fired two rounds. He jerked a couple of times, dropped the backpack in his left hand, and fell backward.

"Come on, Quinnie. Get out of there, come on."

"Oh God, this is so gross. I'm going to need a very hot bath in Epsom salts when we get out of here."

"Let's get moving before someone else shows up." I grabbed the belt attached to Morton's collar. We headed toward Slicked Back, lying still on the floor of the cave. "Maybe don't look at this jerk. He's seen better days."

As we drew closer, I could make out a bullet hole in his forehead. I picked up one of the backpacks and handed it to Quinnie. "Here, take this."

"What's in it, dirty clothes or something?

"Just take it and keep moving. I'll catch up."

I rolled Slicked Back over, pulled his backpack off, and pulled it onto my back. I picked up the other backpack, glanced inside at a bundle of cash, and hurried to catch up with Quinnie.

The light at the end of the tunnel grew larger. We slowed down and approached cautiously. We walked into what was the boathouse that the guy had told us about yesterday. Four snowmobiles rested on racks, and a large empty boat trailer sat in the middle of the structure.

The garage door was open, and the all-terrain vehicle was parked down at the dock. Damien Dambella was on the dock, handing boxes to the guy we'd spoken to yesterday. I couldn't see Phoenix Starr anywhere. We suddenly heard multiple voices coming up behind us. We grabbed the dogs and crouched down behind the snowmobiles. A minute or two later, three guys appeared. I recognized Billy from Tubby's crew. They ran past us, out of the boathouse, and headed down the asphalt path.

Suddenly, the boat started up. Dambella unhooked the chain, jumped on board, and the boat sped out of the small inlet toward the river. Billy aimed his pistol and fired a couple of rounds, but he apparently didn't hit anything.

Dambella did a little dance and gave them the finger just as a loud horn blasted, and two barges appeared. They were riding low in the water, and we could see mounds of what appeared to be coal loaded in them. The barges slammed into the boat broadside and pushed it forward a couple of feet before it suddenly rolled on its side and disappeared beneath the barges. There were six barges in all, the tugboat kept blowing its horn, but it was too late.

What appeared to be a couple of cushions popped to the surface as the tugboat passed. Its engines were now in reverse, and the barges were slowly coming to a stop.

More and more debris rose to the surface, but it was just bits and pieces. Nothing like the boat itself, let alone Phoenix Starr, Dambella, or the guy driving the boat. The debris slowly drifted down the river.

Forty-one

The tugboat had moved the barges closer to shore, and they were now anchored a little way downriver. Three separate boats were tied to the tugboat. One of them was a police boat. There were a half-dozen squad cars on the grounds and officers going through Dambella's house with what I guessed were drug-sniffing dogs.

I'd handed the gun I'd taken from Idiot along with the backpacks, to Billy and two of Tubby's guys. They made a hasty retreat and were now long gone. Quinnie and I were currently sitting in separate chairs in Dambella's living room, answering questions from Officer Porter, a woman with red hair and a no-nonsense attitude. Morton and Muffin were stretched out on the oriental rug, napping.

"And so you were being kept in a room in the basement?" Porter asked.

"No, the room was in the cave underneath the house. Dambella referred to it as the tasting room. I think that was maybe what it was when there was a brewery around here a hundred and twenty years ago."

"You knew Mr. Dambella?"

We both shook our heads. "Never met him and never heard of him until we were kidnapped," Quinnie said.

"I heard his name but never met him in person. I've seen some pictures of him on the internet. He seems to know the mayor, a lot of people on the city council, and important businesspeople."

"How did you get out of the room? You said the door was locked."

"I was able to slip my hand out of the restraint. Whoever was the last person to check on us apparently forgot to lock the door."

"So you escaped from the room in the cave?"

"Yes," I said. "We headed in the opposite direction from the stairs leading up to the basement. Further along in the cave, we could see some light, and we headed in that direction. Then we heard people coming, and we hid in a little hole in the cave."

"It was awful. A rat ran over my shoulders," Quinnie said and shuddered.

"And no one ever saw you?"

"There was a guy on that all-terrain vehicle. He raced past us, heading toward the stairs to the house. A few minutes later, we heard gunshots, and he raced back past us, heading for the river. He had Dambella and some blonde woman with him. Once they went past, we crawled out of the hole we were in and walked toward the light. We saw the boat speed away from the dock, and all of a sudden, it got broadsided by the barges."

The clock on the mantel suddenly chimed six times. "Well, the perfect end to the worst day of my life. It looks like I've missed my flight," Quinnie said. "I was scheduled to fly back to L.A. tonight. Then all this happened."

"I think this might be a good time to bring us to a conclusion. Unfortunately, Mr. Haskell, we've taken possession of your car. I received a call from Lieutenant LaZelle. He's offered to have someone give both of you a ride home. If that's all right, I'll call him and let him know you're free to go."

"Yes, that will work," I said.

"Let me just make that call while you relax here. Glad you're both okay. I know this has been awful, but it could have been so much worse." Porter rose from her chair and pulled the door closed behind her. At least I didn't hear a lock click.

"Let's have them take us to your brother's. I'm sure he's worried."

"Fine with me, I just want to get out of here," Quinnie said.

We waited on the couch for another fifteen minutes. I could hear voices out in the hallway, but I couldn't determine what was being said. After a couple of minutes, the door opened, and Aaron LaZelle walked in.

"Well, once again, you seem to have inserted yourself in a major news story. How are you doing, Dev?"

"Hi Aaron, we're doing fine. Oh, this is a friend of mine, Quinnie Gustafson. We'd just finished walking our dogs when this thing sort of blew up in our faces."

"Nice to meet you, Ms. Gustafson."

"Please, call me, Quinnie. I like to keep as much distance as possible from my brother and his undertakings. Dev has told me a lot about you. The two of you played hockey as youngsters."

Aaron nodded and said, "Yes, and despite that, I still keep him as a friend." Quinnie chuckled at that. "What do you say we get you two out of here?"

"That sounds like a great idea," I said. We followed Aaron out to his car. Another easily identifiable unmarked vehicle. I held the front passenger door for Quinnie and then climbed in back with Morton and Muffin. They both settled down and rested their heads in my lap.

Aaron made a U-turn in front of the garage and then drove out of the driveway and past Phoenix Starr's blue BMW convertible. He nodded at the two officers stationed at the entrance to the property and drove down to Shepard Road.

"Miss Gustafson, if it's all right with you, we'll drop you off first. I'm sure there are a number of things you'd like to take care of. Sorry to hear you missed your flight. Dev told me you had been looking forward to going back to L.A."

"Well, if I wasn't before, I'm certainly looking forward to it now. I just hope I can book a seat tomorrow."

"If you run into a problem, have Dev give me a call. Sometimes we have a little better luck with that type of situation."

Not surprisingly, Aaron knew exactly where to go. As we drove past Phoenix Starr's house, I shook my head and thought, *What a waste.* I wasn't sorry to see Damien Dambella go. That was long overdue, but, as crazy as she was, Phoenix didn't deserve what happened. But then, neither did Sterling Kozlow.

Aaron pulled into the circular drive and stopped at the front door. No one leaning against the house moved.

"Thank you for the ride, Officer LaZelle," Quinnie said. "It was nice to meet you. Dev told me about you, and when we were in the middle of this nightmare, he said you'd never let anything bad happen."

"Thank you, I do my best, but Dev keeps me awfully busy. Very nice to meet you. Have a safe flight home."

Quinnie slid out of the passenger seat and then opened the rear door for the dogs and me. Muffin hopped out, then I slid out, and Morton followed. I was hanging on to the belt I'd stolen from Idiot to use as a leash.

"Dev, don't you want a ride home?"

"Not to worry, Aaron. I'm covered. I just want to make sure everything is okay on this end. I'll give you a call when I'm home."

"Stay safe," Aaron said, gave me a look, and then followed the driveway out through the gates.

I watched him disappear and said, "Would you mind escorting me to your brother's office?"

"Not a problem, as long as you can direct me to wherever it is."

We headed into the mansion. As we approached, both guards seemed to come more or less to attention. One of them opened the door for Quinnie and gave me a look, but no one said they had to pat me down. We stepped inside, and I closed the door behind us. The guy reading the comic book looked up and jumped to his feet.

"Good afternoon, ma'am," he said and forced a smile, then shot me a quick look but didn't say anything.

"Just down the hall, Quinnie," I said as Morton and I followed Quinnie and Muffin. "It's the last door on the left," I whispered.

Forty-two

Quinnie and Muffin opened the office door without knocking and stepped inside. Morton and I followed. Tubby was at his desk, looking at his computer screen. There weren't any naked women giving him a back rub or a massage, although I had to believe they were somewhere nearby, just waiting for his call.

"Are you all right?" Tubby asked as he rose to his feet. His concern appeared to be genuine and focused on Quinnie. I noticed there were three black backpacks lying on the credenza behind Tubby's desk.

"I'm just fine, thanks to Dev. He saved my life in no uncertain terms. They were going to kill us, Jerker, right after they got done raping me."

"Who are they? What the hell are their names?" Tubby growled. He hurried from behind his desk and wrapped his arms around Quinnie.

"Save the drama, Jerker. They're both dead, thanks to Dev." Tubby looked at me for a second and then focused back on Quinnie.

"But my team was there, chased them onto the boat, and then they—"

"And then they didn't do anything. Did they give you the backpacks? There were three of them."

"Yes, I got those," Tubby said and nodded at the credenza.

"Dev took those from the guy who was trying to kill us. Dev dealt with him. He won't be a problem. Did they mention the guy in the room, the one who wanted to rape me? Dev dealt with him, too. The man had a gun, and Dev attacked him and hit him over the head with a chair. Then he hid me in a hole in the cave and blocked the entrance. He was ready to kill anyone who tried to touch me," Quinnie said and suddenly began to sob.

Tubby held her tighter and patted her on the back of the head. "You're safe now. No one is going to hurt you."

"He led us out of the cave once it was safe, gave your guys the backpacks, and let them run away. Then he dealt with the police. You owe him a lot, Jerker. If it wasn't for Dev, right now, your place would be crawling with the police. Instead, a lieutenant gave us a ride back here and told me to have a safe flight home."

"Yes, well, I was just going to, umm, reward Haskell with some cash from one of the backpacks and—"

"Excuse me, sir," I said. "That's very nice of you, but I have a favor to ask you instead."

"A favor?" Tubby said with a look on his face that could kill.

"Yes, sir. You see, I have a friend whose son has gone missing. The kid is seventeen, and he's been on the street for almost four weeks." I pulled Manning's card from my pocket and handed it to Tubby. "If you could maybe help me find him and we got him back to his parents, it might be beneficial for both of us."

Tubby glanced at the card and then looked at me. "Manning? Norris Manning? Isn't he a cop?"

"Yes, sir, a Detective Sergeant in homicide. He's been looking for his son and can't find him. I'm not suggesting you had anything to do with this. I just think you might have some inroads or connections that maybe could help."

"You owe him, Jerker," Quinnie said and sniffled. "Things could be worse. I could be injured and forced to recover in your home for the next six weeks."

"Let me see what I can do. I'll get you a ride home," Tubby said and picked up his phone. He punched in three numbers and waited a moment. "Yes, I'll need someone to deliver Haskell and his dog home. Once you've done that, check in with me. I have something I want you to look into," he said and hung up.

Quinnie gave me a wink and said, "Dev, it's been quite an adventure. Thank you for all you've done. I'm going to go upstairs and see if I can get a flight out tomorrow. If I can get it, would you be available to take me out to the airport?"

"I'd be happy to, Quinnie. Just give me a call. If you don't get a flight, we'll take the dogs to the dog park."

"That sounds much better than walking the river shore after today."

"I'll wait to hear from you," I said.

Quinnie gave Tubby a look. She told Muffin to heel, and they headed out of the office.

Once she left, Tubby looked at me and said, "Aside from not wearing any shoes, are you okay, Haskell?"

"Yes, sir. Thanks for asking, but I'm fine. I guess Dambella thought we'd be unable to get very far if we were barefoot."

"I appreciate you watching over Quinnie. We don't always get along, but at the end of the day, she's the only family I have."

"I understand, sir. I have to tell you, she may not show it, but she thinks a lot of you. By the way, I think it was the smart move that Billy and those guys got out of there before the police arrived. Their presence there would have brought all kinds of unwanted attention to you. For the life of me, I can't figure out what Dambella was thinking. There were a thousand things that could have gone wrong, and I guess from his point of view, that's exactly what happened."

"You and Quinnie actually saw it happen, his boat getting hit by the barge?"

"Yes, sir, it was actually six barges, chained together, two abreast. They were being pushed downriver by a tugboat. Everything happened in a couple of seconds. Dambella gave us the finger just as the boat raced out of the inlet below his house, and boom, they got rammed by the barges and disappeared beneath them. I don't think they'd found any bodies by the time we left."

Tubby smiled and said, "Sometimes, things just work out of their own accord. Frederick is waiting outside to take you home. I'll mention looking for this boy when he returns."

"Thank you, sir."

"And thank you, Haskell. Now, get the hell out of my sight," he said but then smiled.

Morton and I hurried out of the office and down the hall. The Escalade was waiting for us. As we stepped out of the mansion, Fat Freddy hopped out of the car and opened the rear door.

"Nice to see you made it, Haskell," Billy said as I hurried past.

"You too, Billy. Stay safe." I let Morton hop into the backseat, said, "Thank you," to Freddy as I climbed in. Freddy closed the rear door and hopped into the front seat.

"All set?" Happy said, and we drove out of the grounds and headed toward my place. Fifteen minutes later, Happy pulled to the curb in front of my house.

Freddy turned in the front seat and said, "Don't get used to the boss taking a liking to you. You're bound to screw something else up in the next day or two."

"Probably. Hey, Freddy, I got a question for you. How did you know we were at Dambella's? If you guys hadn't shown up, we'd still be hiding somewhere in that rat-infested cave."

"Oh, simple. Her dog told us."

"What?"

"The first night Evil Woman arrived, the boss had us attach a tracking device on the dog's collar. The boss knew where she was, every step of every day ever since she's been here."

"He knew everything?" I asked.

"You mean does he know you took her to bed? Does he know you got her drunk out of her mind? Does he know you had your way with her more than once? Yeah, Haskell, he knows. But when he saw you suddenly being transported down to Dambella's house of horrors, he knew something wasn't right. You're just lucky he doesn't trust your dumb ass. Now, get out. Oh, and enjoy your evening."

Happy waited at the curb until Morton and I stepped inside before he took off.

Forty-three

I filled Morton's dishes, tossed him a biscuit for good measure, and headed upstairs for a long, hot shower. I was stretched out on the couch in the den, wearing a bathrobe and slippers. I'd been sharing a Domino's pizza with Morton when my phone rang.

"Hi, Aaron," was how I answered.

"You said you were going to call me when you got home."

"Yeah, I know. I thought it might be a good idea to grab a shower first, try and wash some of the day off of me."

"You doing okay?"

"I'll survive, but if I never had to go through this again, it would be okay with me."

"I read your interview with officer Porter. Very to the point, Dev. You didn't give anything away."

"What do you mean by that, Aaron? We answered every question she asked."

"Nothing suggesting you may have contacted Gustafson for help."

"Great idea. Only one problem. How, exactly, were we going to contact him? Neither one of us had our cellphones. In fact, Quinnie's phone is still up on my dresser. I've got to get it to her in the morning."

"And yet, somehow, Gustafson's gang knew you were in trouble."

I actually laughed.

"What's so funny?"

"Gustafson's right-hand man, Fat Freddy, gave me a lift home. I asked him about that. Asked him how they knew we were in trouble. He told me her dog, Muffin, told them."

"What?"

"Apparently, as soon as Quinnie arrived, Tubby had them attach a tracking device to the dog's collar. Based on the list of events Fat Freddy mentioned off the top of his head, Tubby knew what she was up to every minute of every day. Quinnie didn't know about the device, and as far as I know, she still has no idea."

"You going to tell her?"

"I can't see anything positive happening if I did, so no, I'm not planning on telling her."

"How's that working out for you?"

"So far, it's okay, but I don't want to push my luck. It's probably a good thing she's heading back to L.A. tomorrow."

"Honest to God, Dev."

"Yeah, you aren't kidding. Oh, one other thing. I gave Manning's card to Tubby. The one with the picture of his son. He's going to check into it. Maybe he'll be able to locate the kid."

"God, if he's even alive. I wish there was something more we could do, but—"

"Aaron, I gotta believe you guys are doing everything you can possibly do. A couple more pair of eyes, even if it's Tubby's group, can't hurt."

"Yeah, you're right about that. Okay, I'll let you go. Glad you're doing okay," Aaron said and disconnected.

Forty-four

I decided it didn't make sense to save the last three slices of pizza, so I ate them. Morton and I headed up to the bedroom just before 11:00. I was asleep in about thirty seconds. My cellphone woke me just after 4:00 in the morning.

"Yeah?" was how I answered and then, still half-awake, followed up with, "Haskell Investigations."

"Got a little something for you, dumb shit. We're out in front of your dump."

"Freddy?"

"Yeah, get your ass out of bed and meet me on your porch."

I was suddenly awake. I pulled on my jeans, grabbed my t-shirt, and slipped it on as I stepped out of the bedroom. I hurried down the stairs and opened the front door.

Fat Freddy was coming up the front steps. He had a kid by the shirt collar and was twisting one of the kid's arms behind his back. The kid had a swollen black eye, a fat lip, and his nose was bleeding, but I still could recognize him from the photo. Cullen Manning.

"Signed, sealed, and delivered," Freddy said and pushed the kid toward me.

"Thank you, Freddy. Really, I appreciate it. I—"

"We're even, Haskell, and good luck. Oh, by the way, we've put the word out. This punk is off-limits. Anyone dealing him will live to regret it."

"Good, thank you."

"Good luck," Freddy said and hurried back to the Escalade.

I pulled Cullen inside and closed the door.

"Who are you?" he said as he ran his hand beneath his nose, smearing blood across the left side of his face.

"Come on, let's get you cleaned up," I said and led him into the kitchen. I sat him on a stool and moistened a paper towel to get the blood off his face. He didn't say anything and let me dab at the blood. His nose continued to bleed. I gave him a couple of Kleenex and told him to plug his nose and stop the bleeding.

I'd given the card with Manning's phone number to Tubby, so I couldn't call Manning. I brought Aaron's personal number up on my contact list and called.

He answered on the fourth ring. "Lieutenant LaZelle."

"Aaron, it's Dev. Cullen Manning just got dropped off at my house. He's a little beat up, but he's here. I don't have Manning's phone number, and I—"

"I'll call him and be over in ten minutes. Do not let the kid out of your sight, Dev. He's liable to run."

"Got it."

"You know my old man? Are you a cop?"

"I've dealt with your dad, and no, I'm not a cop. My name is Dev Haskell and—"

"And you're the guy that drives him crazy," Cullen said and laughed, causing another spurt of blood to run out of his nose.

"Get those Kleenex in your nose, so you're not dripping blood all over my kitchen counter."

"Oh, he's been bitching about you for as long as I can remember. I've always wanted to meet you."

"Well, now you have, so stuff that Kleenex—"

"Relax, dude, I'm on it," he said and wadded part of a Kleenex up and stuffed it in his right nostril. When he'd finished, he said, "Just for your information, I've been clean for six days. So everyone can just take it easy and back off."

"That's really good news, Cullen. There's a bunch of folks who are supporting you and your parents. One day at a time."

"Yeah, I got it. I'm on the mission. Are you recovered?"

"Me, no, at least not officially. But I watch myself," I said, and suddenly, the Fireball Cinnamon Whiskey evening right here in the kitchen with Quinnie popped into my head.

He plugged his left nostril with Kleenex, and he asked for a glass of water. I'd just set the glass down in front of him when someone knocked on the front door.

"Is that the old man?"

"It might be. Let's check it out."

"I'll maybe wait here."

"No, you won't. Cullen, it's great you're on day six. Really it is. But the history is we need to be careful. So, for right now, I'm not going to leave you alone, and you're going to come with me to the front door."

"And what if I don't?"

"I'll deck your ass without a second thought, and then you'll have two black eyes. Your choice. It's after four in the morning. I'm a crabby guy, even on a good day. So don't screw with me."

"Okay, okay. Just would have been nice to be trusted," he said and slid off the stool.

"That's something you have to earn. You keep up the good work, and you'll get there, eventually."

There was more knocking on the front door, and we hurried out of the kitchen. Aaron stood on the front porch looking in. I opened the door, and he stepped in. He glanced at Cullen and nodded, then looked at me and said, "Everything okay?"

"Yeah, going well. Come on back to the kitchen."

"Hi, Lieutenant," Cullen said.

"Cullen. Good to see you. We've all been worried about you."

"No need to worry, I've been clean for six days," Cullen said as he settled back onto the kitchen stool.

"Great news, well done," Aaron said just as we heard frantic knocking on the front door.

"I'll get that," I said and hurried to the front door. Manning knocked two more times before I got to the door. Each time louder than the previous. "Come on in," I said as I opened the door.

"Is Cullen okay? Where is he?" Manning asked, looking around.

"We're all back in the kitchen. LaZelle is here."

Manning hurried back to the kitchen. "Cullen. Oh, Cullen," Manning called as he hurried to the kitchen. He wrapped his arms around his son and held him tightly.

"God, give it rest, Dad. I can't breathe," Cullen groaned.

Manning released his grip, placed a hand beneath Cullen's chin, and raised his head. "Mmm, bit worse for the wear. But thank God you're here. We've missed you."

"I've been clean for six days," Cullen said.

"Oh, well done. I'm glad, no wait, I'm proud of you, son. We both are, your mother and me. Very proud of you."

"So are we," Aaron said. "We're all prepared to keep you on track. You've made the tough decision and carried through with it, Cullen. We're all here to support you."

"Can we go and see Mom?"

"We can, but I've got a spot reserved for you at City Treatment Center. You'll be there for thirty days."

"But I just told you, I've been clean for six days."

"And we want that to continue. There's all sorts of people lined up to help you, Cullen. Let's take our time and do it right."

"Do it right? What's wrong with being clean for the last six days?"

"Not a thing. In fact, it's wonderful. Well done. Now, let's continue that wonderful start by giving you the support and the knowledge you're going to need to continue on that road."

Cullen seemed to think about that for a moment. "Can I see Mom?"

"She's resting, Cullen. This has been very hard on her. She loves you so much, and it's been very painful for her to have to watch what you've been going through. She's all excited about seeing you at City Treatment. You'll have a chance to clean up. I've got fresh clothes packed for you in the car. We'll get the support we're all going to need to see us through this next phase," Manning said and opened his arms.

Cullen wrapped his arms around his father. Manning hugged his son and mouthed the words 'Thank you' to Aaron and me. He calmly moved Cullen to the front door. We watched them pull away from the curb and disappear down the street.

"What do you think?" I asked as we walked back to the kitchen.

"I think it's almost 5:00, and if you were halfway decent, you'd be cooking me breakfast."

"I was about to suggest that. I just want to put the coffee on first."

Forty-five

After a healthy breakfast of pancakes and bacon, Aaron headed down to the office. I cleaned up the kitchen and was on my laptop when Morton wandered down. I let him outside, filled his food and water dishes, and went back to the laptop.

I sent Louie a message explaining yesterday's events. I finished up by saying I'd be there once my car was released. Just before 9:00, my phone rang. I was hoping it might be an update on my car. It wasn't, but even better, it was Quinnie.

"Hi, Dev, hope I didn't wake you."

"Not to worry, I've been up for a while. Were you able to book a flight for today?"

"I've got a 1:40 to L.A. I'm wondering if we could stop by on the way to the airport?"

"You can. I'm not sure where I'll be." I went on to explain my car situation. "So I'll either be here at home, or at the office."

"I was thinking we might come down to your place. Muffin can play with Morton, and maybe you and I could pick up where we left off yesterday afternoon before our interruption."

"Oh, yeah, I can do that."

"See you in twenty minutes," she said and disconnected.

It was more like twelve minutes when Quinnie pulled up in front. She was driving Tubby's dark blue Cadillac CT5, the same car I'd picked her up in when she first arrived. I was standing on the front porch waiting, and she waved and honked the horn as she pulled to the curb. She and Muffin hurried up onto the front porch.

"Let's put these two in your backyard, and we can get down to business," she said and gave me a passionate kiss on the lips.

"Great idea. I just want to make sure you're aware of something I learned yesterday." I went on to tell her about the tracking device on Muffin's collar.

"You know, I'd normally ask if you were kidding, but that is such a typical thing for Jerker to do. You know what? If he's tracking this, he's going to be fully aware of what we're doing."

"Yeah, I know, so maybe we should grab breakfast at a restaurant or something, and he won't get all wigged out."

"I've got a better idea. Let's leave it right on her collar, head up to your bedroom, and drive him crazy."

"Oh, I don't know, Quinnie."

She raised her eyebrows and slowly ran her hand down my chest toward my belt.

"Okay, I see your point, but not out here on the porch," I said, and we hurried inside.

* * *

We pulled into the airport parking ramp just after 11:30. I took Quinnie's suitcase out of the trunk, and we hurried into the airport. She already had her boarding pass, and I walked her and Muffin to TSA security.

"Well, I just want to thank you for making my visit survivable," she said.

"It was wonderful to meet you. Next time you come to town, you and Muffin can stay with us," I said.

That seemed to bring a smile to her face. "No offense, but hopefully, it won't be for another five years. You take care until then," she said. She leaned forward and gave me a kiss on the lips. "Oh, and I almost forgot. A little something from Jerker and me," she said and handed me a little brown paper lunch bag.

I opened the bag and saw a wad of bills, hundred dollar bills.

"Your brother did this?"

"Well, no, not exactly. He was still asleep this morning when I got that out of his office. But I know he'd want you to have it."

"Yeah, I'm sure he would."

"Be good," she said, patted me on the cheek, and hurried down the pre-clearance lane.

I watched until she disappeared. She never looked back. Just to play it safe, I drove home and stuffed the lunch bag under my mattress. I dropped the Cadillac CT5 back at Tubby's. Neither Fat Freddy nor Tubby wanted to see me, and Happy gave me a lift back to my place. I phoned Louie and left a message. "Hi Louie, it's been a crazy couple of days. I'm taking the afternoon off. See you tomorrow." Click.

Aaron called me late that afternoon. "Yeah, Dev. Your car is ready to be picked up. If you want, I'd be happy to pick you up."

"That would be great, Aaron. Much appreciated. I'm cooling my heels at home."

"I'm on my way," he said and disconnected.

I waited out on the front porch. Aaron pulled in front about fifteen minutes later. I hurried off the porch and climbed into the front seat.

"Thanks for doing this, Aaron. I really appreciate it. You hear anything from Manning?"

"Yeah, he's taking a sick day. Cullen is in City Treatment, and everyone's fingers are crossed."

Epilogue

It was three days before I heard anything from Detective Manning. He phoned me late in the afternoon.

"Hi Haskell, Detective Manning. I, umm, wanted to thank you for helping with Cullen. If it weren't for you, I'm not sure where he'd be right now."

"Is he doing okay at City Treatment?"

"He seems to be. We're all in the process of taking things one day at a time."

"That sounds positive. Long may it continue."

"Something else came up you might be interested in," Manning said.

"Oh?"

"You remember I mentioned there was a blonde hair pinched behind the handgrip on that pistol that was placed in your coffee table?"

"Yes, does this mean you found a match in the database?"

"No, at least not in the database. But we recovered the three bodies from the boating accident, Dambella, a woman named Phoenix Starr, and another gentleman named Kenny Greco."

"Grecco was most likely the guy driving the boat," I said.

"Yeah, that's what we figured. But here's the other thing, that blonde hair on the pistol. It's an exact match to the woman, Phoenix Starr."

"Meaning she murdered Sterling Kozlow, her husband?"

"We can't be a hundred percent positive, but it certainly points in that direction. Oh, and the phone call to Kozlow?"

"You mean arranging the meeting at Scuttlebutts?"

"Well, we don't know what the call was about, but the morning he was murdered, he did receive a call from a burner phone. The call lasted all of a hundred and nine seconds."

"So we'll never know who made the call?"

"Not quite. We recovered the burner phone. It was in Phoenix Starr's bedroom. Only one call was made on the phone. It corresponds with the date, time, and phone number recorded on Kozlow's phone. It would appear the wife set him up. Obviously, we found her fingerprints and DNA in his car. Normally, that wouldn't be unusual. In this case, it does give one pause."

I thanked Manning for the call, and we disconnected. Phoenix Starr, I was thinking, *Surprise, surprise*, but then, maybe it wasn't.

The End

Thank you for taking the time to read **Surprise, Surprise!** If you enjoyed the read please take a moment and leave a review. Even if it's just a word or two, it really helps.

Thank You!

Don't miss this sample of Hit & Run The next book in the Dev Haskell series!

Sneak Peek

Hit & Run

Second Edition

MIKE FARICY

Prologue

I was running late and pulled into a parking place in front of the Yarmo Liquor store. A young guy was playing his violin attached to an amplifier at the entrance to the parking lot. He smiled and nodded as I drove past. The amplifier was on a two-wheeled dolly. He looked about eighteen or twenty, and I thought his music sounded awfully nice. His hand-written cardboard sign said he was raising money to help his mother. I watched as a car stopped and handed him a dollar, or maybe it was a five-dollar bill. The driver made a comment and pulled onto the street. I listened for another half-minute and hurried into the liquor store.

"Hey, Lorenzo, how's it going?" I said to the guy behind the counter as I rushed down the far aisle. I grabbed two bottles of Sean Minor Sauvignon Blanc and got in line behind a fat guy buying a case of beer.

"Better give me a half-pint of bourbon, too. What kind you got?" he said.

Lorenzo turned toward the rack of half-pints behind him and read off the brand names. "We got Jim Beam, Dickel, Kentucky Gentleman, Evan Williams, Heaven

Hill, Virgin, Ancient Age, JD Black, and Kentucky Tavern."

"What's the price?"

Come on, man. I got a date tonight, I thought. Lorenzo shot me a look and recited the prices to the guy.

"Mmm-mmm, that expensive? I guess I'll just stick to the beer tonight," he said and handed a twenty to Lorenzo.

Probably not his first night shacking up with a case of beer. I watched him as he waddled out the door. With a massive belly hanging over his belt, I guessed the guy hadn't been able to see his feet in ten years.

"Just these two bottles, anything else, Dev? Maybe a half-pint of bourbon?"

"No, thanks, but I'm good," I laughed. "I'm running late for my date."

"Well then, I better ring you up." He scanned the barcode on the bottles, and I inserted my credit card into the terminal. I input my code and waited for a moment. Suddenly there was a loud buzz, and the terminal screen read 'Card Denied' in red letters.

"That can't be right."

"Pull the card out and insert it again," Lorenzo said.

'Card Denied,' the screen read again. Nothing changed except the buzz sounded even louder.

"Oh, Christ," the guy in line behind me groaned just under his breath.

"Sorry, go ahead and ring this guy up while I dig out another card," I said.

Lorenzo nodded, shoved my wine bottles off to the side, and rang up the next guy. Once his card was approved, he said thanks to Lorenzo, gave me a look and headed out the door. I handed two twenties to Lorenzo.

"Sorry about that, Dev. You might want to give them a call and see what the problem is. That's thirty-five-fifty. You want a bag?"

"Is there a charge?"

"No, Dev, the paper bag is free."

"Yeah, then, I'll take it."

He handed me the change and placed the wine bottles in a paper bag. "Enjoy your evening."

"Thanks. I intend to." I hurried out to my car and placed the bag on the passenger seat. I glanced over at the violinist. He wasn't playing at the moment. Instead, he was talking to two guys who looked like they might be giving him a hard time. One was wearing a black leather vest. The other was wearing a gray hoodie sweatshirt with the sleeves cut off.

The guy in the leather vest suddenly pushed the violin player. He stumbled back but didn't fall. *This is just the way my day is going.* I climbed out of the car and headed in their direction. I wasn't running, but I wasn't wasting time either. The violinist saw me coming. His look caused the other two to glance over at me.

"This ain't got nothing to do with your dumb ass," the punk in the leather vest said. "I'm warning you, dude, 'less you want some of this," he said and slammed his fist into his left hand.

"You been warned, bro," the hoodie sweatshirt said.

I held my hands out to the side and said, "Hey, look, it might be a good idea if you two just left this guy alone. I like his music. Come on. He's here trying to make some cash to help his mother. Probably worked harder today than either one of you has all year. Go on, take a hike, please. No need to cause trouble."

"Little late for that, now, ain't it? Teach him, Bumpy," Leather Vest said to his pal.

Bumpy, the idiot in the hoodie, nodded and spun halfway around, swinging at me. I ducked, grabbed him from behind by the hood, and at the same time kicked his legs out from under him. He seemed to levitate and then dropped to the ground, bouncing his thick skull off the asphalt.

Leather Vest did a little dance and took a swing. I blocked it and punched him in the throat. When he reflexively grabbed his throat with both hands, I kicked him square between the legs, hard. He doubled up, slowly sank to the ground, and curled into a fetal position.

The hoodie slowly rose on all fours. I planted my foot on his shoulder and pushed him down. "It would be best if you two pieces of shit stay right where you are until we leave. I don't want to see you here again. You hear me? I said, did you hear me, dumb ass?"

Hoodie nodded and said, "Yeah, yeah, I got it."

"What about you? You hear what I said? I don't want to see you here, ever again."

Leather Vest groaned and nodded.

I pulled the four one-dollar bills out of my pocket and handed them to the violin player. "You need a ride?"

He shook his head. "Thank you, sir. My car is just over there."

"Thanks for playing. That was really nice. I enjoyed it."

He smiled, nodded, and unplugged his violin. He placed it in a case, put the case on top of the amplifier, and pushed the two-wheel dolly over to an old blue Toyota. I walked back to my car and watched until the Toyota was out of sight. Bumpy and his idiot pal were on their feet. Neither one looked very happy as they limped down the street.

I pulled onto the street and hurried over to Sandie's house. She was cooking dinner, and I figured two bottles of wine would be just the thing to get her in the mood, not that she needed any help.

She lived just up Davern hill from the Sibley Plaza shopping center where Yarmo's was located. Six minutes later, I pulled in front of her brick house, a two-bedroom rambler. I took a couple of deep breaths to get rid of the denied credit card and the wanna-be gangster stress and headed up the sidewalk. With any luck, we'd just skip dinner and head right into her bedroom. I rang the doorbell, wondering if she'd be wearing anything when she answered the door.

One

Sandie was wearing blue jeans and a short-sleeve white blouse with an embroidered pair of lips above her left breast. "Oh, thank God, you're here, Dev. I was beginning to worry."

"Crazy afternoon. Brought your favorite Sauvignon Blanc. Maybe we just start with that and see where we end up? We could have dinner at midnight," I said, handing her the paper bag.

She lowered her voice and said, "Sounds great. I only wish. My folks are here. They're in town for a memorial service, and they're going to be in the spare bedroom for a couple of nights."

"They're staying with you? Here? Tonight?"

"Oh, calm down. You'll love them."

"Can't wait to meet them," I lied.

She gave me a warning look and said, "Come on, they're in the kitchen." I followed her through the living room and into the kitchen. "Mom, Dad, this is Dev Haskell. He's the private investigator I was telling you about."

Sandie's mom turned on her kitchen stool. She was a nice-looking woman. I guessed late fifties or possibly sixty, orange hair, brown eyes. "Oh, well, we've heard so much about you. Nice to finally meet you. I'm Eleanor, but everyone calls me Elle."

The man with the crewcut next to Elle slid off his stool and held his hand out. "Bert Thomson, Sandie's overly protective father. Nice to meet you, Dev." His introduction sounded more like a warning.

"Nice to meet you, sir," I said as we shook hands.

"Grab a seat, Dev. I'll put this wine in the refrigerator. You want a glass?"

"I'll have whatever you guys are drinking."

"So, Sandie told us you're a private investigator," Bert said.

"Yeah, I've been doing that for a number of years."

"Were you a cop before that?" Bert asked.

"No, I know a lot of folks on the police force, but I was never on it."

"Chase a lot of bad guys?"

"Just the opposite, actually. I double-check work histories on employment applications. Occasionally investigate someone for an insurance company. You know, false medical expenses, that sort of thing."

"Sounds like he should check out your brother," Bert said.

"That's enough, Bert. Don't pay any attention to him, Dev," Elle said.

We chatted about everything and nothing. Bert ran a small concrete company up in northern Minnesota. Elle was a third-grade teacher, looking forward to retiring in twenty-two months. Sandie took dinner out of the oven, lasagna and garlic bread. We ate in the dining room after Bert led us in prayer. It was a pleasant enough dinner. After I helped clear the table, we had chocolate brownies for dessert. We chatted in the living room for another half hour, and after saying how nice it was to meet Sandie's folks, I said goodnight.

Sandie walked me out to the car.

"Thanks for coming, Dev. Sorry my folks were here. I mean, I love seeing them. I just wish they would have called first. I was looking forward to a night with just the two of us."

"Hey, relax. It was nice to meet them. They seem really nice."

"Hope you didn't feel interrogated."

"No, I get it. If you were my daughter, I'd want to know who you were going out with too. You know parents, they still think we're fourteen, and they need to know what we're up to."

"Or worse, they do know and don't like it. Well, thanks for being so understanding." She stepped forward, gave me a big kiss, and said. "I'll make it up to you."

"Counting on it," I gave her a hug and headed home.

Morton, my golden retriever, met me at the front door. I followed him into the kitchen, grabbed his leash, and we took a long walk through the neighborhood. Once home, we settled down in front of the TV. After watching a movie I'd seen before, we went up to bed and slept through the night. I was up before my alarm went off.

I was washing the breakfast dishes when Morton wandered downstairs an hour later. He stretched as he entered the kitchen and then stood next to me for his morning head scratch. I let him out into the backyard, filled his food and water dishes, and he was back inside ten minutes later.

We were in the office well before my officemate, Louie Laufen, turned up. When I saw him park across the street behind my car, I filled his mug with fresh coffee and set it on the picnic table he used as a desk. Our office is on the second floor, and you have to climb a rickety set of stairs to get up to that level. I could hear the stairs creak as Louie slowly made his way up to our office.

He opened the door and stood in the doorway, catching his breath. He was red-faced from the stair climb. Not surprisingly, since he could stand to lose maybe a hundred and fifty pounds. He gave me his standard wave and settled into his desk chair. He never says anything for the first five minutes after his arrival. He catches his breath, sips some coffee, and, I think, debates internally whether he really wants to work.

"So, it appears you survived your hot date with Cindy last night."

"Actually, it was Sandie, and yes, I survived since it was anything but a hot date."

"Oh, God, was this one of those 'we need to talk' nights?"

"No, fortunately, nothing like that. Her folks showed up unexpectedly, and they're spending a couple of nights at her place. Apparently, they're down here for a memorial service. Needless to say, other than the lasagna she made, there was nothing hot happening."

"Oh, sorry to hear that. I know you were looking forward to the night."

"Hopefully, I won some points by being a nice guy. Her folks seemed nice enough. What did you do?"

"Just the usual, left The Spot right around 9:00. Grabbed some fries and a couple of quarter pounders on the way home and settled in to watch the news."

"Sounds about like my night, well, except for the quarter pounders," I said and glanced out the window behind my desk. A guy was climbing out of a dark blue Ford Mustang. He'd parked in front of my car, wrote down my license plate number, and came across the street to our building. A moment later, I heard the stairs creak at a much faster pace than Louie made.

The door opened a moment later. "Hi, I'm looking for Dev Haskell."

"You serving a court order?" I asked and focused on the envelope in his hand.

He smiled and said, "You're Mr. Haskell?"

"Yeah, give it to me."

"Not a court order, sir."

"Then what is it, a restraining order? Can't be an eviction notice. I own my place."

"I believe it's an invitation, sir, but the envelope was sealed, and I can't be sure. It's from Mr. Grumley."

"Grumley? I don't know anyone named Grum—wait a minute. You don't mean a guy named Arthur Grumley, do you? I went to high school with a guy named that. More or less the class prick."

He nodded. "Yeah, that sounds like Mr. Grumley."

"Tall guy, glasses, brownish hair?"

"Sounds like him. Grumley stands about six-two. He does wear glasses. His hair is brown with blonde highlights. I think it's probably dyed. End of my knowledge."

"You work for him?"

He shook his head. "No, sir. Just delivering this for him and charging his firm, by the way."

"His firm? He's a lawyer?"

"No, some kind of tech guy."

I glanced over at Louie, who was nodding and typing away on his computer. I took the envelope from the guy. "Okay, thanks, I guess."

"Thank you, sir," he said and headed out the door.

"You don't know who Arthur Grumley is?" Louie said.

"Actually, I do know. Unless he's changed, he was a spoiled little rich kid who thought very highly of himself and was a real pain in the ass in high school. We called him Arty-Farty. Haven't seen him since graduation, and based on what that guy said, it sounds like he hasn't changed."

"I'd say that's fairly accurate. Along the way, he parlayed his family's inheritance or trust fund into an online marketing company, Grumley Creativity. They got some pretty big-name clients, sports teams, pro golfers, and a couple of NASCAR Racers. Take a peek," Louie said and turned his desktop screen toward me.

I stepped over to read what he'd found. He was right. A number of big names were listed as clients with photos and then testimonials from them. I shook my head.

"Amazing, the guy I knew in high school was a real self-absorbed jerk."

"Well, I'm guessing so are these people he's listed as clients. It's probably a perfect match. What's in the envelope?"

"Oh, yeah, I guess that would help." I slipped a pen knife into the envelope, a number ten business envelope with the name Grumley Creativity and a PO box address in the left-hand corner. I opened it and pulled out a sheet of paper. An address in block letters with a phone number was centered and, below that, a handwritten note.

I read the two-sentence note to Louie, "Haskell, hoping you can join me tomorrow for a 1:00 p.m. business lunch at my place. Call if you can't make it." The address was on Quinlan Avenue North in Stillwater, a town twenty minutes east of the city on the St. Croix River.

I turned the sheet of paper over, thinking there might be something on the back, like a map or an indication of what the business meeting was about. There was nothing.

"So, are you going?"

"Why in the world would this guy want a business meeting with me? I don't know or need anything techy."

"Dev, maybe he's got someone hacking into his system or breaking into his house. Maybe it's some kind of investigation that he'd like to keep quiet, and he thinks you're the best guy for it. God, meet the guy and have a free lunch. If nothing else, you can always say no. On the other hand, since he's a millionaire, what if it was some kind of deal that led to all sorts of opportunities?"

Two

I left the office at 12:15 the following day, allowing plenty of time to get to Stillwater and Arthur Grumley's place. Good thing, five minutes from my office, I hit a highway construction zone. It took ten minutes to get through a two-mile stretch. I eventually made it to Stillwater only to learn, by following my GPS instructions, that Quinlan Avenue North was, at no surprise, on the north end of town, actually still within the town's limits but not in any sort of heavily developed area.

A 'private' sign directed me to the paved trail that led to Grumley's house. I made my way through a forest of birch trees for four or five minutes and suddenly pulled into a large open area overlooking the St. Croix River fifty feet below. The house looked to be a hundred years old, a massive two-story brick structure with a slate roof, copper gutters, four large chimneys, and an attached four-stall garage. A parking area with angled white lines was in front of the mansion, just off the circular drive that led to three outbuildings. Four cars were already parked there. I pulled into an open space between two of the cars.

I climbed out of my car, looked around, and walked over to the granite steps leading up to the front door. Or was it the back door? I climbed the steps, and when I rang the doorbell, I could hear it chiming inside.

A moment later, a man opened the door. He looked to be about forty and was dressed casually in slacks and a nice shirt. "You wouldn't happen to be Devlin Haskell, would you?" he said.

"Yes, I am. Believe me. No one else would want to be me."

He laughed at that and said, "Mr. Grumley is expecting you. He's in his office. If you'll follow me, please," he stepped to the side so I could enter. Once he closed the door behind me, he nodded and said, "This way, please."

The place reminded me of Tubby Gustafson's house. Only it was easily twice the size. At least there weren't a bunch of armed guards out in front of the place, and I hadn't been patted down before I entered. Still, there was an elegant entryway with white marble tiles on the floor. Walnut paneled hallways led off the entry in three different directions, and a massive, elaborate staircase rose up to the second floor.

We walked halfway down one of the halls, and he stopped, knocked on the door, and opened it. "Sir, Mr. Haskell is here for your luncheon appointment."

"Oh, wonderful, right on time. Thank you, Tony. Dev Haskell, it's been a long time, my friend, a very long time," Grumley said, stepping around from a large, carved antique desk. He wore a gray three-piece suit with a red tie. He looked essentially the same, a few pounds heavier than when we were seventeen but certainly not fat. His brown hair had blonde highlights like the man said yesterday. He stepped toward me with his hand outstretched. "Thank you for coming. I really appreciate it."

"Happy to oblige, Arthur. I have to tell you, your note really surprised me. We haven't seen one another since high school, and even then, we didn't talk very much."

"Well, we ran in different groups. Come on, sit down and let's catch up over lunch." He indicated a polished wooden table with a wave of his hand. We walked over, and I pulled out a side chair. Grumley settled into the gold embossed chair at the end of the table that looked more like a throne than a dining chair. "So tell me, Haskell, what have you been up to?" As he spoke, a dachshund appeared out of nowhere. Grumley picked it up and placed it on his lap.

"Oh, I did a semester of college, but wasn't really wild about that. Spent some time in the service. Started my own investigative firm and have been working at that ever since."

"Yes, which is one of the reasons I contacted you. I'd like you to take a look at something for me, but we can get to that later," he said as a door on the back wall opened and a dark-haired woman walked into the room carrying a silver tray with food.

"Oh, perfect timing, Carmen. Thank you."

She smiled, nodded, and set the tray next to Grumley. Two plates loaded with what looked like roast chicken breast, vegetables, and mushrooms were on the tray.

Grumley took one of the plates, passed it to me, and said, "Help yourself."

I grabbed the plate as Grumley reached for the bottle of white wine on the table. The label on the wine bottle was in French. He filled his glass and then filled mine, although not quite as full as his. He raised his glass in a toast. "To old times," he said.

"Yes," I agreed. I raised my glass toward him and took a sip. It was actually pretty good. I took a bite of the chicken breast. It was delicious. "Mmm, this is very good."

"Oh yes, we import it from France, Bresse poulette," Grumley said using a heavy French accent. "I own a farm over there just outside of Bourg-en-Bresse. We raise chickens, the world's best, literally. Once I had this dish, I knew I just had to play a part."

"Of course. Why not? Are you over there often?"

He smiled, shoved another forkful of chicken into his mouth, and said, "Mmm, not as often as I'd like. One of the problems with running an award-winning business. You always have to stay ahead of your competition." Grumley fed the dog from his plate. For the rest of the meal, he'd eat two forkfuls and then feed pick up a small piece of chicken between his thumb and forefinger and feed the dog.

The lunch was excellent, the wine was perfect, and the dessert, creme brulee, was the best. I listened to Grumley for the better part of forty-five minutes and three glasses of wine, telling me how wonderful he was and how everything he did was incredibly fantastic. Once Carmen cleared away our dishes and set another bottle of wine on the table, he finally got down to business.

"Well, I suppose you're wondering exactly why I contacted you, Haskell."

"I thought it was to introduce me to this wonderful chicken dish. By the way, I'd love to get the recipe."

He gave me a look and shook his head. "Actually, no, Haskell, that was just one of the many benefits of dealing with me. The reason I wanted to meet with you is to discuss the possibility of you performing an investigation on my behalf."

"Are you having an employee problem, or is someone attempting to hack your system?"

"I think those are two areas a bit out of your range. No, actually, this is more of a personal matter. You see, a number of years ago, a woman forced herself on me and became pregnant."

"What? I mean, I'm sorry. That's just such a surprise." *Because you're such a self-impressed jerk, what woman would have the hots for you?*

"I know what you mean. One of life's surprises, in fact, maybe the only time I ever really made a mistake. But be that as it may." He reached into the inside pocket of his suit coat and pulled out a folded sheet of paper. "I'm keeping the original, of course. But you may keep this copy should you decide to take on the case," he said, unfolding the piece of paper and placing it in front of me.

I glanced at the wrinkled, yellowed paper. It was a copy of a birth record as opposed to a birth certificate dated December 6, 2003. The record was from Seton House, a home for unwed mothers that had been operating for at least a hundred and fifty years. The line for the father's name had the word 'None' typed in. The mother's name was blacked out. The line for the child's name had two words 'No Name' typed on the line. The baby was listed as male, with a weight of seven pounds and six ounces. There was a case number along the top of the certificate.

"Did you black out the mother's name?"

"It's really not that important. What I want is the name of the child. As you can see from the certificate, he was born the year we graduated from high school. I happen to know he was adopted from the hospital when he was two or three days old. Given that the birthdate is on the certificate, it would seem to be a logical path to discover who adopted him and what his name is. He would be nineteen now, so no longer a child. I'm sure I could find this out myself, but, obviously, I'd prefer to keep my involvement private."

"How long have you had this thing?"

"Yeah, I know. It's a Xerox copy. The mother gave it to me a month or two after the birth. She wanted me to see that I wasn't mentioned. Only saw her one time after that."

"Have you tried to contact the biological mother?"

"No point in trying. She passed away some years ago. All I have is this copy of the birth record. That's why I immediately thought of you. I'm not interested in the mother. As I said, she passed away. I would like to see if the boy is okay. If he needs financial help or something, maybe I could play a small part. Of course, I'd like any knowledge of my involvement to remain private. To that end, I've had a contract drawn up," he said and reached into the inner pocket on the left side of his coat. He pulled out an envelope and handed it to me.

Just like his lunch invitation, Grumley's address was in the upper left-hand corner of the envelope. It was also in the middle of the envelope along with a postage stamp. I opened the envelope and pulled out a five-page contract. I quickly went through all five pages. The fifth page had two signature blocks. Grumley had already signed and dated his name.

"Would you like a pen, Haskell?"

"Thanks, but I always have my attorney double-check things before I sign. I don't see a problem, but I want to play it safe."

"Very well, don't let me keep you from your lawyer," Grumley said, pushing his chair back. He set the dachshund on the carpet and stood. "I figured that might be the case. Just mail it back to me once you've signed it."

I slipped the contract back into the envelope and stood. We shook hands for a half-second. Grumley pulled his cellphone out and pushed two numbers. A minute later, the same guy who had answered the front door stepped into the room. "Sir?"

"We've concluded our meeting, Tony. If you would be so kind as to show Mr. Haskell to the door. Wonderful to meet you and catch up after all this time, Haskell. That unsigned contract will be valid for forty-eight hours. I look forward to hearing from you."

"I'll get back to you. Thank you for lunch. Very delicious."

"Of course, it's French," Grumley said and then added a phrase in French that was lost on me. He could have been telling me to get screwed, and I wouldn't have known.

I followed Tony out of the room. He led me back to the entryway and held the door for me. "Thanks, Tony. Nice to meet you."

"Enjoy the day, sir," he said, then closed and locked the door as soon as I stepped out.

Three

I asked Louie, "So, what do you think?"

He shook his head and flipped the pages back on Grumley's contract. "It seems reasonable enough, except for the part where he gets the title to your house and one of your fingers if you don't find this kid by the end of the week."

"What, he has that in the damn contract?"

"Just joking, Dev. Calm down. The thing seems reasonable enough, maybe a little bit of overkill as far as keeping quiet about him. That said, it's not uncommon in this kind of circumstance that a biological parent doesn't want their name mentioned. There could be a variety of reasons. Maybe the kid or the family that adopted him has serious problems. He could have a wife who would be upset to find out he'd fathered a child. It could be any one of a number of things. You said he's wealthy?"

"Appears to be very wealthy. Some tech thing, Grumley Creativity is the company."

Louie nodded and said, "Oh yeah, we looked it up online. Not that it means anything. Anyway, I don't see a problem with signing this thing. Did you discuss fees?"

I shook my head. "No, never came up, not even in general terms. He liked to tell me how successful he was, and I was happy to listen and make some mental notes."

"What'd you learn?"

"If what he said is true, and I've no reason to doubt him, he's worth millions. He's also the same person he was back in high school. Very impressed with himself and not really interested in anyone else."

"Well, good luck. Maybe increase your fee and see if he blinks. Nothing like a good-paying client to make the world seem sunny and bright."

"So you don't have any problem with me signing this thing?"

"No, the main thing is you have to keep your investigation private. You can't mention his name. If you do find the kid, about all you can do is turn the information over to Grumley. I know he told you the mother is dead, but if you find out her name, you might want to verify that. Just make sure you don't mention Grumley's name if you learn who she is and she's still breathing. Once you sign that contract, make a couple of copies before you send it back to him."

"Of course," I said, turning to the back page, signing and dating the contract. I brought my fee schedule up on my laptop, raised everything by thirty percent, and printed off three copies. I raised the lid on my printer and made two copies of the contract with both signatures as well as the birth record. I placed the contract back in the envelope, added the sheet with my fees, and sealed the envelope.

"You going to be here for a bit, Louie?"

"Yeah, I'm here until I head over to The Spot for a beverage. You want me to keep an eye on Morton?"

At the moment, my Golden Retriever, Morton, was stretched out on his pillow. He was sound asleep in his mid-afternoon nap. "He'll be out for another hour or so. Hopefully, I'll be back by then. I want to go over to Seton House and see what I can find out about this birth."

"Seton House, time to update, Dev. They closed their door back in 2016."

"What? They're a home for unwed mothers. What do you mean they closed their door?"

"Just that. The news report said they were merging with some other organization later that year. Apparently, being an unwed mother isn't as difficult or as embarrassing in today's world as it was twenty years ago."

"Merging? That can't be right. Let me check it out." I Googled Seton House. Yeah, unfortunately, once again, Louie was correct. They closed their doors in 2016. Seton Services were now a part of Catholic Charities, and they were located over on University Avenue. I could only hope they might be able to give me a name on the birth record.

Louie smiled and said, "I'll watch Morton while you see if you can get some answers."

"I think I already know what the answer is going to be, but I'll check it out just in case."

The Catholic Charities Seton building on University Avenue is a three-story concrete structure. The entrance is actually in the back under a blue awning, so I pulled in next to the building and parked. The door buzzed open a moment after I pressed the bell. I walked in and headed for the reception counter.

"Good morning. If you'd sign in, please," the woman behind the counter said. The three-ring binder used to sign in asked for my name, car make, color, and license. Once I filled in the information, she handed me a visitor's badge and said, "How may I help you?"

"I have a birth record from Seton House, dated 2003," I said, handing a copy of the birth record to her. "There's no name for the father, and the mother's name has been blacked out. I'm trying to find the child, now an adult, if he's alive."

"I'm afraid we can't help you. The mother apparently did not want her name to be known, which is why it's been blacked out."

"If that's the case, why wouldn't it just say none, like where the father's name should be."

"Most likely because she didn't provide the father's name. She may not have known his name, or he asked that his name not be given. That's not at all uncommon."

"Is there someone I could talk to regarding this?"

"I can see if someone is available. If no one is available, you'll have to make an appointment."

"Okay, hopefully, someone can see me."

She input a three-digit number on the phone and a moment later said, "Hi, Gary. I have a gentleman out here with questions on a birth record dated December 6, 2003. Would you be able to meet with him? Yes, he did. All right, thank you," she said and hung up.

"He's just finishing up. If you'd like to take a seat, he should be out in five or ten minutes."

"Yeah, okay. That's great. Thank you," I said and sat down.

Gary Carlsrud introduced himself five minutes later. "Come on back to my office, and let's go over this," he said.

I followed him back to a room furnished with a desk, a credenza, and two file cabinets. A pair of black plastic chairs were placed in front of his desk. I took a seat as he settled behind his desk and said, "I understand you're adopted and want to find information on your biological parents."

"Not exactly," I said as I handed him the birth record. "My name is Dev Haskell. I'm a private investigator. I've been hired by the biological father, who wishes to find his son. Based on the birth record from Seton House, the child would now be an adult, age nineteen."

He pursed his lips and said, "Unfortunately, the father's name isn't listed here. Who crossed out the mother's name?"

"I thought that was done by Seton House."

He shook his head, "If we did it, the same format as the father's would have been followed. The word 'None' typed in."

"Then I'm not sure. It may have been the father who blacked it out, but I honestly don't know that."

"Here's the problem," he said, handing back the birth record to me. "As it stands, we've no way of substantiating if indeed your client is the father. If you knew who the mother was and she requested the information, we might be able to obtain it. I'm afraid you're dealing with state laws here that are very specific."

"So you can't provide me with the information?"

"I'm afraid not. At least not without the documented father and/or mother requesting it. If his name isn't listed on the birth record, we can't supply the information. If you could get the mother to—"

"Unfortunately, she passed away some years back."

"Oh, dear. I'm sorry, but there's really nothing we can do."

I thought about that for a moment and couldn't come up with anything. "All right, Gary. I appreciate your time."

"Wish I could tell you more, but that's it. The laws are very black and white and with good reason in these instances."

"I get it. Okay, thank you. I'll see myself out."

He smiled and said, "Don't take it the wrong way, but I have to escort you." He walked me to the door beneath the blue awning, we shook hands once again, and I stepped out into the sunshine.

Four

I climbed back into my car in the parking lot. I wasn't that far from the police station, so I pulled out my cell phone and called my pal Aaron LaZelle, my lieutenant pal in the police department. I called his private number.

"Hi. This is Aaron. I'm unable to take your call at the moment. Please leave your number, and I'll get back to you as soon as possible."

"Hi, Aaron. This is Dev. Amazingly, I don't have a problem. Give me a call when you're able. I think it's my turn to buy dinner. Which McDonald's do you want to meet at? Thanks," I said and headed back to my office.

Morton was still asleep when I returned.

"That was fast. I'm guessing you didn't get any information," Louie said.

"You guessed right. Since the father isn't listed on the birth record and the mother's name has been blacked out, there's nothing they can do. I left a message for Aaron LaZelle to see if he would have any ideas."

"What about the county or the state?"

"Even if they could help, the best they could do would be to give me a list of boys born on that date. I looked it up. There's seventy thousand babies born every year in the state. Cut it in half, so thirty-five thousand boys. A birth certificate, if you can get it, costs twenty-six bucks. I don't have the information or the biological connection to obtain a birth certificate, so that's out. Unfortunately, I don't even have the information to physically obtain a birth record. But I checked online, and birth records are only available up to 1934, so that's not an issue. I'm starting to think I may be screwed on this," I said.

"And the baby was born at Seton House in 2003?" Louie said.

I thought about that for a moment. "That's the premise I was working under, and for a number of years, they would deliver the babies, but at some point, they moved the delivery to St. Joseph's hospital just because they were in a better position to deal with any potential problems that might develop during delivery. You know, the hospital would probably have records, maybe. Why didn't I think of this before? You know anyone over there at St. Joseph's?"

Louie shook his head. "No, I don't. Although, if you could find someone there, possibly they could help. I don't know. It sounds like a pretty slim chance."

"It sounds better than the one I didn't have a few minutes ago." I thought for a while, drumming my fingers on the desk before I came up with a name, Maureen

Connolly. We'd dated a few years back for three or four months before she'd dumped me. She was a nurse at Regions Hospital, not at St. Joseph's, but maybe she knew someone there. I called her number.

"You have reached Maureen Connolly. I'm unable to take your call right now, but if you'd like to leave a message, this is a secure line. I'll get back to you just as soon as I can. Thank you and have a nice day."

"Hi, Maureen, a voice from the past, Dev Haskell. I'm just calling to see if you might be able to connect me with anyone working at St. Joseph's hospital. I believe you're still at Regions but hoping you might know someone. Hope all is well with you. Thank you."

I called Grumley next. Just like every other call I'd made, I got dumped into voicemail. "Arthur Grumley," the recording said, and then I heard the beep to leave a message.

"Hello, Arthur. This is Dev Haskell. I signed the contract and mailed it back to you along with my fee list. Any questions, please feel free to call me. I'm working the case now, attempting to obtain the county or state birth record. Feel free to call with any questions."

As I disconnected, Morton stood, stretched, then gave me a look and walked to the door. "Duty calls," I said to Louie and grabbed Morton's leash. We took our usual route, three blocks around the neighborhood. Morton sniffed every other fence gate and left a personal message on the three fire hydrants along the way. I kept trying to come up with some way to obtain the birth record for Arthur Grumley's biological son, but nothing seemed to make sense. Once back in the office, I unhooked the leash from Morton's collar and tossed him a biscuit. He hurried over to his pillow in the corner so he wouldn't have to share just as my cell phone rang.

'Maureen Connolly' came up on my cellphone screen.

"Hi Maureen, thanks for returning my call. Gee, it's been years since we talked."

"Hi Dev, let me just state I've been happily married for four years. We have a darling daughter almost two, and I'm pregnant with our son, who is due in three months."

"Oh, that's wonderful news. I'm very happy for you. Who did you marry?"

"A perfect gentleman from Wisconsin, William Nelson. He's a prosecutor with the city attorney," she said, sounding as if she was giving me a warning rather than just providing information.

"Great, good for you, Maureen. You deserve someone nice."

"Yes, I certainly put in my time on the other side of that equation."

I decided not to pursue that last statement. "Umm, the reason I called is I'm working on a case for someone. A biological father, who is attempting to get the birth records of a child, a newborn boy who was adopted a day or two after his birth almost twenty years ago. The problem is, the father isn't mentioned on the birth record, and the copy I have has the mother's name crossed out."

"Does he know who she is?"

"I believe so, but she apparently passed away some years ago. The child was born in 2003. He would be 19 years old now. My client is a wealthy individual, and he wants to see if there's anything he can do to help the child. The mother was receiving care from Seton House when she was pregnant, and I believe they had moved the delivery services to St. Joseph's hospital prior to the boy's birth, so I'm thinking they might have the birth record. But with the father not mentioned on the birth record and no name for the deceased mother, it's been impossible to obtain any record."

"So, how do you expect to find anything at St. Joseph's?"

"It's a long shot, but the date of birth was December 6, 2003. Even if there are no names on the birth record, I'm thinking the adoptive parents might be listed. I was hoping you might know someone there that I could talk to and explain the situation." There was a long pause.

"Hello? Maureen?"

"Yeah, give me a minute, I'm thinking. Well, I kind of know someone there in accounting, but I don't think she would be much help."

"Would it be all right if I called her? Maybe she would know someone I could talk to."

Another long pause. "Well, I suppose you could try to call her. I better not give you her private number. Her name is Monica Bennett. But like I said, she's in accounting, so she wouldn't be in the records department."

"I'd like to try her. It's better than nothing, and I've really run out of options. If she can't help, I'll just have to contact my client and tell him we've hit a wall."

"And this is so the biological father can help the adopted boy?"

"Yes, it is."

I heard her take a deep breath, and then she gave me the number. I wrote it down, repeated it to her, and said, "Thanks, Maureen. I really appreciate your help. Wishing you all the best on your delivery. Healthy mom, healthy baby."

"Thank you, Dev. If you talk to Monica, please don't mention my name. I don't want her to think I'm passing her name out to everyone. And I hope you won't take this the wrong way, but things are really going well for Bill and me. I think it would be best if I didn't hear from you again, ever."

"That's not a problem. I won't…" but she'd already hung up.

Louie glanced over and said, "Did you get a contact?"

"Yeah, at least I think so. I'll find out in just a moment." I dialed the number and listened to three rings.

"St. Joseph's Hospital. How may I help you," a woman said.

"Hi, I'd like to speak to Monica Bennett. I believe she's in accounting."

"One moment, please, and I'll connect you." Apparently, Maureen had given me the general number. Still, I had a name, so that was better than when I'd started. The phone rang four times, and I was ready to leave yet another message when suddenly a woman answered, "Accounting."

"Hi, I'm calling for Monica Bennett."

"Speaking."

"Hi Monica, my name is Dev Haskell. I'm hoping you can help me. I'm trying to get the birth record for a man born at St. Joseph's and adopted two or three days after his birth."

There was a long pause before she said, "I don't think I'd be able to help you. I'm in accounting. What did you say your name was?"

"My name is Dev Haskell, and I—"

"Dev Haskell? Did you date Maureen Connolly for a while?"

"Yeah, off and on. But that was some time ago, and she—"

"I'm sure you don't remember, but we met at a party. A wedding shower actually for me and my ex."

"Do you live in a condo overlooking the river?"

"Well, we did. It belongs to my ex. Thankfully I don't live there anymore. Everyone in the place was older than my parents, way older. It's nice to hear from you. Still, I don't know how I could help you. As I said, I'm in accounting. How'd you get my name anyhow?"

"Oh, I remembered meeting you at the wedding shower," I lied. "I didn't realize you were in accounting."

"I try to keep it quiet," she said and laughed. "We should get together sometime. It'd be fun to catch up."

"You busy tonight? I'd love to buy you a glass of wine."

"Tonight, yeah, I can do that. You know where the A-Side Public House is?"

"I do. In fact, my office isn't too far from there."

"See you there at 7:00?"

"I'll be there. They get busy at night, so I'll call in a reservation for 7:00. Oh, this will be great, Monica. I look forward to seeing you again and catching up."

"Thanks for the call, Dev. See you tonight," she said and disconnected.

Louie looked over and raised his hands, suggesting, *So, what happened?*

"She's going to meet me for a glass of wine tonight."

"Yeah, I got that part, but can she check the birth records?"

"It doesn't sound like it, but maybe she can line me up with someone who can."

Louie shook his head and said, "It sounds like you're grasping at straws."

"That's exactly what I'm doing."

To Be continued . . .

Thanks for taking the time to check out <u>Hit & Run</u>, the next Dev Haskell tale. Things are about to go crazy for Dev, you should grab your copy and check it out.

Books by Mike Faricy
Crime Fiction Firsts

A boxset of the first four books in four crime fiction series:
    Russian Roulette; Dev Haskell series
    Welcome; Jack Dillon Dublin Tales series
    Corridor Man; Corridor Man series
    Reduced Ransom! Hot Shot series

The following titles comprise the Dev Haskell series:
    Russian Roulette: Case 1
    Mr. Swirlee: Case 2
    Bite Me: Case 3
    Bombshell: Case 4
    Tutti Frutti: Case 5
    Last Shot: Case 6
    Ting-A-Ling: Case 7
    Crickett: Case 8
    Bulldog: Case 9
    Double Trouble: Case 10
    Yellow Ribbon: Case 11
    Dog Gone: Case 12
    Scam Man: Case 13
    Foiled: Case 14
    What Happens in Vegas… Case 15
    Art Hound: Case 16
    The Office: Case 17

Star Struck: Case 18
International Incident: Case 19
Guest From Hell: Case 20
Art Attack: Case 21
Mystery Man: Case 22
Bow-Wow Rescue: Case 23
Cold Case: Case 24
Cash Up Front: Case 25
Dream House: Case 26
Alley Katz: Case 27
The Big Gamble: Case 28
Bad to the Bone: Case 29
Silencio!: Case 30
Surprise, Surprise: Case 31
Hit & Run: Case 32
Suspect Santa: Case 33
P.I. Apprentice: Case 34
Rebel Without a Clue: Case 35
Puppy Love: Case 36

The following titles are Dev Haskell novellas:
Dollhouse
The Dance
Pixie
Fore!
Twinkle Toes
(*a Dev Haskell short story*)

The following are Dev Haskell Boxsets:
Dev Haskell Boxset 1-3
Dev Haskell Boxset 4-6
Dev Haskell Boxset 7-9
Dev Haskell Boxset 10-12
Dev Haskell Boxset 13-15
Dev Haskell Boxset 16-18
Dev Haskell Boxset 19-21
Dev Haskell Boxset 22-24
Dev Haskell Boxset 25-27
Dev Haskell Boxset 28-30
Dev Haskell Boxset 1-7
Dev Haskell Boxset 8-14
Dev Haskell Boxset 15-19
Dev Haskell Boxset 20-24
Dev Haskell Boxset 25-29

The following titles comprise the Jack Dillon Dublin Tales series:
Welcome
Jack Dillon Dublin Tale 1
Sweet Dreams
Jack Dillon Dublin Tale 2
Mirror Mirror
Jack Dillon Dublin Tale 3
Silver Bullet
Jack Dillon Dublin Tale 4
Fair City Blues

Jack Dillon Dublin Tale 5
Spade Work
Jack Dillon Dublin Tale 6
Madeline Missing
Jack Dillon Dublin Tale 7
Mistaken Identity
Jack Dillon Dublin Tale 8
Picture Perfect
Jack Dillon Dublin Tale 9
Dublin Moon
Jack Dillon Dublin Tale 10
Mystery Woman
Jack Dillon Dublin Tale 11
Second Chance
Jack Dillon Dublin Tale 12
Payback Brother
Jack Dillon Dublin Tale 13
The Heist
Jack Dillon Dublin Tale 14
Jewels To Kill For
Jack Dillon Dublin Tale 15
Retirement Scheme
Jack Dillon Dublin Tale 16
The Collector
Jack Dillon Dublin Tale 17

Jack Dillon Dublin Tales Boxsets:
Jack Dillon Dublin Tales 1-3
Jack Dillon Dublin Tales 4-6

Jack Dillon Dublin Tales 1-5
Jack Dillon Dublin Tales 1-7
Jack Dillon Dublin Tales 6-10

The following titles comprise the Hotshot series;
Reduced Ransom! Second Edition
Finders Keepers! Second Edition
Bankers Hours Second Edition
Chow Down Second Edition
Moonlight Dance Academy Second Edition
Irish Dukes (Fight Card Series)
written under the pseudonym Jack Tunney

The following titles comprise the Corridor Man series:
Corridor Man
Corridor Man 2: Opportunity knocks
Corridor Man 3: The Dungeon
Corridor Man 4: Dead End
Corridor Man 5: Finger
Corridor Man 6: Exit Strategy
Corridor Man 7: Trunk Music
Corridor Man 8: Birthday Boy
Corridor Man 9: Boss Man
Corridor Man 10: Bye Bye Bobby

Corridor Man novellas:
Corridor Man: Valentine
Corridor Man: Auditor

Corridor Man: Howling
Corridor Man: Spa Day

The following are Corridor Man Boxsets:
Corridor Man Boxset 1-3
Corridor Man Boxset 1-5
Corridor Man Boxset 6-9

All books are available on Amazon.com

Thank you!

Contact the author:
- Email: mikefaricyauthor@gmail.com
- Twitter: @Mikefaricybooks
- Facebook: Mike Faricy Author
- Website: http://www.mikefaricybooks.com

Published by

MJF Publishing

Milton Keynes UK
Ingram Content Group UK Ltd.
UKHW020646220124
436466UK00019B/806

9 781962 080514